THE CLOCKE - ST(
ANGEL HAA

RHAPSODE

ERIC SCARBORO

**CAUTION**
Προσοχή
prosochí_

Say:  pro - soy - chay
Noun: care, caution, regard, note, heed, notice
prophylaxis, precaution, prudence, wisdom, discretion, gumption, sageness
warning, monition, premonition, *nous*.

## CONTENTS

### THREE PRELUDES

| | |
|---|---|
| THE TAKE-SEE | PAGE 5 |
| THOMAS WEDDERBURN'S HOLE | PAGE 15 |
| THE CONFLUENCE ROOM AT UNTHANK HOUSE | PAGE 21 |

************

### THE PROLOGUE

| | |
|---|---|
| THE MADE-UP DAY | PAGE 26 |

************

### ACT ONE: THE BOY

| | | |
|---|---|---|
| 1. | OUT OF BOUNDS | PAGE 39 |
| 2. | THE EMPTY SHOP | PAGE 43 |
| 3. | THE PERFECT DAY | PAGE 49 |
| 4. | STRANGE DAYS INDEED | PAGE 55 |
| 5. | AN INSPECTOR CALLS | PAGE 63 |

************

### ACT TWO: THE MAN

| | | |
|---|---|---|
| 1. | IN THE MIDNIGHT HOUR | PAGE 68 |
| 2. | TEA FOR THE TELLER-MAN | PAGE 71 |
| 3. | THROUGH THE BACK-GLASS | PAGE 75 |
| 4. | FACING THE MUSIC | PAGE 78 |
| 5. | ALL TOMORROW'S PARTIES | PAGE 84 |
| 6. | ALL OF THAT BAD NEWS TO MY DOOR | PAGE 94 |

| | | |
|---|---|---|
| 7. | IN A BIG COUNTRYDREAMS STAY WITH YOU | PAGE 105 |
| 8. | THE FOG ON THE TYNE | PAGE 109 |
| 9. | NORTHERN SOUL | PAGE 113 |

************

## ACT THREE: THE TASK

| | | |
|---|---|---|
| 1. | INTO THE VALLEY | PAGE 120 |
| 2. | MARCHING MEN | PAGE 126 |
| 3. | GOING UNDERGROUND | PAGE 131 |
| 4. | PARK LIFE | PAGE 136 |
| 5. | PLAYGROUND TWIST | PAGE 141 |
| 6. | FRANKIE'S TALE | PAGE 144 |
| 7. | PARTY FEARS TWO | PAGE 148 |
| 8. | MAGIC NUMBERS | PAGE 155 |
| 9. | MORNING HAS BROKEN | PAGE 167 |
| 10. | ASHES TO ASHES | PAGE 169 |
| 11. | REASONS TO BE CHEERFUL | PAGE 172 |
| 12. | HERE COMES THE SUN | PAGE 176 |

************

ILLUSTRATIONS                PAGE 180

************

ASPECTS OF THE PLEROMA       PAGE 181
Explanations, sources, thoughts and strange feelings.

I hope you enjoy this enough to want to read it to children, whether you are adult or children already. Regardless I suggest that you read one chapter ahead if you are reading to young children as there are some terrible goings on in this story, and you may not want to induce nightmares.

The story involves natural magic and time. No waving stupid wands around or wearing pointy hats, this is *real* and *natural* magic.

If you are a child or children then keep your wits about you: there are several strange events in the tale and you had better enjoy the story if you start remembering them and try to guess what may be happening in the little, hidden stories that also take place.

There is a lot of debatable information to be found in the notes in the back pages, also.

There are twists and traps and danger and fun, so you should ask the adults reading this to you as many questions as possible.

Some of the answers of course, may only be fully apparent in books two and three. Some of them you will have to work out yourself.

I can say no more – Begone!

## PRELUDE
### προανάκρουσμα
### proanakrousma

Say. Pro - aná - krews - ma

Prelude-noun
Prelude, import, importation, introduction, input, insertion.
Prelude-verb
Enter, insert, import, introduce, induct.
Precede, forego, go before, to prelude.
Also *forebode*.

# THE TAKE-SEE

## Treacherous doings on the quayside, coffee with Johnny.

Newcastle 1880. The quayside was it's usual lively self, the sun setting and a sea-fret working it's way inland along the river valley, slowly covering the waterway and flowing up both banks. People thronged along the waterfront, those finished work for the day and those just starting for the night. There was much to-ing and fro-ing in and out of the boats, ships, barges and bars, the structures on the water much more trustworthy than those on the land.
 And also more sturdy.

Further up the hill were to be found the grander sandstone buildings occupied by the bankers and shipping agents, keen to attract money from the engineers and architects of the brave new Newcastle. Beginning the climb to respectability was Milburn House, it's interior modeled on the decks of a ship, instead of floors of a building.  In between the old riverside and the new 'castles in the air' lay a murky crosspatch of dark, cramped alleys, and the rotting buildings that choked them.

The only direct path from river of sweat and coal up to river of money and gold, lay up Dog Leap Stairs. On a clearer day or night one could look up and see the towering peak of St Nicholas' Cathedral at the top of the wooden flight. On a bleak night like this it might be possible to see a quarter of the way up the stairs. Even so there were several points on the ascent where it was best to be well-known, or travel in company, or to brandish a knife in plain sight.

A low-bowed boat slid across the smooth surface of the Tyne toward the Newcastle bank. When docked and tied a single passenger stepped ashore, attracting the attention of several men slumped against the wall of the Guildhall, and several women, young and old, stood under the lamp at it's side entrance. Seeing that he carried no baggage, and made straight to the carriages outside the Red House Inn, they quickly lost interest.

He approached a hostler and after a brief discussion strode not to the first, fine-looking carriage but to the fourth carriage in line. A shining black Landau with the hood advisedly up. The driver was Lucas Grundy, a churlish looking fellow, with a three-cornered hat bearing a blue feather totally out of keeping with his miserable manner. He sparked into life upon catching a glimpse of the wallet shown to him by Mr Abraxason, who asked,

"I wish to go to the Penny University Coffee House, do you know where it is?"

"Sixpence sor. Taking fee's sixpence. But for seven pence I can show you the sights of the city." Grundy replied.

"I didn't ask the price." asserted Abraxason. The surly man considered and slowly wiped his mouth with his dirty woolen glove, before spitting a stream of chewing tobacco into the gutter.

"Aye I know where it is."

"I wish to meet a man who may be there or he may not be."

"None of my business sor. Less you wants to be took to a private detector-finder. *Young* man is it, you require?"

"I have little time to waste. If he is not there, I do not want to walk back here to take another carriage. I will need to meet him at his home in Winlaton village."

"If I were to return back to the Penny for you sor, how might I be sure that you would be waiting.    Time is money after all."

"I do not require you to return. I need you to wait outside for me. Wait for me until my travelling is done."

"Can't be done sor. Why who's to say I mightn't miss a take from here to Sunderland or Bortley. I has a living to earn."

"Then quote me a fee for the service I require."
exclaimed Abraxason.

"A fee for taking me to the coffee house, and waiting to see if I need any further journey. In fact waiting to see how long I will be before I need you again. Not a take-fee, a 'take-see' fee."

"A take-see fee? Alright then, five shillings!"
he suggested, knowing that this ridiculous fee was exorbitant.

"Done!"
said Abraxason, climbing into the back of the carriage.

The climb up to the ledge that the new city was being built on was slow and laboured, needing to be by way of several gentler, meandering streets. Eventually the carriage was moving smoothly through the darkened streets of the old city towards Haymarket and the Penny University Coffee House, wheels rattling efficiently on the cobbles. Only the occasional gas lamp outside a public house on Mosely Street, lit the way, the streets looking black and slick with rain. Behind them down the bank, the quayside disappeared below the fog cover which now stretched to the far side of the river, ebbing and flowing slowly from bank to bank like a living thing. Within  minutes they arrived at the windows of the brightly-lit Coffee House.

"That'll be two shillings and sixpence sor."        demanded the driver.

"Surely not."
retorted the passenger, stepping out from the Landau.

" You did understand the terms of our deal didn't you?"

"I ask only half the fee, two and six, as is fare."
he said, clearly *not* understanding.

"The take-see fare, as I see it, is to be payed at the end of the travelling. My man we are only partway, perhaps not *yet* even half. Wait for me here."

He turned and walked to the Coffee House entrance, the discussion obviously over for him. The driver was puzzled. He had *hoped* to claim the full five shillings and depart as soon as his passenger was out of sight, spending a full day's wages in one almighty drinking session back in The Nag's Head on the

Gateshead bank and afterwards spend some time with his occasional womanfriend, the delightful Nippa. Now he had been refused half. He had the suspicion that he had been gipped. He decided he could wait a while to see, after all a quick and easy return downhill to the quayside and the money would be his anyways. The real hard work he and the horse considered to be done.

After about ten minutes Abraxason emerged in company with a man of at least seven feet height, made all the more immense looking by virtue of the tall, white top-hat he wore. This could only be Coffee Johnny himself. The driver made a promise to himself that he would now behave impeccably.

Coffee Johnny looked up and declared in his booming voice,

"We're in luck. A carriage, unoccupied. Coachman, take us to Winlaton."

Abraxason strode alongside him, matching his giant stride yet walking at his normal leisurely pace.

"No such thing as luck, Johnny. I bade the driver wait for me here while I looked you out. And payed him a take-see fare. He is bound by his agreement and could not, as a gentelman, leave any sooner."

Turning to the coachman he said,

"Could you, my man?"

The driver just shrugged. His view was that the driver did the driving and passengers were like boxes, to be carried silently where they had to go. It had been a long day and he was ready to sound the retraite. Johnny squeezed his huge body into the Landau as it settled, complaining, on it's springs. The coachman looked down anxiously, but not daring to complain.

Abraxason leaned up to the driver.

"Do you know where Kingsmeadow is?"

The driver hesitated, although he had heard clearly, and there were not two such places he could be confusing.

"Aye sor, I know of the place. What of it?"

"I have not decided yet which, but you will be calling at an island when we are done. Kingsmeadow or Blaydon island. One of the two I imagine. And I would like you to find a crossing near enough to drive within sight of the five wand mill. Such a sight bestows luck on all would pass it, I am told."

The driver considered carefully, summing up Adam in his mind in as simple terms as he could. He reckoned to be able to handle the littler man but Coffee Johnny was a different matter. He knew of no man could take him if Johnny was soused let alone sober.

Abraxason joined Johnny in the cramped cab. Though he already took up most of the inside, Johnny was surprised to find that once Adam had sat, they somehow both seemed to have ample leg-room. Much more than he alone seemed to have had.

"Ahhhh. Thank you."   he said,    "Most gracious of you Adam." and stretched his feet out and onto the seat opposite.

"The least I can do for you my friend..."

"... have you met the Tenlocks?" asked Adam Abraxason.

"Not yet. They'll be staying in the colony at Bensham Bank I imagine. I understand they are … colleagues of yours? Engaged in the same line of business?"

"Indeed they are. Jews by birth and knowledgeable people. I would like them looked after, if you can. They face the most irrational hatred sometimes."

"But of course. I'll call in on them in the next couple of days. Sunday perhaps, when there will be plenty about to see me, and plenty to pass the word that they are friends of mine."

"My thanks. And perhaps tomorrow you might help me locate someone. He may be staying in Wolsingham. A Greek - a breeder of rare and exotic birds"

"Surely. …as long as it turns to be a simpler business than that affair in Darlington."

They fell silent for a moment as old friends sometimes do when there is simply too much to catch up on. Recalling one of Johhny's more famous exploits, Adam asked,

"So, Johnny, tell me, how *did* you lift the horse, rider and all, from the bog?"

"Why, sheer brute strength, would you believe."
came the reply, at which they both laughed.

"I also have a journey to make soon to Unthank House, through the Devil's Causeway by Rothbury. Best to set off at first light. I take it I can stay this night with you in Winlaton?"

"Of course. You are always welcome." replied Johhny.

"However, you normally seem in such a rush, always moving on, did you not plan to travel *tonight*? You have the coach. It would teach the driver well to find himself in the middle of the county in the middle of the night. He is well known as a surly fellow."

"This driver will be otherwise occupied, I fear. Did you have a good look at him?"

"No, only in passing. I think he may be the same coachman I heard took your messenger and package some months ago."

"As I thought. It seems that neither messenger or package arrived. Most inconvenient.

"Someone ran off with something … of …value, then?"

"Not the messenger for certain. He would be a trusted fellow, working off a debt and with much to lose and little to gain, for he believed the package only to contain papers, which in a way it did."

"Special papers then?"

"Special enough, and far too dangerous to be loose among the unskilled. Still, I will settle that matter one way or another as soon as we arrive at our destination."

The carriage passed east along the river banks, with Kingsmeadow island to the south and Blaydon more so, without stopping, the driver giving a scowling glance at both as they went by. He crossed the Newburn Bridge and did not turn left to take in sight of the five wand mill as he had been instructed.

"Far too bloody late and cold." he muttered.

However, within ten minutes he realized he must have made a wrong turn in the fog that hugged the riverbank, for ahead, rising like spirits from the mist were the five wands of the mill on Windmill Hills. Reining around he set off again for Blaydon and the hill up to Winlaton. The fog now so thick he could not see the horse rump in front of him. He navigated by public house and reckoned he could find his way past the Old Fox in Blaydon, the Red Lion in the square and up past the Bisley to the Highlander at Winlaton, in his sleep. He didn't like the coincidences of the evening or the way it was turning and was ready to be shot of his customers. He considered the situation and his passengers.

The strangest feeling crept up his back and brought goose-bumps up on his arms. Had he not taken this same ride before? It seemed very familiar.

Dismissing it, he returned his mind to his passengers. The first man he was quite confident he could handle. He had finished off a few over the last two years that looked much handier than he did. However the famous Coffee Johnny himself was another matter. He doubted there was a man in the north could take Johnny when he was soused, let alone sober. Besides it broke the rules he had set himself. *Never* take anyone well known. *Never* take anyone heading somewhere important. *Never* take anyone who had been seen-off on the journey. It had done him well so far. Indeed it had led to his luck with the paper. A Northumberland County Chronicle (incorporating The Day Ahead). Took it off that quiet fellow he done in going up to the Beach House at Beadnell. He remembered tossing it onto the back seat once the fellow's throat had been cut and him dropped in the Dene at Jesmond. Next day he had picked it up to idle through and thought he was seeing wrong things. The paper gave details of *that* very day's Racing and Boxing results. Taking it into the light near the window of his room he saw it cast a faint pink glow. He threw it into the corner, ready for the fire should it turn cold. Thank the Lord it hadn't. Next day he had wondered how accurate this prank had been and picked it up to read. It gave again, that new day's winning runners. The first four named winners he checked with Walter Shoesmith that evening, upon him just returning from Hexham course. All had won. Next morning he looked at the paper again, cursing his luck for not having read it soon as he came by it. He could have made a good few shillings the easy way.

To his amazement, the paper bore a new headline. He had looked around. There was no other paper in the room, he never bought one and seldom bothered to take any other mistakenly left in the cab. He held it to the window light. Again it glowed pink. Turning to the sporting page, he could not believe what he saw. The results of *that day's* racing. This was no prank for no one had been in his room over night. He assembled what meager funds he could.

His first win had been modest. A few shillings. He soon fell into a routine. He would rise, quickly take the paper from the old wardrobe where he hid it, and he would select a couple of good odds winners. He continued to work in the afternoon and evenings, having the sense to keep his good fortune to himself and not raise any suspicions with unusual behaviour. Something he had adopted as a custom a couple of years ago when he began his second career of disposing of untraceables who came his way. He had given the matter much thought and developed a plan. He would accumulate money slowly over a year or so, giving no clue as to his sudden extra wealth. He would meantime arrange to *be bequeathed* a large sum by a distant relative or unknown benefactor. He would then purchase a property in a respectable part of town and open a business. What it was didn't matter, he had no intention of spending more than the briefest effort on it and it was free to run at a loss if need be. He would employ someone to run it for him, as cover for his increasing fortune. He, meanwhile, would live the life of Riley, frequenting sporting events the length of the county, possibly even losing the odd, large and highly publicized wager. Probably run ten or twenty acres, with a dozen horses. Maybe even hire a trainer and become a sporting man. And certainly keep and rear birds, finches mainly like the old fellow Joe Aviary at Potter's Way had taught him as a lad. All he had to do was to put up with annoying people like his current passenger, for a short while longer.

    In the cab a short silence had descended as it sometimes may between good friends reunited who simply have too much to say and can't decide where to start. Eventually Adam said,
    "So then Johnny, tell me. Exactly how did you manage to lift that horse *and* rider clear of the bog?"
    "Why sheer brute force I would imagine!"
he replied and they both laughed.
    "And not even a glimpse of petticoats did I see."
He seemed bemused for a few seconds and asked,
    "Have I not told you this already ? Strange the tricks your mind plays when you have a magician for a friend."
    The Landau having risen above the incoming fret, visibility was slightly better as Johnny leaned from the cab and hailed the driver.
    "A little ahead, my man, stop at the white gates on the left."
    The cab slowed to a halt, the driver breathing hard with the effort of the climb up to the village. Johnny and Adam stepped out onto the gravel.
    "I'll meet you inside Johnny. For now I'll settle with this fellow and meanwhile, no matter what we say in it, your good wife will no doubt insist on a fuss being made."
    "Hah, that she will."
he said and strode away to the white-walled cottage.
Adam turned to face the driver.
    "And now, coachman, for the final reckoning."
he said calmly, fixing him with an unmoving stare.
    "As we agreed then, five shillings," the coachman demanded, only later adding an arrogant,
    "Sor!"
" But no fellow, the *fee* is not due. For did you not promise to accept a take-see fare? I have not declared my travels to be over."
    "I made no such agreement…" he scowled.

" .. now… now… let's settle what is fare between us."

"At your invitation then."

continued Adam, reaching deep inside his inner pocket, his hand re-emerging clutching a silver-framed, black handled spy-glass. His Guy's Eye. He held it to his eye and began examining the cab, a curious act in the dead of night.

"At your invitation to settle what is fare, you will return to me what is mine, a paper, the contents of a package removed from a courier of mine some six months ago."

This night was turning sour as three-day-old milk. Taken by surprise the driver feared the game was up, but flight was still possible. He acted instinctively, as had served him well in battle many times. Gripping the reins tightly he suddenly cracked them forward and bellowed at his horse

"Heeeaaarrrggggh!"

No thing happened.

He stared unbelieving into the empty space where he thought his horse had been.

"What the.where the …how in…my nag. What have you done with it?"

"All things being level, I decided the horse was hardly to blame for your crimes. Indeed by the look of it's well-struck rump I believe it is more sinned against than sinner. Accordingly I freed it to graze the rest of it's days on Windmill Hills, as we passed."

"Wey, how am I to earn an honest living now?"

Adam laughed at the very idea.

"Let's just say you now possess the first horseless carriage."

The driver sputtered in complaint, not really forming any words as such, more a stream of curses. Then he managed some composure.

"You'll do well not to threaten me. Do you know who I had in this very carriage, just this very morning? Why none other than the Magistrate himself Sir James.. "

Adam cut him off.

"More to the point, do you realise I may be the last fare you ever carry?"

Adam leaned forward, peering through his spy-glass.

"Ah there it is. In the seat-box. Hand it over."

Admitting no thing, the driver saw a way out. He would need to be quick, in case the giant returned. He lifted the lid on the seat-box, placed his weight on all toes and reached into the box, seconds later whipping out two very old, long-barreled pistols one of which he held squarely over Adam's heart.

"Step aside now," he said "as I'll be taking leave of you and you'll be taking no thing from me, less you'd like a hole through you from my dragons."

Adam didn't even blink. Not once.

"Lucas Grundy, I announce your guilt; the abduction and murder of seven innocent individuals, guilty of no crime save naively trusting you to provide carriage safely and without malice, and the simultaneous theft from their person of all then-present valuables, including a courier of mine Arthur Sibbet, and the package he carried, bound for Beadnell Beach House, in this very carriage

The fog now so thick he could not see the horse rump in front of him.

some six months ago. How do you plead?"
Astonished, the driver could only act in desperation now. He would have to shoot his passenger here, in the open, but thankfully *in* the dark, and make off with his prize. His anger rose, the gun trembling in his hand with fury alone.

"Why you…. black… dark… you are one of them… black… dark… dark magicians you... you… black-arts!"
he fired straight at Adam's chest from barely two feet away.

Inside, Johnny had informed Elizabeth of the guest waiting outside. As predicted she had set about making up the spare bed and setting up a supper. The shot woke Johnny, who had removed his boots and sat by the fire only minutes before. Elizabeth stuck her head in from the scullery and stared at him. There rang out a second shot. Johnny leapt to his feet, grabbing both boots and making for the front door. It was locked. He had come in the side way and turned now to go back out the same, worried about his friend whom he had left outside.
The smoke of the pistol shot cleared. Adam stood as he had, calmly, grimly, smiling at the coachman.

"I'll accept that as an admission of guilt. Lucas Grundy, on behalf of the blameless souls of the seven departed victims, I refuse to loose you from our agreement. You will remain my take-see driver, at my beck and call, wherever and whenever I require you. You will neither accept nor offer fare or carriage

from or to any other individual, or cause them harm, unless I decree it."
Adam reached forward into the seat box, and withdrew the paper and the satchell it had originally been held in. He pushed the driver once, gently in the chest. He fell slowly, helplessly back into his seat. Turning away from the cab Adam said

"You may wait for me to summon you, on Blaydon Island, or Kingsmeadow, as you choose." Chuckling to himself he added,

"Be aware that it may well be the last choice you ever make. Worry not about your empty reins. You will have the pull of many chargers when in my service."
He beamed a smile at the condemned coachman, and said,

"Begone!"
The coachman instinctively jerked his reins that led to no horse and the carriage jolted forward. It wheeled around in the clear space at the head of the lane and sped away into the distance, seeking the hill down to the river. Johnny came dashing up the side of the cottage, his shirt loose and his boots still in his enormous fists.

"I heard gunshot. Maybe two."
he said, looking at the receding coach.

"Nothing for such as you and I to worry over." said Adam.

"I would not have done the deed here if I were to place you or yours in peril."
They turned to walk back to the cottage.

"Consider only that a wrong has been righted."

"I meant to say," offered Johnny,

"…when we spoke before, Kingsmeadow and Blaydon Island. You know,

I am sure, that they are one and the same, Adam."

"Of course I know it Johnny Oliver. Any man who didn't would surely be taken for a tourist." laughed Adam.

"A what? A two-er wrist?"

"Tour - ist! A visitor. A guest to the region."

"Ah, a holy-day caller. I hear they have them on the coast, mainly from Whitley Bay, down as far as perhaps… Whitby."

"Ah yes Johnny, Whitby. But believe me, that is a story for another time. Another time entirely."

## Continued
Συνέχισε
synechise

Say: syn - ay - chis - ay

Continued, verb.
Continue, keep going, keep on, carry on
persist, go on. *To remain.*

# THOMAS WEDDERBURN'S HOLE

## Ice and Rock, Fire and Revenge.

Darkest Northumberland. Down a muddy path came a well-wrapped figure. Hood up and furred collar pulled forward, there was nothing of it's face visible. Only the warm breath hanging in the cold morning air gave away the fact that the garment was currently occupied. Black trouser bottoms with an outer vertical stripe up each leg and the brightest purple and white shoes completed the outfit, although there was no telling how much was also worn underneath. The sun was up on an early spring morning but the enigma descended out of reach of it's warming rays and into a frost pocket. The path skirted Thrunton Woods, weddershins, until it reached what seemed to be it's lowest point, the path ahead beginning to upturn again. The figure turned to face the hill. Behind, lay true north, directly up the hill lay true south. A gravelly lay-by had been dug into the steep slope and a rusted sign at one side, pointing up, indicated the way to 'THOMAS WEDDERBURN'S HOLE'.

The enigma began climbing. Effortlessly walking up the muddy, crumbling, scrambly path that too few others had bent through the grass and the bushes. Too upright, the traveller seemed, not needing to grab a tree root or branch where you or I might cling on anxiously, the hill having become a virtual cliff. Some sixty yards up a clearing of sorts appeared. Two huge slabs of displaced rock having evolved around each other to form a gaping hole and giving the look of a pair of thick, rocky lips. The lower of these was inscribed with a T and a sloping W next to it, like a three, reversed.

An echoing, hollow voice delivered the following mantra,
"MY FAITHER HAS SOME WINTER FRUIT THAT IN DECEMBER GREW,
MY MAITHER HAS A SILKEN GOUN THAT WAFT GUID NEVER THROUGH,
A SPARROW'S HORN YOU SOON WOULD FIND - THERE'S ONE ON EVERY CLAW,
AN TWO UPON THE GOB OF IT, AND YE SHALL FIND THEM ALL.

THE PRIEST THAT STANDS WITHOUT THE YETT, JUST READY TO COME IN,
NO MAN CAN SAY THAT HE WAS BORN, NO MAN UNLESS HE SIN,
FOR HE WAS WHOLE TOOK FROM HIS MAITHER'S SIDE AND ALL,
SO WE'LL BOTH LIE IN OUR BED, AND YE'LL LIE AT THE WALL."
A cold breeze from very far away stirred inside the hole, rustling the

grasses as it emerged. The figure dropped the heavy hooded coat, kicked off the shoes and stepped from the trousers. He was completely white. Featureless white like a hole cut through a drawing, showing the page below. His face consisted of shining, black eyes, two nostrils and a pair of dark lips, framed by a tangle of hair, similarly seeming as transparent as his skin.

The icy wind blew into his face. He strode to the hole, bent, and scrambled inside.

At a different place, not connected to the hole by distance, but by something else, footsteps appeared in flat, smooth snow at the base of a mountain. Whatever lay below and around that site, it was hidden by densely packed, slowly churning cloud tops, as far as the eye could see. There was only Mountain, and a sea of air. The white figure was lost among the drifting snowscape, detectable only by the faint motion of hair, the outline of eyes and features, and the footprints, which were quickly covered over as though the mountain wanted to erase all trace of this visitor. He walked around the base of the mountain, again weddershins, holding before him a silvered compass in a hand invisible but for black polished nails. The compass had three dials, each still, each pointing to a different direction. He walked for a long time if we may say that, as time was not the same there as we know it. Eventually one of the compass needles began to spin clockwise. In less than another pace the other began to move, weddershins. Slowly the third drifted to a heading of it's own and held steady. Following this direction, the outlined man set off up the slope.

High above, the wind screeched around the mouth of a ragged cave, on a ledge above a sloping plain, blank save for a few charred stumps, and stones as smooth-topped as glass. Our figure paused near a pair of such stumps and exhaled.

Inside, huge nostrils slowly steamed, causing drips of water to fall and run into the cave corners from stalactites as old and weathered as dragon's teeth. Lazily, a huge and ancient head tilted, sniffed at the air, lay still, then sniffed again.

Old vocal chords cracked, having almost seized solid with disuse. A rumbling cough and a blast of hot air spat out the debris from an ancient throat, and two yellowed eyes slowly slid open.

*"By my tail, my throat aches. Pardon me if I don't boil you in your skin. I haven't flamed anyone in such a long time... ah my throat diam swells. Be patient. Your roasting will come."*

With that the dragon casually raised it's head, almost to the roof of the cavern, and gazed out into the almost endless white.

*"And yet, you may provide me with a little sport. Fancy! Here of all places, an invisible man comes to play with me before I bake him in his invisible skin."*

There still being no reply, the beast rolled it's head towards the cave entrance.

*"So. How is it to end for you, hidden one? Did you come merely to look? To wonder?"*

It's body moving as slowly as a cat in treacle, it's head stole out of the shadows

*"...to admire? .... to pity?"*

As he had spoken his huge chest slowly expanded, the scales scattering light like oil on water. Now he suddenly leased a wide, flat spray of fire, completely covering every inch of the opening and out across the snow and ice.

When the flame died away and the steam of the melting snow had been whipped off by the howling wind, the cave was once again silent. The dragon crossed it's front legs, nonchalantly.

*"Well?"* it said.

"I WAS HOPING FOR A MUCH WARMER WELCOME THAN THAT." came the echoing reply.

*"Oh and you shall have one. However   it occurs to me that I have so few visitors here, I might drag this out a little. It'll   help to fill the …. Time."*

"WE COULD IN FACT DISCOVER THAT WE HAVE MUCH TO TALK ABOUT. OLD FRIENDS WE BOTH REMEMBER, FOR INSTANCE." called the echoing voice above the shrieking wind.

This was a cunning approach. It is not advised to broach a subject in conversation with a dragon. The chimera should always feel that he has initiated the conversation, and that he has manipulated it to his advantage. Assuming of course, he doesn't kill you outright as soon as smell you.

*"Old friends? What would you know of my old friends? Any of them   you are likely to have come across are also likely burned to cinder or to have   passed through my innards."*

The unblinking yellow eyes were slowly scanning the field of snow outside, looking for the tiniest movement.

"OLD FRIENDS MAY NOT BE THE CORRECT TERM. FORGIVE ME. I BELIEVE I MAY KNOW SOMEONE WHOM, THOUGH IT BE COMPLETELY BEYOND THEIR CAPABILITIES OF COURSE, ONCE WISHED YOU HARM."

*"And whom might that be? Who could reach me   here in this cold deathly no-place?"*

The dragon was sifting his words now, not admitting that he was marooned here on the ice mountain with no way down. Not wanting to confess that each second was filled with plotting his vengeance as soon as he had escaped this scale-numbing dungeon. Which, obviously, was any day now, and entirely at his own leisure. Not wanting to ask how this intruder had managed to locate him, yet he wondered if it were possible that he might know the way down if he knew the way up.

"I CAME ACROSS ONE OF A FAMILY. A FAMILY OF NAME THAT MAY DISPLEASE YOU. MAY I HAVE PERMISSION TO SPEAK THE NAME IN YOUR PRESENCE?"

Seeing the tiniest of movements in the snow, the Dragon suddenly lurched it's head forward to it's full reach, belching out a solid bar of flame, as water from a hose. The figure was silhouetted in white against fierce red fire. A white outline unmoving, in the heart of the conflagration.

When the blast subsided, the white legs of the figure could be seen on bare rock, which was still hissing and steaming and cracking into flakes.

Featureless white like a hole cut through a drawing, showing the page below.

*"And so you think yourself shielded? You imagine that there is only one way I might end you?"*

"I AM WELL AWARE THAT SUCH A FAMOUS DRAKE AS YOURSELF MUST HAVE MANY ABILITIES THAT CAN HASTEN MY DEMISE. HOWEVER, I SHIELD MYSELF ONLY TO LIVE LONG ENOUGH TO BE ALLOWED TO BRING YOU NEWS."

… echoed the outlined man, cleverly turning the situation back to the subject he wished to discuss while at the same moment flattering his host. The beast considered for a minute or so then demanded,

*"Well then, get to it!"*

"THERE IS A RUMOUR THAT, OBVIOUSLY UNTRUE OF COURSE, STATES THAT YOU ARE SOMEHOW... CONFINED TO THIS PLACE. UNABLE TO LEAVE OF YOUR OWN FREE WILL. RIDICULOUS I REALISE, BUT OFTEN TOLD AMONG MEN WHO SIMPLY HAVE NO RESPECT."

*"Incredible. Why I was just this very morning pondering an excursion."*

"OF COURSE. HOWEVER, THIS IS AN EXTREMELY DISTANT LOCALE, AND EVEN ONE SUCH AS YOURSELF WOULD FIND THAT AN EXCURSION TO ANYWHERE INTERESTING TAKES A LONG TIME AND SOME CONSIDERABLE EFFORT. NO?"

The beast considered how respectful this latest comment was, and decided that he could allow the conversation to continue, for the moment. He nodded.

"IT JUST SO HAPPENS THAT I HAVE COME BY KNOWLEDGE, PURELY BY CHANCE OF COURSE, WHICH MAY ALLOW ME TO MAKE THE JOURNEY DOWN FROM THIS DISTANT, MOUNTAIN TOP, IN A VERY SHORT TIME. I SIMPLY WONDERED IF YOU MIGHT BE INTERESTED IN MY OFFER TO SHARE THIS KNOWLEDGE? IT IS A *VERY* COLD, *VERY* DISTANT PLACE, IS IT NOT?"

Ruminating, the drake assembled the facts. This person was offering a way down from this icy prison. He could not be harmed by flame. He doubted if he would be easily vulnerable to claw or jaw. And he had been respectful.

*"Perhaps I would. In return, what favour may I bestow upon you?"*

"WHY THAT IS A VERY KIND OFFER. LET ME THINK. HMMM. SOME HUGE TASK THAT ONLY ONE SUCH AS YOURSELF MIGHT MANAGE. HMMM. I HAVE IT. THE FAMILY I MENTIONED. THEY SEEM TO BE THE CHIEF PERPETRATORS OF THE BLATANT LIES BEING TOLD ABOUT YOU. PERHAPS IT WOULD BE FITTING IF YOUR FAVOUR MIGHT INVOLVE RETRIBUTION UPON THIS FAMILY? IN THE CIRCUMSTANCES IT WOULD NEED TO BE DONE... STEALTHILY."

*"I believe we may have a deal. The terms of which are thus. I shall allow you to save me a little time and effort by revealing your way down this mountain... just in case it turns up to be a... quicker... way down from the frozen rock upon which we stand. The way I normally choose, being of course more interesting and scenic to the dragon's eye, yet I must confess that a boring route might on occasion prove useful. In return, my first task on reaching Albion will be to ease the removal from he mortal world of the required family members of the.....?"*

"OF THE ABRAXASON CLAN."
"I see. Then it is so. All that remains is for us to declare the agreement to be royal, by the sharing of our names. Agreed?"
"AGREED."
"I am known among men as Dorcanus Fouljaw."
"AND I AM KNOWN TO MY ENEMIES AS THE FRACTURED MAN."
"The deal is sealed. And skillfully wrought if I may make so. And very fortunate for you… purely by chance as it happens! However I believe your deal to be a weak bargain. The excursion I pondered this very morning? It is an excursion I have pondered many times. In fact the extermination of the Abraxason clan was the very first task I intended to undertake in any road, the very next time that I roused myself to descend the mountain.
Which, obviously, was any day now. And entirely at my own leisure."

\* \* \*

Thomas Wedderburn had, so some local legends went, been a Border Reiver, plundering farms and villages across the shifting Scottish / English border. He had somehow discovered this hidey hole, hidden well away from any approach by horseback and giving lofty views of the flat plain to the north. With a thick mass of old woods up the cliff front and behind, he considered he had the perfect bolt-hole. Unfortunately his love of a woman (from Fowberry Tower possibly) had led him to give away the secret of his sanctuary. One wet miserable night he returned from his reiving to find the hole occupied by two soldiers laying in wait. Though he killed them both by stabbing at them each time they tried to emerge, he was wounded once in the arm and bled heavily. He went to ground in the hole, having tumbled the men down the hill face. Above, the captain and three men waited till he was at ground, before surrounding the hole. Thomas Wedderburn was not of a mind to surrender and the hole was soaked in oil and he was burned to death, the cave 'mouth' seeming to belch out smoke and flames. When they subsided, he was dragged out and shot. His 'hole' can be visited near Thrunton Woods a few miles north from Rothbury. Just off what's now known as the A697, the passage was once called 'The Devil's Causeway.'

# THE CONFLUENCE ROOM AT UNTHANK HOUSE

## An impossible meeting.

Somewhere up on the darkened Northumberland moors, many miles north west of Newcastle, a hat with a blue feather flew through the trees eight feet above the forest floor. As the trees thinned it could be seen to be worn by a scruffy, scowling head. Bursting into a meadow, scattering sheep, it became clear that he drove a carriage which like himself had seen better days. A carriage that gently rose and fell regardless of the rough, untenanted Northumberland countryside. Inside sat a man dressed all in black, his grey hair beginning to turn silver and threatening one day to entirely cover his head. His carriage had seen better days, the seats now leaking horsehair and the seat backs oiled dark from too many dozing traveller's slumbering heads.

Normally such a vehicle would be drawn by a horse, but this seemed to have no obvious propulsion at all. The reins were empty. The driver, a scowling, miserable, filthy specimen gripped his end of the reins regardless, old habits too hard to break, and often cracked his whip into thin air, forcing every atom of speed from the unlikely wagon that he could. He'd long since passed the big house at Cragside, streaked through the streets of Rothbury and now over the hill to Callaly. He thrust his impossible cart into the woods at Little Ryle and out through the other side. Down the bank he surged to the house at the end of the country lane, too grand, too large to ever look at home here. Driver reining in and pulling back the wheel brake at the last moment, the carriage surfed to a halt on the gravel, jolting sideways at the last. As it came to rest, the cab door swung open and out dropped the late passenger, landing lightly. Closing the door and stretching his arms as though he had just risen from a favored armchair he raised a hand in thanks to the driver, who simply muttered under his breath. He flipped up a silver shilling, which the driver attempted to catch in his outstretched, snapping fist, and failed. The coin dropped back into the hand that issued it.

"Begone!"

stated the traveller, turning to the large paneled door. The driver flicked his reins angrily and the carriage reared round to set off away up the hill and into the forest.

No lights were visible to either horizon and only a near full moon and a handful of bright stars could be seen through the barely moving clouds. This was Unthank House. Above the door arch, there was carved into the stone a single, sharp-beaked bird. Not of prey but of carrion. A vulturine creature that had likely seen very lean times. In the darkness his hands moved quickly, never seeming to actually touch door, lock, handle or knocker until there was a loud, dry clunk. He turned the handle once and entered. The hall was pitch black. The sound of a door creaking open made his head turn to the left where a pool of warm light spread into the hall. A young, fair-haired girl was carrying a lamp and a small box. There was a full-length mirror behind her as she walked and, in the gloom, she appeared to have walked out from the glass itself.

"You're back late… " she said,

" …take a lamp. I've left the stove on in the scullery and something you can heat up to eat, in the larder."

"Thank you, that's very kind." he said,

"… I'll have it soon. You should go back to bed now, I'll see you in the morning. I'm going to the Confluence Room."

He stepped through a pile of papers at his feet and looked down puzzled.

"They arrive almost every day now."
the girl said,

"At home as well. You should look at this one."
she added, handing him an envelope.

Taking it, he picked a lamp from a hook near the door and lit it with one of the matches that poked from the box alongside.

He made his way through a large central hall, to a corridor of several doors, entering the last. He placed the lamp in the centre of the table therein while he used the matches to light wall-lamps, then placed the first lamp on the floor near the door. The room had no windows or other doors. It contained only a single battered chair and a truly ancient, round, wooden table on which were three mirrors. One truly antique, no more than polished metal, one in a neat wooden frame, the third seemed to hover above it's base.

He placed his hands on the table, and lowered his head, breathing slowly, calmly. After some minutes there appeared to be more light in the room than there should have been. He raised his head, turned to the mirror on his right and said

"Hello Adam."

This mirror was lit by the face of a young man with jet-black hair, who could have been his son.

"Hello Adam." came back the reply.

In a second or two the centre glass lit up slightly and the face of another man appeared. His hair was brushed back at top and sides with patches of silver white hair above his ears. Apart from that he could well have been his father or brother. Once again he exchanged greetings with the reflected face. They waited in quiet for almost a minute, before the last mirror lit up weakly. Here was shown the face of a very old man, skin as thin as poppy petals, gray hair whispy and shoulder-length, but with the sharpest eyes you could imagine.

"Hello Adam." he said again.

"Hello Adam." again came the reply.

"I Adam Abraxason invoke a confluence from Unthank House."

In deference to age, the eldest was allowed to speak first. The man sat at the table held the floor and directed the meeting, indicating who should speak next. All three apparitions told of situations they were involved in, as though they were speaking of someone else, a friend perhaps, leaving out carefully any references to particular persons' names and dates and times. Each of the others offered suggestions or asked pertinent questions. Occasionally one of the mirrors would dim, as though something secret had to be held back from one of those others at the meeting, as if something was about to be revealed that could not be allowed to be seen or heard.

The youngest of the gathering, the first face to appear in the glasses, spoke last.

"I have a situation developing that may need some attention." he said.

"My sister is spending a lot of time with a young man name of James Hill. It appears she is utterly infatuated with him. I have not mentioned this before. However I believe now that this is actually turning into a permanent passion."

The eldest spoke.

"And is this man good? Does he reciprocate the devotion?"

"Indeed he does. It has been necessary to 'hint' at the solitary and hazardous nature of our family business. He has declared that they are to be together, regardless. Further, he has told me to either give my approval graciously, or to never visit them again."

"Then you can see that they must be together?" asked the elder.

"Of course, Adam."     replied the youngest.
"My concern is how to proceed. What levels of protection and disinterest I should invoke."

"I believe none are necessary. Surely she can more than protect and shield them herself? Should a child ensue from the union then that is a different matter. A sleeping guardian-familiar or two, a deadman's alarm perhaps? An iron circle?"

The seated Adam added,

"Perhaps a distress trigger hidden in the Eddys? Quarterpage could help."

"Yes all of this eventually."     spoke the old man.

"For now, they will of course be relocating?     Somewhere north perhaps?"

Adam hesitated before offering,

"I have already begun looking...."

The elder cautioned him,

"This seems to be becoming a trend Adam. Caution wherever possible."

This seemed to be the last word on the subject. All fell silent. Adam then indicated that the meeting was over. The eldest face faded from sight, followed by the next oldest and then the younger. Adam sat for a moment or two, breathing deeply, head lowered. Abruptly he rose from the chair and proceeded to blow out the wall-lamps. He looked around the room, which now did not seem to have a door. He bent to pick up the lamp he had placed on the floor. When he stood again, lifting the lamp in front of him, the door was there, as it had been when he entered. Leaving the Confluence Room, he made his way out of the corridor and across the hall to another door. Once inside he sat on a chair between a bed and the desk which held only a flat sheet of glass, and where he placed the lamp. He sat silently, reflecting on the day's events. Hearing a rustle, he retrieved the envelope from his pocket and saw that, unlike the others which had arrived, it was addressed to him.

"Curious. Who could know where a magician lives?"

After a few minutes there was a flickering light visible under the door from the hall. And a low buzzing.

"Ah," he said, "At last."

Then he reached forward and down behind the desk and flicked two switches. There was a low buzzing and the glass screen on the table started to glow.

"So then. Adam Adamant or Dad's Army?

… as if something was about to be revealed…

# PROLOGUE

## THE MADE-UP DAY

In a house on Ellison Villas on Mount Pleasant in Deckham, Gateshead, James Hill and his son Tom were sneaking around downstairs. It was a Saturday morning in August 1955. Upstairs, Harmony Hill (nee Nightingale) was pretending to be asleep. Not easy considering the racket the two downstairs were making as they tiptoed around, quietly (they thought) preparing a surprise Birthday breakfast for her.

James was handling the boiled eggs, boiling the kettle and adding the tealeaves to the teapot. Tom being only seven, had buttered the bread, laid out the tray and put another two slices under the grill
to toast. The leaky kitchen roof plink-plinked into various assorted pans, cups and old tin cans that were scattered around the floor. James had turned around to face the table with three teacups in his hands, just washed in the sink, and kicked over two of the old tins. Water splashed everywhere and one of the tins bounced through the doorway and across the living room floor.
He turned to Tom and hissed

"Shhhhh!"

They both stifled laughs.
Tom carefully picked up the tins and put cloths down to soak up the spills.

"I'll get Aggy and Hermes Dad."

he whispered, and removed the cloth over the birds' cage.
Aggy and Hermes (Agamemnon - a red-chested, male Bullfinch ; Pyrrhula Pyrrhula, and Hermes - a brown and yellow female Linnet Carduelis Cannabina) began the loudest morning celebration song ever heard in Gateshead. James and Tom both turned to each other to hiss in unison

"Shhhhhh!"

before this time erupting into laughs they failed to stifle.

"You'll wake her."

whispered Dad, before sniffing, turning slowly around in the kitchen and shouting,

"The toast!"

He then grabbed the smoking grill pan and dumped it onto the sink-bench, wafting the blackened slices with a tea-towel.

Tom took a seat at the table to finish wrapping up his Mam's presents and grimaced as he put down the scissors, realizing that he had made a lovely job of cutting the wrapping paper... *and* the corner off the tablecloth. His Dad James, meanwhile, was making a surprisingly loud job of scraping the toast from black to patchy brown and white. Both unfortunately had their hands full when the kettle began to whistle.

Upstairs, Harmony had buried her head under the eiderdown to enjoy a good giggle. She was hoping she would be able to pretend to wake up at the right moment, *and* keep a straight face. Eventually, she heard the clinking noise, that cups, saucers and spoons make on a tray no matter how carefully you carry them, coming up the stairs. She closed her eyes and acted for England.

To the west, in Cumberland, soldiers were pouring thick concrete deep into the pits of the soft earth. Much further west, on an island, more sinister foundations were being built upon.

To the east, in the North Sea, un-seasonal winds swirled and began to gather storm clouds fifty miles off the coast. Inside them lurked something equally as concrete as that which was being planned in Cumbria, and as fantastic and dreadful as the events on the island.

Having eaten her 'toast' and under-done egg and having drank luke-warm tea, smiled and said 'mmmm, lovely.', Harmony was opening her presents and wondering how long it might take her to tidy up the aftermath of her surprise breakfast. Her presents at least, were thoughtfully presented. Tom and Dad having made an effort over the last
month to watch out for anything that she may have looked at in a shop window or talked about having seen in a newspaper. New shoes from Shepherds, black, brushed suede effect *and* in her right size five: a much-wished-for book, Catcher In The Rye, to add to her small bookshelf; Fats Domino's forty-five, 'Ain't That A Shame'; and a brush and comb set with marble effect handles.
"Dad helped me pick it,"         said Tom of this last gift,
"There was a one with a looking glass *as well*, but we decided that this one was best."
"Tom, James, I love it, and my other presents."
she said, combing out her long, dark hair.
"I'll finish my tea and read five or six pages, *while* I enjoy my lie-in"
"And then, after I've had a look at the paper," said Dad,
"…we'll take a walk down to the park. They say it's going to be a glorious weekend."

About an hour later they left for the park, bread for the ducks and Dandelion leaves for the rabbits, wrapped up in newspaper, in a bag Dad carried along with sandwiches and a bottle of Lemonade. As they locked the front door, a tiny, thin, blonde girl and her Mam were passing the front garden, the girl singing
"… lived by the sea, and frolicked in the morning mist, in a land called Honalee…"
They were returning from the shopping parade known locally as The Front and carrying two shopping bags.
"Oh that reminds me."  said Harmony,
"Can we call into Dummler's on the front, and order a joint for tomorrow? We can pick it up on the way back. That way they won't be sold out when we return and we don't have to carry it around with us."
At the Front, Dad called into the papershop and came out a few minutes

later with a comic (rolled up in a magazine, rolled up in a sheet of brown paper) as a treat for them when they sat on the grass in the park. While he did this, Tom's Mam popped into the Butcher's.

"I'll not be a minute Tom. Do me a favour and nip next door to the Baker's. Ask for half a dozen white buns, and a stottie."

Being a truly glorious day, the park was packed. The park had tall, metal fences all around the outside, with five gates set into them. As the locals said, 'One for each point of the compass.' One lap of the park always had to include the bird and rabbit cages. It seemed everyone had arrived fully equipped to feed the already-stuffed rabbits and the never-full hens and peacocks, before they looked for a good spot to rest. Tom noticed a black rabbit that he hadn't seen before. Pure black without even a trace of white in it's coat or eyes. Noticed because it just kept eating. Kept eating *everything* that the visitors could push through the bars.

They managed to find enough room to sit on the top of the green with a view of the swings, slides and lake. Tom could see a steady stream of people through the 'top gates' at the end of Avenue Road. Down by the lake, dozens of Dads showed dozens of kids how to fish with nets on poles. The string-handled jam-jars remaining mostly empty. Before the lake, a mass of kids were churning the paddle-pool into a tempest, finding fun in the play-storm. There were always at least twenty waiting in line for a turn on the banana slide, the shuggy-boats and the teapot. Behind Saltwell Towers, the rabbits and peacocks in the enclosures continued to be fed all afternoon, whether they liked it or not. Dozens of family groups circled the lake, leaning over the metal rails to feed the ducks and swans. The boats on the lake had a twenty minute queue and there was hardly room for another blanket to be spread out on the green. Tom wondered if they would see Franky the Fireman, the park's resident tramp, limping around the pathways. His dad pointed out that he was rarely seen when the park was full like this. He thought that he couldn't stand to be around kids and families. From where he sat, the lake looked like a huge, horizontal mirror, showing back the sky and the island in the centre where the swans nested. Sometimes Tom would lie with his back to the lake and roll his head back so that he was looking at it upside down. He tried to imagine climbing onto the reflection of the island which was, in this position, the right way up.

As they sat together, Tom's Mam again began to thank them both for a lovely Birthday.

"I'm absolutely made up boys, I really am."

"Well not bad for a totally made up day." said Tom, who then abruptly clammed up, wondering if maybe he'd said the wrong thing.

"It's alright son, Mam understands what you mean. and she did pick it herself. Didn't you?" said Dad.

"It's fine Tom, really." she insisted.

"I grew up in an orphanage, because nobody knew where I came from. So, obviously nobody knows when my Birthday really is. That's why I could make one up. Who else picks their own birthday? And who could have picked a

4.5.56  Thomas Hill                                   SHIPCOTE SCHOOL

$9 \times 1 = 9$   The rule of nines.

$9 \times 2 = 18$   $1+8=9$

$9 \times 3 = 27$   $2+7=9$

$9 \times 4 = 36$   $3+6=9$

$9 \times 5 = 45$   $4+5=9$

$9 \times 6 = 54$   $5+4=9$

$9 \times 7 = 63$   $6+3=9$

$9 \times 8 = 72$   $7+2=9$

$9 \times 9 = 81$   $8+1=9$

The reflecting eights.

| 9 | $1 \times 8 + 0 = 8$ |  |
|---|---|---|
| 9 | $2 \times 8 + 1 = 17$ | $1+7=8$ |
| 9 | $3 \times 8 + 2 = 26$ | $2+6=8$ |
| 9 | $4 \times 8 + 3 = 35$ | $3+5=8$ |
| 9 | $5 \times 8 + 4 = 44$ | $4+4=8$ |
| 9 | $6 \times 8 + 5 = 53$ | $5+3=8$ |
| 9 | $7 \times 8 + 6 = 62$ | $6+2=8$ |
| 9 | $8 \times 8 + 7 = 71$ | $7+1=8$ |
| 9 | $9 \times 8 + 8 = 80$ | $8+0=8$ |

Lives of a cat.    The mirrored eights.

Thomas, your number work is excellent but where have you found these tables? You were not asked to copy any of this down. I certainly do not have time to check any of these so I can not mark them as correct or incorrect.
                              Mrs McCluskey.

A page from Tom's Mathematics Jotter.

better day, eh? Or anywhere better to spend it than Saltwell Park with my two favourite boys?"

She looked around the packed field.

"And even though I'm your step-mum, I couldn't have had a cleverer little lad if I had the pick of everybody here, which is just about everybody in town it seems, …..so…."

And here Tom's dad joined in what was obviously a family ritual,

"… that makes you, the-best-little-boy-in-Gateshead!"

'Not long now.' he thought. 'When I'm ten. Surely when I'm ten they'll stop doing that'.

Tom lay back on the blanket and stared straight up into the bright, blue, lunchtime sky, and dug his hands into the grass. He was hanging on. He often had the feeling that he was about to float right up into the air and spin off into space. He remembered a headline from one of last week's newspapers,

'USSR PLAN SPACE BASE AT ZARYA' and wondered if any one was already up there. He imagined gigantic, booming rockets blasting into space. His vivid imagination allowing him to feel like he was part of the scene, looking up as the rocket trail split the sky in two, the long, sleek craft bearing the Russian insignia and the code ZA 865.

There was a low rumble in the distance.

Tom sat up and looked around. On the horizon, huge dark clouds were piling up. He hadn't noticed them, or their reflection, when he had been looking at the lake just a minute ago. In the paddle-pool, someone had obviously taken a glass of juice or a bottle of something into the water. Having dropped it, it was proving difficult to find and it looked like someone had stood on it. The light blue bottom of the pool darkened purple as though a cloud of blood from someone's cut foot was sweeping through the water in the currents of the departing children. A mirror image of the sky above. All around people began packing bags and slipping on shoes, ready to beat a quick retreat. Having a twenty minute, uphill walk back home to face, Mam and Dad decided they also should be on their way. Tom had had two hours sun and that was really enough for one day, they thought.

Their timing wasn't bad at all. The first spits of rain came on as they turned the corner from Split Crow Road into Ellison Villas. The same little blonde girl they had passed as they went out, was sitting on her doorstep looking down the length of Ellison Villas, watching as they came along the path, her voice carrying along the too-quiet street.

"Don't know why, there's no sun up in the sky…. Stormy Weather…"

'She always seems to be around' thought Tom, 'but I've never asked her name'. In fact, he concluded, 'I've never been able to even talk to her.'. Just as they stepped through the garden gate, there was a loud split of thunder that rattled all the windows in the street.

As they hurried into the living room, they could see that Aggy and Hermes were agitated. Tom decided to cover them for a while and move them away from the window, which didn't quiet them at all, while his Mam quickly placed out pans and tins on the Kitchen floor, ready for the downpour.

Dad switched on the radio, and just caught the chorus of Les Baxter's 'Wake The Town And Tell The People'.

"Well, haven't heard that on the radio for ages. Still that's us home earlier than expected."
said his Dad.

"Oh and guess what?" shouted Mam from the kitchen.

"We forgot to pick up that joint!"

The afternoon seemed to close in around them. Gathering storm clouds were reported on the radio as wreaking havoc around the region: various lightning strikes had hit power stations and floods were cutting off many of the main roads through Gateshead and Newcastle. The radio presenter joked that everywhere else was enjoying fine weather and that the north east seemed to be a place to avoid today. Shortly after a few minutes of The Goon Show episode 'The Policy', the radio itself ceased to broadcast, words and music replaced only by hissing and swirling static.

James and Harmony made the decision together. He would wrap up and go to the phone box near the Shakespeare pub. He would ring and tell their friends Jean and Ken, and Dorothy and Tommy and of course the Tates and the Rowell's, not to call around that night as planned. They could have a celebratory drink next weekend instead. As he left, high above, yellowed, ageing eyes watched him from behind cloud cover. The clouds swirled around above him as though he were trapped
inside a giant walnut whip.

When James came home some twenty minutes later, he was panting and very cold, and looked awful. Handing Harmony a newspaper package he told his tale,

"I got through to them all, lucky they have the phone in really. When I came out of the phone box, at the last minute I had a thought that I was already more than halfway to the front. That's your joint, by the way, wrapped up. I had to knock at Dummler's to get him to open up, he'd shut for the day. So anyway, I waited for a drop in the wind and rain. When I left the phone box I turned right to the Front, not left to come back round here. I had only taken two steps when the wind whipped up from nowhere. The rain was stinging my eyes and I could barely keep them open at all."

"Let me stoke this fire up love." said Harmony,

"James, go get your dad a towel."
James continued as soon as he could see that Tom was out of the room.

"Thing is Harmony, I heard something behind me, a horrible cracking and a thud, even over the rain. When I had a look, a tree had crashed down not four yards away. The box was flattened, overhead wires were ripped down…. If I'd turned left to come straight back home and not gone for the joint…."

They stared at each other, not knowing what to say, and then knowing what to do, and collapsed into a hug. Tom came back just then, with a towel. The birds were chirping loudly away, Aggy and Hermes seeming determined to get out of their cage. Tom's Mam said,

"I'll close the curtains, wish we had storm shutters like we had in France. I think we're in for the night."

Tom's Dad looked puzzled,

"I didn't know you'd ever been to France."

"Mmm? What? France? No I haven't. what makes you ask?"

He didn't get a chance to reply as the front door boomed like a giant had knocked.

"What the hell?" he cried.

When they had tried to open the door and found it jammed in it's frame, they went to the front window to have a look outside.

"Look at that!" shouted James.

"The garden wall's blown over onto the front path. It must have buckled the door."

"It'll have to wait James, you're not working out there tonight."

The wind continued to shriek at the doors and windows, and moaned a warning down the chimney. They were beginning to feel like prisoners. Mam stepped into the almost unusable kitchen which had a larger collection of drip-catchers than ever before, and returned with a cardboard box. Just in time as it worked out. It was barely 5pm on an August afternoon when the electricity cut out, and the room was plunged into semi-gloom. Harmony reached into the box and produced candles,
saucers and matches.

"Start lighting those." she said.

"Tonight we dine by candlelight. As a special Birthday treat from me to you two."

For the rest of that made-up day, the three of them made their own entertainment. Paper-ball Olympics, sock-grenade battles, I-Spy, shadow shapes on the living room wall and toast done over the fire with butter and jam. They were all determined to cheer each other up, none of them really sure that it was only the storm that was on their minds.

Tom spent an hour on the rug by the fire, reading his old stack of Beezers, Toppers and Hotspurs, keeping his DCs back for later, should the electric come back on before bed-time.

The Numbskulls in the Beezer were trying to keep their *man* occupied while he was stuck inside with a cold. He'd read this comic a dozen times and couldn't remember this story. The brain's numbskull had sent a message to the throat numbskulls, telling them to push an umbrella through his nose to clear the man's snots. Tom laughed. Why would a throat numbskull have an umbrella?

By the time that nine o'clock came around, they were all feeling the wear of a hectic day and more or less went off to bed at the same time, hot-water-bottles in hand, thanks to James' ingenious plan of resting a pan of water in the embers of a dying fire. Tom was allowed to bed down in the guest room at the front of the house, to be nearer Mam and Dad, and all were soundly asleep before ten.

In the churning cloud above, something old and sly beat it's ancient wings, searching memory, trying to reach just the right pulse. Lightning reached down, through the descending mist, flooding the back garden with a blink of blue light, as bright as that afternoon had been, and shattered the back kitchen door. The family were all asleep in the front two bedrooms upstairs. They didn't wake. Had they, their only easy way out was through that very back door. Directly above, thick, heavy clouds were spiraling apart as enormous, thick, leathery wings snared the air.

Two specks of amber light peered through the darkness. The clouds were lit incandescently by a sudden, orange glow. Clouds became steam and a clear channel opened. Claws of dirty, yellow ivory tucked beneath a belly of dense, scaley armour as thick as dinosaur hide. A belly that had seen much fuller times and longed for a feast. Into the gap surged the fire-beast. With one enormous slap cracking the damp air, it tucked it's wings to it's sides and dipped it's long, bony, smouldering snout towards earth. Dorcanus (a black-and -green-backed male Fire Drake: Dracus Canus Rex), swooped down through the skies of his ancestral hunting grounds, glad to be back.

Far below, the wind whistled through the blasted, smoking, back doorway, into the living room, slamming the door to the stairs. Agamemnon thumped into the doors of the cage, Hermes hanging onto a safe perch behind. Eventually the cover slid off as the cage was buffeted by the draughts. Through the window, the garden was lit by a dramatic burst of orange light from above. The caged birds cast enlarged shadows up the walls and along ceiling. Shadows that none of the family would have recognized.

Shadows that didn't belong to little birds. Dorcanus belched a fireball every few seconds, lighting his way down through the storm. Ancient eyes narrowed, focusing in on the Street, house, the garden, the blasted door. He thrust out a wing which instantly snapped into shape, clutching at the air and sweeping him sideways. Old routines took over. Not for nothing was he once called 'the sly flame', among many other things. He circled once and then once the other way, and thought, *'Their homes are now more solid, yet they leave themselves defenceless. This will be an easy feast. Long-awaited, but poor sport.'*

On the ground, Aggy had wrenched himself free of the cage and was frantically circling the room. The cage door had snapped shut behind him and Hermes was unable to follow. The back garden was yet again lit, this time there was heat as well, and it was getting closer.

Only yards above the garden, Dorcanus hefted both wings above his head and reared up, landing with a thump on the gravel and flowers. He stepped forward into the tiny yard, and down from the raised-garden. His thick, heavy tail

crumbled down some of the bricks of the raised-garden wall, just by grazing along it. He saw no defences. He would force his way through the shattered back door, likely taking the some of the walls with him. Once inside he would feast. He took a clawing step forward.
Something flashed at him and fell back. He looked from side to side, puzzled.
Again something pinged off his long snout and fell back. He had to make an effort to focus his old eyes, to peer into the space immediately before him. A tiny red bird was hovering in the doorway.
He began to lumber his creaking shoulders forward. The bird again dashed at him. This was folly.
Why didn't it cower, hide, fly away? No matter, he had a meal waiting inside for him, with starters and pudding, and enders.

     Loyal, plucky, absolutely hopelessly outgunned, Aggy retreated to the doorway. Yet again he swooped at the beast, this time sticking his pin-sized beak into the oily yellow gristle of it's left eye. Dorcanus, flicked his head, grumbled, and spat a liquid trickle of fire that completely engulfed tiny Aggy. He span, burning, to the gravel.
Dorcanus ignored him, the tiniest morsel, not worth stooping for, instead peering into the back bedroom windows, seeing them unoccupied, he then crouched to crane his neck and head level with the living room window.
Inside, he saw that another bird fluttered, this one, by fortune, locked up, *'not wanting to make a pointless sacrifice for the beings who had caged it.'* he thought. He sniffed. Something else was in the soaking air. He sniffed again. Some tiny trace of some old scent. Some old scent from long ago that maybe he should remember. Some survival instinct took over. He stepped cautiously back.
Danger?      Here?      How could there be?
Through the constant splatter of the downpour, he strained his eyes and ears, his nose and tongue, his throat diam. He clawed the gravel, raking through memories. Something stirred at his feet.
The bird?    The sacrifice?

     Slowly he followed the trail of smoke to the puttering squirming shape before his claws. It shifted in the flames it fought against, struggled to break through the guttering flames and out of it's own ashes.
Dorcanus reacted automatically, casually through lack of any pity, belching another, bigger, hotter ball of fire. When it cleared, the bird was staggering to it's feet. Craning neck up, stretching wings far too big for it's puny body, unfurling fabulous new feathers.
Some ancient, genetic fear took hold, and before he could stop himself, Dorcanus had spewed a huge ball of flame that lit up all the surrounding houses and trees. Realising instantly his stupid mistake, he staggered back trying vainly to take to the sky in the tiny enclosure. There wasn't room to fully extend and flap his wings. He tried and succeeded only in bringing down the Kitchen walls, and trapping his tail in the broken bricks and stones.

     Thunder boomed dully all around. Aggamemnon rose in front of him, stretching, growing, swelling.

Barring the broken doorway, now standing almost eye to eye with the monster. Becoming stronger from the flames.

Dorcanus reeled. A trap! A concealed fire-bird! A damned Phoenix!

He was too old for an aerial battle against a Phoenix. He could not flee nor could he drown it in conflagration.

He must take it now here, on the earth, in the cursed wet and the mud. He slashed horizontally with his right front claws, vertically with his front left, rearing high on back legs to tear diagonally down with both. The fire-bird was too quick, too young or too new-borne. It darted between the killing talons that raked the air. Leaping aloft it arched back it's head and itself became a swirling blur of fresh, razor-sharp claws, ripping at the Fire-Drake's head. Old, thick, dark, green blood spurted down the beasts' chest. It gave out a terrifying roar of pain that had not been heard for centuries.

The blood spattered shattered stones and broken brick, sparking them into flame as it did to virtually all it touched. A split and ruptured gas pipe burst into life, lighting up the yard and garden, giving an unreal, blue tinge to the red and white roses and both of the fabulous, warring creatures. The scene was a strobe-lit theatre of battle, furious slashing movements too quick for most human eyes to have followed. The surrounding curtains of walls and trees lit by light red, then yellow, then green. Dorcanus made a last mighty effort, his old battle nous returning, and he charged forward, butting Aggamemnon into the remnants of the kitchen, scattering pots, pans and crockery.

Agamemnon's powerful, hooked beak tore a hole in Dorcanus' neck. Steaming blood and fire-vapour sprayed what was left of the benches, rotting them. He staggered back into the yard.

So this was it?

This was the battle he did not win?      Here, among the rain and the mud and the men?

He could *not* win, he was too weak. Throat Diam separated from the noxious oils and breath of his chest. His opponent was unlikely to show '*... what was the word?... stupidity? ... madness? ....*

*no .... mercy?* '

That was it.     He could not win.      However he did not have to lose.

With the last of his strength he lurched sideways and leapt, clawing his way up the building to the rooftop, and he screamed,

"*FRACCCCTURRRRE! CURSE YOOOUUUU!*"

in a voice as old as mountains. There he leapt again into the air, arced back over himself and plunged down. At the same moment Aggamemnon leapt upward at him. With a hideous screetch and an agonized howl the two met high above the garden. They tumbled over one another, Fouljaw's fangs biting deep into wing, fabulous feathers flurrying out like brown-gold leaves in autumn. Aggamemnon himself piercing claws into the exposed neck and waiting for the moment... waiting... waiting... until he could thrust his beak into the drake's exposed

Diam.
Foul, dying breath, flammable blood spraying the air and roaring gas-pipe.

There was a blinding, white explosion of heat and light.

Then silence.

After the steam cleared, melting into the swirling mist sucked into the vacuum left by the rising heat, the yard was empty. Lit only by the still burning gas pipe.

There was no sign of Aggamemnon or Dorcanus.

Throughout the night, the rain slowly subsided, the clouds gradually drifting off to sea.
At the top of the street, only one little blonde girl at a window, unable to sleep, had any idea that something had happened. Muffled booms and howls, a furious blazing lighting up the thick gloom like a seascape by Turner. She assumed it had been a dream and went to bed.

Lights started coming on in the neighbouring houses.

The family had been awoken in the early hours by a man clutching an umbrella who lived in the street behind. James himself had smothered the flames of the leaking pipe, capped the end, and checked for further leaks. The phone box obviously not working, he had then walked down to the police station in Swinburne Street to ask for help.

In the morning, a hot August sun slowly steamed away the rain from the pavements and roads.
A week later work began on rebuilding the kitchen extension. 'A gas explosion' the Gas Board insurers said. No-one was able to explain the missing bricks in the back wall. Some of the burnt flowers returned by themselves, in time, as is the way with nature. Some had to be replaced. Thereafter, the roses never flourished in that garden, which was bountiful with Magnolias, Rhododendrons and acid-loving Blueberries. Most peculiar of all, Aggy was missing, yet Hermes was found, cold but still safe, in the cage. With the door firmly shut.

## AVATAR
είδωλο

Say; av - a - tar
Noun.
a manifestation of a deity or released soul in bodily form on earth; an incarnate divine teacher.

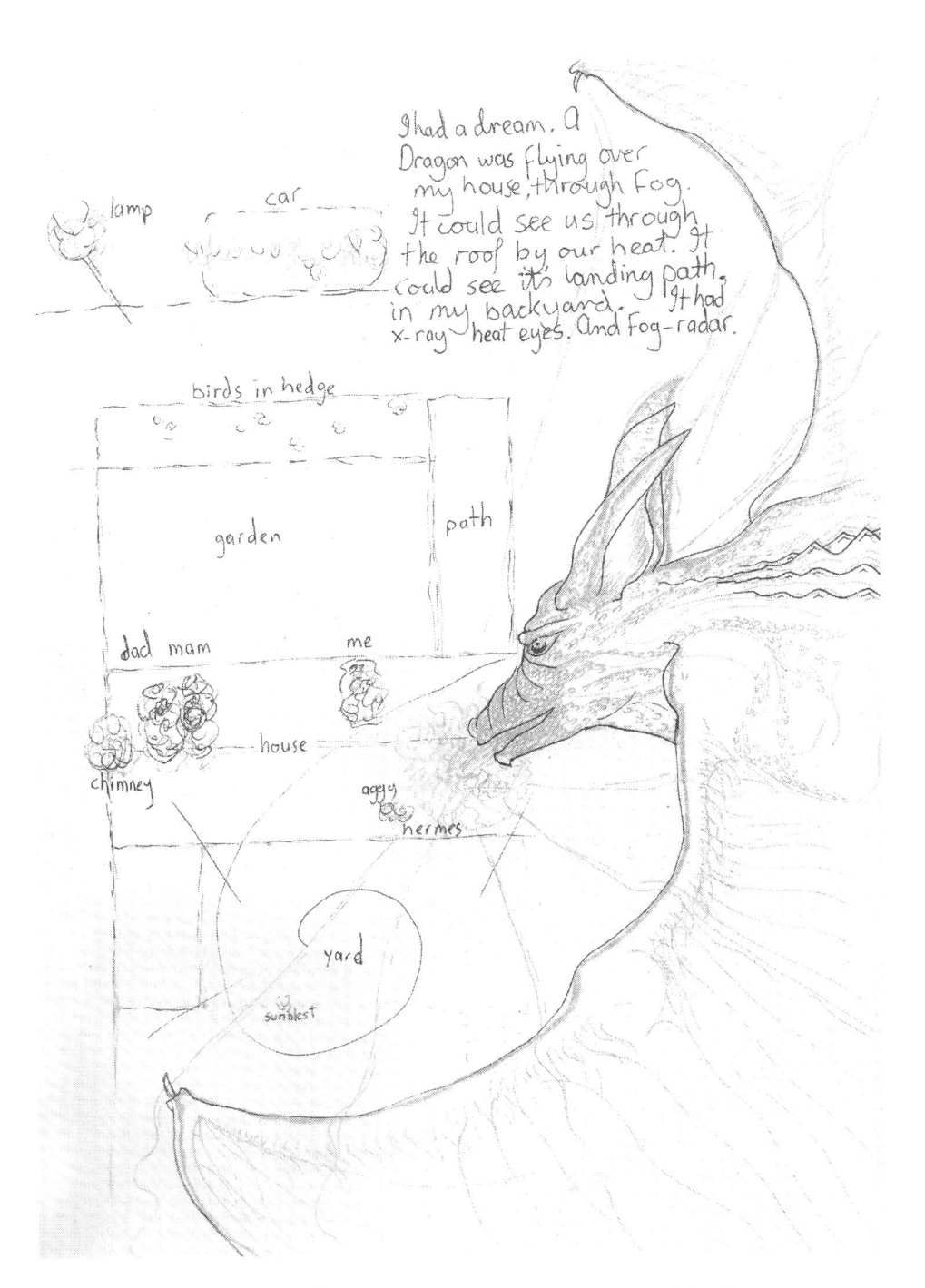

*I had a dream. A Dragon was flying over my house, through fog. It could see us through the roof by our heat. It could see its landing path, in my backyard. It had x-ray heat eyes. And fog-radar.*

After Tom had a fever, aged seven, he remembered this dream.

## ACT ONE

## THE BOY

### BOY
Αγόρι

Say; A - gor - ee.
noun
a male child or young man.
synonyms: lad, schoolboy, male child, youth, young man, laddie, stripling, *sunny-boy.*

# CHAPTER ONE

## OUT OF BOUNDS

**We meet a young man without a mirror, who is scared of his own reflection.**

## Wednesday, 9th May, 1956.

I'm Thomas Hill. I'm seven, well eight on the twelfth of May, 1956 which is this Saturday. I go to Shipcote School. Yesterday, Tuesday, at school, it happened again. I was asked to take a note to Mr Fleetwood's office. The Assembly Hall is out-of-bounds while the workmen put in a new inter-whatever-it-is, so I had to cut through the Reception Hall, what with the Dining Hall being used for gym between eleven and twelve. Dad had said not to, *ever,* because of the mirror, but I had to take the note. Unless I climbed out of the classroom window, ran along the yard and climbed the drainpipe to his office, Mr Fleetwood, the Head, wouldn't get the note. And if he didn't get the note, he'd come stomping down the lines, next morning Assembly, in the Dining, shouting my name which he knew well by now, his feet going Tap-CLOMP Tap-CLOMP Tap-CLOMP.
He has a false leg from the war see, which is why the upper-schoolers call him Mr Fleetwoodenleg, although I heard Kevin say that someone he knew lived next door to Nurse Bramble and she said that his leg is only wood from the knee up.

So I was nervous to start with, what with having the note to take and on top of that I had to get past *the mirror.* It's massive. Right in the middle of Reception, nearly up to the ceiling and wider than.... a settee! Thick frame as wide as my hand, with a carved wooden eagle on top that has eyes that follow you around the Reception as though you were a rabbit it was eyeing for breakfast.
We haven't any mirrors at home and I don't really know what to do with them, but I couldn't help having a look. Even after what happened *Yesterday.* See, first morning the workmen were in we had to march into here from the class-lines in the yard and wait to enter the Dining for Assembly. On the way to school I had stopped to look in Batty's window on the Front to see if any new DC's were in. There weren't but I spotted a new Marvel Character whom I thought was called The Mighty Thor.
I knew he was the God of Thunder and thought I might try some Marvels myself one day. Well I got to school and got to school late. So I was standing in Reception at the back of 'the lates' waiting to go into Assembly and I didn't notice that the line had moved and gone in. I hadn't noticed I was staring at the mirror. What I saw reflected wasn't the Reception.

The mirror showed me something else. A tall man in black clothes. He had grey in his hair and was standing in a room that… didn't look like any room
Dad had said not to, *ever,* because of the mirror, but I had to take the note.
in the school. It was dark but seemed to have lots of mirrors and shelves and

The mirror showed me something else.

stacks and piles of odd stuff that completely filled it up. Mostly stuff I didn't recognise but some that I sort of did. Like a motorcycle helmet on the shelf behind him. Except it was all silvery and had a piece of black glass where the goggles should be. Who could see out of black glass? And on a desk in front of him was a stick wrapped in heather or leaves or something.

He was talking and I heard some of what he said. I think it was,

"… and so, all she could do was *think* his name, never *say* it. This of course made her think it all the time, and she went quite mad."

In the middle of this he glanced up for a second as though he had seen me, but then carried on. I'm sure he was talking to two cats although one of them might have been a fox. Then I heard the Head's voice growl in my ear

" Hill, what are you doing out here boy?"

That's when I realized that the line had gone in and left me standing there. So that's how the Head came to march me into Assembly and up onto the stage, where he made me stand by the piano while he paced up and down  Tap-CLOMP   Tap-CLOMP   Tap-CLOMP.

He turned to look at me from the far side of the stage, hands on hips, with all the teachers sat between us.

" <u>MISS - ES     AT - KIN - SON</u>!  I believe this boy is one of yours?"

Misses A just nodded nervously.

"Well then it appears that we now have to start a new line - for the lates that are too late even for the late-line.    That line will be here - in front of this very piano. <u>MISS - ESS STUD - MAN'S  PIANO</u>!"

I didn't turn round but I knew that Mrs Studman was glaring at me, like she would have when she peered at the enemy through the slit in her tank during the war.

"And the very first of the later-than-the-lates is our very own Thomas Hill, from Mrs Atkinson's."

I looked down at the assembled school. I didn't have many allies there. Only Kevin and maybe Barbara, but at that moment it seemed like I had the sympathy of them all.

"Mrs Atkinson, he shall carry your notes to my office  -  for a month!"

Every kid in school gasped. Something heavy hit the floor and I wouldn't have been surprised to find out it was someone fainting. Maybe even one of the teachers. I looked at the shocked faces of my classmates and the *astonished* faces of the uppers. I felt my face reddening as silence descended on assembly and all eyes turned from the Head to me. Feeling uncomfortably hot, I took a deep breath, pushed my bottom lip out and blew cooling air up over my face, making my fringe flick up in salute. The entire school burst into laughter. And so, there I was on this morning, Wednesday, carrying notes to the Head's office and trying to

get past the mirror, again. Without looking directly at it I could tell that it reflected the Reception, as it was supposed to, so I chanced a quick look.

Me.             Just me.             In Reception.

That mirror's lies had got me into so much trouble and now here it was, telling the truth but with no one around to see it.

I stared at my mirrored eyes.    For too long.    I didn't like the way it made me feel.  I didn't know who I was looking at.
Suddenly, the Reception in the mirror started to shake. Oddly, my reflection didn't. It stood still.

There was a muffled bump and again it shook. This time I felt vibrations under my feet as well. I had a terrible feeling of not being able to move although I wanted to desperately. I wanted to run but my legs were as heavy as tree trunks. Somewhere there was a growling noise. I tried to shout for help but my voice wouldn't work. There was a loud boom and the mirror shook for a third time. I looked up at the eagle, trembling back and forward like it was preparing to launch out and down at me. Looking up made me dizzy but I was sure that the mirror was coming away from the wall. I saw a black arm reach out from behind me and I was swept up and out of sight of my reflection. The boom faded. The arm belonged to a man in a tatty black suit with grey hair. He looked at me for several seconds.  I turned away as I heard the Secretary's door opening. Mrs Archer came out and almost walked into me.

"What on earth! Thomas Hill what the goodness are you up to?"

"Nothing Miss. I'm taking a note to Mr Fleetwood Miss."
She glared for a moment.

"Well get on with it then, it won't take itself. I think I may have to have words with your parents"
she said and looked around the hall.

There was only me and Mrs Archer there.

I'm Thomas Hill.        I'm seven, well eight on the twelfth of May, 1956, which is this Saturday.

I go to Shipcote School.

I'm frightened.

# CHAPTER TWO

## THE EMPTY SHOP

**Thomas sees something in an empty shop but, thankfully, hears nothing under a full moon.**

## Thursday, 10th May, 1956

    Last night I told Dad what had happened, that I might be getting reported, apart from the bit about the man in black and the mirror. Dad always said I was to stay away from mirrors. Next day he kept me off school and went out to 'see someone'. I stayed home with Mam. Well not my *Mam,* but *my* Mam. She's called Harmony and was a Nightingale before she married Dad, James Hill, and became Harmony Nightingale Hill. My first Mam was called Venus Abraxason Hill, but she died. Her pictures were very beautiful. My Mam is also very beautiful with long shiny black hair. I don't know how she takes care of it as we don't have any mirrors at home, not even a little one in Hermes' cage. Or how Dad shaves.
    'We're getting one this summer,' he keeps saying. Each time he cuts his chin.
    'Honestly?'
Mam always says, laughing,
    'Some women complain about their cookers or want fancy holidays. I'd just like a mirror!'
    'I know,'   he says,   '…but I've told you about that. Go to your Hairdresser's.'
    And usually it's fine, and sometimes they might have a row, but not for long. About the time I get sick of it, like magic, they pack it in and make up. Mam had to go to the shops so we walked down to the Front. She said to put my hood up in case anyone saw me. If anyone did, I was to say I had cold. I felt very silly as the sky was clear and blue and the sun shining. On the way we passed the Black gates that lead up the hill to the Witche's house. On the Front we went to the Fruit Shop for a banana and the Baker's for buns.
    We passed the papershop on the way which was sometimes worth a look for comics, although they never had as good as Batty's and laid the comics on the counter instead of stood up in a proper rack. I sneaked a peak at the counter. They had Marvelman. First time I'd seen him in ages and I felt so happy but wasn't sure why. The Miller Studio comicswere… odd. The cover colours were gentler, the insides were black and white and very cartoony and they were slightly smaller. If I was in there with Mam or Dad I would get right up close to really see the colours and smell the inks. Marvelman had a magic word - KIMOTA - which turned little Mike Moran into Marvelman. At the Saturday morning pictures for kids at the Ritz, I had seen a serial where Captain Marvel did the same but his word was SHAZAM. Somehow I just knew that, one day, they would make a

film serial of Marvelman as well. I wondered if I would have a word one day and what it might be. Did
you just make them up? Or did you have to keep guessing until you found exactly the right word?

That would mean *everybody* had a secret word.

The papershop had a stand outside that had the day's headlines on it behind a wire mesh, to tempt people to buy newspapers I suppose. As we approached I saw that the headline was ATOMIC STATION TO OPEN. Mam walked past to go the Bakers so, hoping for a better look at the pile of comics on the counter, I glanced into the shop as we passed. The doorway was blocked by a man in dark clothes so I couldn't see. However as I looked away, the window showed me the headline board, back to front. I had to look again. The board read CIMOTA NOITATS OT NEPO. CIMOTA? It was almost like the word. The WORD that Marvelman said. I wondered if there really could be magic in the world, just maybe you could only find it in reflections, or by looking at things differently. I was so fascinated by this that I didn't really hear what Mam said just then, but when I looked around she had gone into the Bakers, so I stood in the doorway.

Mam met someone in the Baker's so she started talking. The Baker shouted to me,
"Hey Hilly! You off school again?"
I hadn't been off for ages and didn't know what to say. I didn't want to lie to him about the cold so I wandered outside, pretending I couldn't hear him. The next shop was empty and then there was Dummler's the Butchers. Not just empty. All dark inside so I could see myself in the window, like in a mirror. I saw a black dog cross the road behind me. It was huge. There are always dogs hanging around because of the Butcher's so I wasn't concerned. Everyone knows Links, the stray. He steals sausages when the Butcher's not looking and gets chased. It'd be better to feed him and keep him as a guard dog and a pet. He gets called links because links are sausages I think, although I call him Patch because of the brown spots on his white skin.

He wasn't around and I noticed the black dog reflected behind me again. He was watching me and I got the feeling he was big enough to sit on. Just then Mam came out the Baker's and so I didn't turn around to look at the dog.
"Why didn't you come in?"    she asked.    "Dick was calling you. Did you not hear him?
He only wanted to give you a jelly diamond off the ice cakes."
I'm sure she knew I was embarrassed so she let it go at that and gave me a cuddle.
"I'll not be a minute in the Butcher's."    she said,    "Stay here. I'll get ham and pease pudding for the buns for dinner."
I was back in front of the empty shop again, trying to remember what it had been when it was full. I couldn't. All I could remember was that the

Butcher's was next to the Baker's. I couldn't remember any shop between them. Stepping closer, I peered through the dusty panes looking for clues. Empty bags or shelves or a counter or a sign.  Nothing.  I saw the big dog's reflection again, in the street behind me.  It *was* huge!

Big enough to sit on I thought, but then abruptly stopped myself. I had imagined sitting on it, and it riding away with me clinging on to it's back for dear life. Running so fast I couldn't get off or breathe or even shout for help. I dared to look into it's reflected eyes and I felt ill, just like when I looked into my eyes in the school mirror, but worse.

Lots worse. It stared, never blinking, daring me to look away or turn and face it for real. It began to cross the road. Padding toward me, each enormous paw thudding into the ground. Just then the light was somehow different for a second, like the sun blinking. Within seconds there was a boom and the window before me shook violently. Almost at once the pavement was covered in large dark spots as big as Patch's. They joined up like a jigsaw as the rain began hammering down. The thunder boomed again, the window rattled and it came down like bats and frogs. I turned to see the dog stomping towards me and our eyes met. I thought, 'If it comes right up to me I'll jump on it's back and it'll get me out of the rain.'

Then it stopped and looked down. The rain had made a river flow down the gutter, no more than six inches wide, but the dog seemed unsure what to do next. It lifted a powerful paw but was somehow not able to step across.

At that second Mam popped her head out of the Butcher's doorway and shouted for me to get in out of the rain. I was drenched. They both looked at me like they couldn't believe how wet I was, like the rain was somehow my fault. The Butcher said,

"Best stay in here for a few minutes, let it blow over."
He walked to the window.

"Don't understand it. It was a lovely spring morning not minutes ago."
"The dog'll get wet."   I said.
"What dog? Links? Well he can get wet, he's not welcome in here."
"No the other one, the black one."   I replied.

They both went to the doorway and looked up and down. There was no black dog.

By the time we walked back home up Split Crow Road, the sky was clear and warm again. As we got to the front door, Dad was coming up the street from his meeting at the school. In a few minutes we were sat down at the old kitchen table having our buns, and Dad began his tale.

"Mrs Archer apologized for shouting at you, first off. Also told me you were in the reception hall. Apparently the noise in the Reception Hall was from the builders hammering on the walls in the Assembly Hall. That must have shook the mirror. I also spoke to a Mr Courtney, the building firm boss. Canny fellow. Dresses a bit odd for a builder, wears an old black suit, even on site. He'd just come from another job so his hair was covered in dust - plaster or cement. Makes him look older than he is. Apparently he picked you up as he thought you were in

the way, and then went straight next door to see to the builders."
Dad looked at me for a few seconds.
"You never mentioned him."
"I just forgot Dad."
Mam and Dad shared a look and Dad said quietly to her,
"No, it wasn't him."
Then he looked at me, very serious but calm and deliberate.
"Look Tom, keep away from that mirror, like I've told you to.
*And* tell us if you see anyone dressed in black, OK? NOT Mr Courtney but anyone like him. Black suit, black hair maybe a little grayer by now. Alright?"

I said OK and didn't intend to lie to him. He should have been in a real bad mood, what with having to take the morning off, but he was just being concerned. I didn't mention the other man I'd seen in the mirror that first time, although Man told him about the Black dog and the drenching we took at the shops. I also didn't tell him them that I was carrying notes for another three weeks. Not saying something isn't the same as deliberately telling a lie. It was my birthday soon and I didn't want to be in trouble so I just promised myself that I'd be careful. In fact I was surprised that it hadn't been mentioned to Dad when he went down to the school. If they had told him, surely he'd have asked me about it. I hoped the builders would be finished soon and I wouldn't have to cut through the Reception any more.

Dad didn't go to work that afternoon. He sent me out in to the back garden while he and Mam had a talk. I sat on the steps to the upper flower garden so I could see in through the window. They were very serious with each other but not angry. After a while he put his coat on and put his cap in his pocket at Mam's insistence. He looked very serious as he kissed us goodbye and said he was going to 'see a man about a dog' which I think means something else but I'm not sure. When he had gone, Mam bolted the door and said that we were in for the day. It was fine. We listened to the radio, Mam joined in drawing with me and after tea I went off to bed with a handful of comics. I read my favorites strips first which is to say Kelly's Eye, The Steel Claw, Robot Archie and The Spider, then Alf Tupper The Tough of the Track, and The Q-Bikes, and left the funny stories for last when I wouldn't have to concentrate so hard. Kelly's Eye was a diamond that Kelly wore around his neck and it protected him. As good as a magic word, in fact you didn't have to say it, it just worked. I wondered if my word was something like 'diamond'. But slightly different like CIMOTA was with atomic. DONAMID or DIMANDI. NO,... DIAM ... ?
Or SHAXAM? Or MAZASH?

I also wondered why The Spider, Claw or Archie didn't have words. Or maybe they had already said them once? That's probably why I dreamed about visiting them. I arm-wrestled Lewis Crandall - The Steel Claw, and had tea and cakes with Robot Archie. Then I went to school and The Spider was the Head! Late that night I was woken up by a noise in the living room. Or maybe it was *that* old clock. No, Mam and Dad were arguing, downstairs. Dad must have gotten back really late. It was just after Midnight. From where I lay I could see a

dozen bright stars and the moon in the sky. I guessed it would be full in a day or two. The passage light came on and I heard steps. Dad looked in and whispered,
"Tom, you awake?"
I pretended I was just waking up and hadn't heard the argument.
"Sorry it's so late." he said
"I just got back. Been to see a friend who knows about dogs. Got some advice, just in case that black dog comes back, what with you telling Mam it was big and all."
He spoke slowly and calmly.
"Just,… I'll be out at work when you get up for school so……. what to do right, with big dogs. Some big dogs, don't like water right?"
He paused here for a few seconds to look at a battered, faded piece of paper he was holding, then continued.
"And you know how dogs chase sticks? Well if you can get a dog to chase a stick and it can't get back to you, because you cross a stream or a pond or something … well then, you'll be safe. Specially if it's a stick with something on it right? Something smelly that dogs can't resist."
"Alright Dad," I said "But where will I get a stick from?"
He rummaged in his pocket.
"I got this from a friend." he said "Put this in your coat pocket for school."
And he dropped onto the bed a stick. A stick covered in leaves or something.
As I snuggled back into bed the door closed and the landing light went off. The bed spread was lit by blue-white moonlight. The candlewick pattern became hedges and the panes like fields and hills.
The dog-stick like a huge fallen tree. It reminded me of the tree that had smashed the telephone box last year. I could smell the leaves wrapped around it.
Why couldn't I just have a word instead?
"LIGHTNING." I whispered. "THUNDER."
Nothing happened.

Everything was quiet.

I hoped I wouldn't hear a dog barking outside.


## LAELAPS
### Λαῖλαψ

Say; Lay - laps
Noun; Storm-wind, squall.
Myth; a dog (usually female) so swift it always caught it's prey.

Padding toward me, each enormous paw thudding into the ground.

# CHAPTER THREE

## THE PERFECT DAY

**Big lads, a girl, birds, rabbits and a mouse all make friends with Tom.**

**Thursday, the tenth of May, 1956.**

I had another dream, but this one wasn't very nice at all. I sometimes dream that I can fly and this dream started out like that one, but this time I could barely get off the ground. I couldn't concentrate enough to fly up or to fly very fast. And I needed to as there was something I couldn't quite see but I knew I had to get away from.

In the end I sank into the ground like the path was quicksand. I was very relieved to wake up a little early. I walked around the bedroom, touching my things, comics, soldiers, pencils. Even the oldclock. Just to make sure they were real and I wasn't still dreaming. I stood at the window to look out into the back garden. It was looking like a sunny day again and the birds were in the trees waiting for breadcrumbs and breakfast leftovers. I always leave something even just a little bit of
toast crust. Sometimes there's a little mouse called Sunblest who dashes out of a hole at the bottom of the wall of the raised flower garden, but he wasn't there today.

I could hear Mam downstairs in the kitchen making tea and toast. I decided to get myself ready and go downstairs without being called for. I would much rather have stayed under the warm covers, but if I dropped off there was always the chance that the dream might come again. My third option, and I felt this as a strong urge, was to sneak out and run away, but I didn't know why or what exactly I would be running away from. In fact I could run straight into it without knowing and make things worse. I decided to go down to see Mam because it seemed the least selfish of the three.

She was in the new, back kitchen. The old one that always seemed to have a leak somewhere, even when it wasn't raining, had been rebuilt after the gas explosion (When we also lost Aggy, friend of our other canary, Hermes). So I couldn't hear the plink-plink of dripping water anywhere. I noticed that the steam from the kettle, teapot and eggs in the pan had steamed up all the windows. I sat quietly at the table, careful not to squeak the chair legs across the floor so I could sit and watch her for a moment.

She always made cooking seem like magic, how everything came together, all ready at the same time. A few seconds later she leaned out of the door and shouted

"Tom!"

I jumped in surprise.

"Oh there you are. I didn't realise you were up. Sleep alright?"

"Yes thanks Mam."

I didn't want to talk about the bad dream. I never did. Just like I never talked about the clock either. In my room there was an old mantle clock on my chest of drawers. It had been my Gran's or Granddad's or something, and it had never worked. I used to open the back door, which had a little brass plate with the maker's name, AXIOM on the inside, and keep my 'passport card' and my little cars and soldiers in it. My 'passport card' was given to me by a little girl. She had bought a packet of cards at the papershop. A packet of footballer cards with a piece of flat, dry chewing gum in it. She looked through the cards as I was walking up to Batty's Toy Shop, and she was saying ' Got. Got. Got. Haven't, Haven't. Got. Got. Got.'. Then she sort of screwed up her face, looked at me, and said 'Here.'. She gave me a card and walked away.

A little flat, oblong card with a silver picture on it and a word I didn't know.
When I got back home and dad came in from work I asked him what that word on the card meantand he said 'passport'.

I also have a favourite soldier called little Tommy. Not named after Me or Dad's friend 'uncle' Tommy but because English soldiers used to be called Tommy. I sometimes hear kids in the street playing war games like 'Japanese and English'.

When they call to each other they always shout things like 'Help! I'm wounded Tommy!'.
Sometimes the reply comes back, 'Try to make it back to base Jim.' indicating that there is also an American in the game. Little Tommy is different to the other toy soldiers. They are all the same green colour, but he is painted all colours and doesn't have a surfboard to stand on for a base. I imagine he's cleverer than the rest because he doesn't seem to be holding any weapons and must use his brains instead. I don't really use them for fighting games. My favourite three are Tommy, Jim and Hiro. If I'm thinking about something important I usually find myself talking to them.
One day I had decided to fix the clock and took it to bits.

The cogs were easy to figure out but it was still too hard to fix. I put it back together as best I could but I knew it wouldn't work as there was *something* missing, I just couldn't say what. However, if I was awake at night it sometimes started ticking by itself. It only lasted half a minute and then ended in five chimes. One night it woke me up and the curtains were open. I didn't know if I was still dreaming or not. The sky seemed inside out, like a negative of a photo when you hold it up to the light. The stars and the sky were the wrong colour, and they were moving. It was my breath in the air that made me realise that it was snowing. The flakes were whirling past a light outside. They seemed to be alive, darting and dashing into the spotlight and back out again. A change in the wind would send them all jumping to the side and then back again. I tried to pick one and follow it but it always looped around once too often and was lost in the shoal. For a while I stared at the light instead. I stared until my eyes were fooled. They started to tell me that I wasn't tucked up in bed, but flying through space, stars whirling around me, too many to count and never stopping. It was like being hypnotized. I mean in both ways. It did get me off to sleep but before that, it was also like being asleep *while* I was awake. Somehow I always knew that the chimes happened around midnight. I didn't know what to say about it and nobody ever asked 'Does that old broken clock in your room still start ticking in the middle of the night?'

Dad had an old watch that someone had given him that also didn't work. It was constantly set at six o' clock. He told me it had stopped the second the owner had died and it never worked again.
How tidy to die at exactly six. I hope he had his tea first.

Mam placed my boiled egg and toast on the table and I tucked in, the egg soft and yellow, white hard, still hot and with a little hill of salt. Mam sat really close and cut up my toast into soldiers. She took a tiny, burnt piece of the crust and placed it in between the bars for Hermes, who trilled in delight.
"Only two days to your birthday Tom."
"I know Mam, I can't wait. Will Kenny and Alex come around?"
Kenny and Alex were two boys from Cromwell Street who sometimes knocked to see if I was playing out.
"Yes I'm sure they will. Is there anything particular you'd like as a present?"
"Well a comic from Batty's, maybe Superman or Flash or some pencils or paints."

I left some crusts so I had something to put out for the birds. Sunblest was there and he stood up on his back legs and looked at me. I threw a special crust into the corner just for him and he dashed after it and out of sight. I stood at the back door as the birds came hopping along the garden path towards the crumbs.

I realized I was stretching the morning out and hoped that Mam would say 'Oh look it's gone nine o'clock. Too late for you to go to school, you'd better just stop off now.'

This was such a normal, happy part of the day. Nights could be scary and lately school was getting to be strange, but here was always safe. I think Mam knew what I was thinking because she said,
"Come on, I'll walk you as far as the school gates. Let's go a couple of minutes early. We can look in Batty's and you can tell me which comics are best for a little boy's birthday."
She gave me a paper bag with biscuits in for milk-time. As I put it in my pocket I remembered the stick Dad had given me and I dashed upstairs to get it.

Batty's was open and there was a new title - Challengers Of The Unknown - which I pointed out to Mam in the revolving rack, and also a Rip Hunter - Time Master, which you hardly ever got to see, just in case Superman or Flash were sold out at present-buying time. Batty's was the best shop in Gateshead even better than the big store, Shepherds, which was so big *it had it's own money,* special coins you could only spend at Shepherds. Batty's had cars and bikes hanging from the ceiling and in the top corners airplanes hung ready to zoom around, as they probably did at night when the shop was closed and the blinds might be down. It also had a *very top* shelf. This was where toys were put that parents were putting away for Christmas. You could see quite clearly that the shelf was filling up as the year went on, but no-one had any idea if any of the toys were being kept for them or not. Even the counter was special. Most shops had a counter where the shop-keeper stood, and where goods were wrapped up. Batty's had a glass counter which was full of model cars, soldiers, and farm animals.

The counter was sealed, obviously to prevent all the animals getting out at night. There were also some displays. A train set on a table top and a farm on another. Surprisingly the display was full of mistakes, very unusual for Battys. There was a train Station without a name sign and someone had mixed together different brands of toys so that standing at the station was the farmer's big black dog which was exactly that. Too big. It towered over the cows! I wondered if maybe it was meant to be a horse, but decided that it would be much better if the makers just got together and made all their toys proper sizes. You can't play with a set where the chickens are bigger than the farmer.

Mam kissed me at the gates and I walked slowly into the yard.

Barbara from my class asked me to play Montekitty, which is a girl's game like Two-Baller, so I said 'no thank you' but I watched anyway and she explained the rules. I saw the uppers were watching me from the top yard and I thought they would start laughing at me for being with the girls. However when they saw me looking they waved and called my name. I waved back to an excited cheer from them.

It was the best I'd felt in my life.

Later, Mrs Atkinson read the test results and I was best in class at both tables and sums.

At milk-break I swapped biscuits with Barbara. She liked my custard creams and I pretended to like her ginger nuts.

At dinner-time we had steak and kidney, mash and carrots and gravy followed by Eve Pudding and custard. Beautiful.

After dinner, in the yard, the uppers' ball came over the fence into our yard. The uppers wouldn't let anyone else get it and called for me to kick it back into their yard.

Third lesson was hard work, but mainly writing and drawing about dinosaurs. Maurice Mitchener was the best drawer in class and I saw him looking over my shoulder to see how I was shading in my Brontosaurus. I wondered if really he was just the best copier in the class.

At afternoon break, I spotted a man in black at the fence, but it could have been anyone's dad so I wasn't bothered.

In last lesson I was allowed to chose the book for the story. This drew a couple of groans but they turned to cheers when I went to the bookshelf and picked Aesop's Fables.

Dad met me at the gates, which he only ever normally did on a Friday,

In my room there was an old mantle clock on my chest of drawers.

and only then if he could finish on time. I could see in his haversack that there was a bag from Batty's. Mam had tea ready for us - bacon and eggs, beans and buttered bread with banana and custard. Mam and Dad had cups of tea but I was allowed Villa lemonade.

    Afterwards, instead of turning on the radio, Dad and I walked to Saltwell Park, fed the rabbits, and had a slow walk back. Dad had been scribbling in an old paperback for a day or two, and he decided to show me what he had made. He held the book towards me, gripping the spine in his left hand and bending the pages back in his right.

    "Look in the bottom corner.    Ready?" he asked.

    I nodded and he started fanning the pages at me. He had made stickman drawings in the bottom corners. Each one changed slightly and when they were flicked at just the right speed the stickman came to life. I watched as he took off the top-hat he was wearing and pulled a rabbit from it. The rabbit jumped down, the man jumped into the hat, the rabbit picked the hat up and put it on. Then he hopped off the edge of the page. Dad said it was called a flicker-book and I called it my very own little cartoon. It reminded me of the time when Dad had taken me to The Tatler, in Newcastle, which showed nothing but cartoons all day long. By the time I had had a bath and lay down in bed I was ready for sleep. The moon was low in the sky which still had a touch of blue around the horizon, as though the edges of the day weren't quite painted out. Altogether I felt I had had the best day I could have hoped for, and my birthday was still to come the day after tomorrow. I slipped into a warm, happy sleep with not a care in the world.

Of course I didn't know that next day I wouldn't be here anymore.

# CHAPTER FOUR

## STRANGE DAYS INDEED

**Something hatches. Tom beats a bully without a single punch, and makes the Head laugh.**

**Friday, the eleventh of May, 1956. Time, 7.22 am.**

I must have slept soundly. For the first time I can remember in ages I was awake to hear the front door clash as Dad went out for work. I leapt from the bed and ran to the front passage window. Dad was just closing the gate as I waved. He waved back, a big smile on his face. Standing in the doorway of the Mount Pleasant Club halfway down Cromwell Street was a man in a black suit. I looked sideways to see Dad disappear around the corner to Split Crow Road and when I looked back the man was nowhere in sight, the doorway empty.

My breath had misted up the window so I rubbed it clean with a squeak. There was a voice behind me.

"Tom, come away from the window."
It was Mam.
"Go back to bed it's too early."

Reluctantly, I went back to bed. Mam, however stayed at the window. I was tucked back up under the covers when I heard her close the passage window curtains. The bed was still warm. So warm I wondered if someone had been in it while I was out. Sometimes I just like to lay and think. I wonder if I'm supposed to do something special. If that's why I'm here. But mainly I wonder how long I have to wait to find out what it is that I'm supposed to do. And how I'll know. I thought about other people and how most of them just seem to… I don't know… just seem to *do* things. I mean, they just seem to *act*. To know how to live. Sometimes I think I'm the only person in the world who thinks about things, and everyone else just seems to do things but not think about them first.  I thought about the man. I only saw him for a second but he seemed…. tired. Or perhaps just worn out. Clothes torn and ragged and worn out. And the way he was standing, like he was hurt maybe.

I dozed back to sleep but awoke with a start.  Mam's voice! She had shouted from the kitchen. No, not shouted. Screamed or cried.
I was downstairs in seconds.

She wasn't hurt thank goodness, or anything like that. She was just sitting at the kitchen table laughing, but laughing in that way some people do when they are scared or shocked. Hermes was singing a rising, dipping song, like he had a lot to say. She had her hands cupped together.

"Come and see." she said,  "The eggs. I was going to do breakfast. They must have been near the hot water pipes and the boiler.  In that basket on the table. I usually cover them up with a tea-towel.  Look!"

As I edged forward she opened her hands a little.
"It's a chick!"   we both said together.
"I'm the one it saw first when it hatched, at least when I lifted the tea-towel. It thinks I'm it's Mam."

Lovely as it was, despite it's lack of yellow fluffiness, and it's faintly red, raggy feathers, I wish she hadn't said that. For a second I felt like I was being replaced. Like there was something special about this chick. Like Mam might love it more than me, or instead of.

Eggs were off the menu that morning, obviously, so I just had toast. I was so preoccupied with the chick that I ate all my toast and forgot about leaving any crusts. I did look out of the back door but there was no sign of Sunblest. It took me a while to work out what it was *but* something was different. It was the sky…. the light…. the wrong *kind* of brightness.        And it was quiet.

No birds. I could hear no traffic or voices or footsteps or shouts.

Mam had made a nest with a tea-towel and was trying to feed the chick with bread and milk. Grabbing my coat I said goodbye and left for school.

In the yard there was a big crowd waiting for me. They rushed forward to surround me, all jabbering like starlings but no-one saying anything. Pushing through came a lad from the next year up, face as red as a tomato. I think he was called Ronny Thompson. He had the previous longest record for note-carrying. A week.
"Right then Tom, I'll fight you tonight after school."
And then he stomped off. The gathered crowd gasped.
"What if I want to fight you now?"           I said,
"Or next week?"         "What if I don't want to fight you at all?"
Not believing their ears the crowd fell ominously silent.
He turned back towards me, his red face paling slightly.
"What do you mean?"
"Well for starters, why are we fighting?"
"To see who's the best!"
"Well then, I challenge you to a test of tables."
The kids that were out of reach of him laughed. The ones within reach hid their smiles behind their hands.
"That's not a fight! - that's stupid!"
he spluttered, not liking how this was going.
"No it's not."       I said.      "It's clever."
Everyone laughed, whether in or out of reach. His red face returned.
"I'm bigger than you so I say it's a fight!"
"Right then I'm littler than you so I say it's now."
His redness faded, to be replaced by an expression that showed nothing but bafflement.
"Now?                       I can't. I'll get sent home."

Another big laugh ran around the gathering.

"Well then," I continued,

"So a fight is out. And I'm younger than you so you should know more than me. So. It's a test of tables. What's three nines?"

"Easy." he shouted, "Twenty seven!"

"What's eight nines?" I asked him in a hurry.

"Erm….fifty six! No, erm…. Aye, fifty six."

Even some of the bottom years giggled. How could he not know the rule about the nines?

"How many ounces in a pound? Hundredweights in a ton? Yards in a mile?

Pounds in a stone?

Quarts in a gallon?"

He was lost. I quickly finished him off.

"How many bananas in a flock?"

Our audience now must have been everyone in the yard. They all laughed. He was completely flustered. Ominously his fingers slowly curled up into fists and he gritted his teeth. A booming voice stopped everything dead.

"Ronald *Geoffrey* Thompson, seventy two Woodbine Terrace! Go home tonight and learn your tables. There will be no fight today."

The boy walked off looking both embarrassed *and* disappointed. The crowd, cheated of it's treat drifted away. When they had cleared, there was just me and, a few yards away, Barbara and Kevin.

"That was just stupid Tom, getting him more mad." Barbara said.

"Was that a teacher who shouted?" I asked.

"No, just someone's Dad I think. He was over by the fence with a black coat on but he's gone now."

She stomped off, looking over her shoulder to shout,

"*I'm* not being late!"

Kevin at least looked relieved that I had escaped a thumping.

"That was great Tom." he said.

"How do you do things like that?"

"Like what?" I said.

"Well come on," he replied,

"You're always doing that sort of thing. It's like you know what people are thinking sometimes."

Kevin's a good friend. He's not in my class because the teachers think he's not clever, but he's good at what's important. He's good at being a friend and being reliable.

"Well all I know is that I had to do something or else I was going to get walloped. And I wasn't going to spend all day worrying about it."

I went off to my class with Mrs Atkinson and he went off to Bagley's.

At milk-break Barbara sat at another table and ignored me. I'd forgotten my biscuits so I had to ask the teacher for a class biscuit. Now they'd be saying I was poor. I'd probably be getting free dinners with a pink ticket next.

Dinner was liver and onions, followed by rice with the jam already in. Disgusting.

After dinner, in the yard the man in black appeared at the fence. I was determined I was not going to be afraid of him and so I walked straight up to him and said,
"Thank you for stopping the fight."
He seemed in pain and was muttering,
"….should've known….should've been ready…..worse than bloody Darlington… Look, everything's going to be alright. Don't worry. You did get that message from your Dad?"
I nodded, thinking he meant the stick.
"Good. I have to go now, but I'll come back.   I'm your uncle Adam. Hello."
He turned to stagger across the street clutching one arm to his side. There was an excited babble building up in the playground behind me. My friend Kevin tugged on my coat sleeve.
"Tom, do you know who that is?"       he asked.
"No, exactly the opposite."
"Anyroad, we've to go in straight away. The teachers say there's a mad dog in the yards somewhere, so it's indoor play."
I walked off with him but turned to look through the railings.    The man was gone.

Across the street two men were delivering a large mirror to a house. I had to look twice because at first glance I couldn't tell which way it was facing. It seemed to be showing a huge stone wall and there were flames and smoke. I thought I knew the brickwork of the wall. When I looked the second time the men had turned the mirror so it was only showing blue sky.

As we crossed the yard together I heard a rumble of distant thunder and wondered how far that sound could carry. There wasn't a cloud in the sky.

Assembly was cancelled. The Head wanted less people moving about I suppose, so registers were taken in our rooms, just like at afternoon starts. Mrs A seemed in a good mood, but she was smiling too much and too long, like she was really worried about something. She asked me to go to the Head's office to get a note. The Reception was very quiet. I could hear my footsteps crystal clear on the polished, wooden floor. And the reflected sounds of those steps, coming back to me from the walls.
They echoed after me, a split second apart from my own.
They seemed too loud, so I walked more slowly, taking soft gentle steps.
I stopped completely.
I could hear other steps. Padding along behind me.
Something big, something heavy, trying to keep close to me.    They stopped.
Nothing now but my breathing. With an enormous effort I held my breath.

I could *still* hear the breathing.     Faster than mine.     Panting. Like a ….dog?

I hoped that was a draught I could feel on the back of my neck.

    I looked around the Hall, but just with my eyes, without moving my head. It *seemed* like there was no-one there but me. I stepped forward slowly. Twenty steps to the Secretary's office another five to the Head's. I took them one by one, pausing between each, taking far too long, the whole world far too quiet, and at each step I doubted I would take another.
Eventually I was within three steps of the Head's office door, and dared to turn back to the Reception behind me.

Empty.

    What was I worried about? My imagination, that's all. However as I turned back to the office door, Something in the mirror stopped me. I saw a strange black shape, with a gleaming, coal black eye.
    Looking across my shoulder to where it should be, I exhaled with a sigh of relief. I was spooked by the reflection of a coat left by on a chair by the front door. Found in the yard probably what with everyone dashing in early. Nothing more than one of the upper's goal-posts.
Suddenly the Head's door swung open and he barked at me,
    "Hill boy! Where have you been?"
He stared down at me and I tried to not show how scared I had been just seconds before. He paused, took a good long look at me and said,
    "Come in come in then, no time for loitering!"
I didn't ever get invited inside. No-one got invited inside unless… they were in *real* trouble.
    The room was all dark wood and smelt of cigars…. or something rich like oil or leather. There was a tall bookshelf packed with shiny, leather bound volumes, many of them with gold lettering written sideways down the spine. From the ceiling there hung three aeroplanes. Another, half assembled, sat on his desk. He saw me looking around and seemed to relax.
    "Ah, spotted the models have we? Well? What do you think?"
What I thought was 'I wonder who would win? These models or the display in Batty's?'
    "Lovely sir, are they yours?"
    "Of course! You think the caretaker sneaks in here at night and plays war-games? You imagine he stands on this very desk, reaches up and stages a dog-fight?"

He laughed.     I laughed.     For the first time all day.
    "That's better boy, just what we need. Whole school seems to be wound

up around something. Anyway, this'll cheer them up, take it to all classes. The note *was* to say to all classes that the builders are finished and we shall have Assembly as normal on Monday.
However it now *also* says that what with this dog loose in the yards I'm cancelling afternoon break. Meaning… all afternoon lessons are also cancelled to be replaced by drawing, quiet reading and board games. Well? Here's your note. Get on with it."

He sat back on the corner of the desk and scratched at his shin.

His shin! I couldn't help staring. So it was true. His leg was wooden from the knee up!

But…. how could it be?

He saw my puzzled look. He leaned back and chuckled.
"Ah, the leg? No it isn't wooden. Up *or* down from the knee. But yes, it is from the war. Fighter pilot you see. Got into a dog-fight over the French coast. Pan-caked down in the channel. Can't bend the knee."
He stopped as though considering whether he had said too much, or possibly if he should say any more. Then, resting his hands on the desk, he seemed to have decided.
"Your first day here. Had a chat with your Dad. Fine fellow. I take it everything's fine at home? All tickety-boo?"
Tickety-boo sounded good so I nodded.
"Good. Good. This note carrying business. I daresay it's made you a little more… popular?"
I nodded again.
"Well," he continued, "…what better way to keep an eye on you than have you pop along to my office every day, eh?"
I smiled. He was looking out for me. He was looking out for me and had cleverly managed to have the whole school look out for me, while fooling them that I was in trouble, and *not* a teacher's pet.
"And by the time this intercom is finished, you won't have been carrying notes long at all anyway. Certainly not as long as I announced to the assembly. Well get along with that note then, and… let's see more of that smile eh?"
I left the office and the rich smells behind and stepped into the quiet of the Reception. A strange day. Everything so good and fun yesterday, everything going so wrong today. But now, well, we had a fun afternoon to enjoy, *and* everyone would see *me* taking the good news note around all the classes.
Bright sunlight lit the floor of the Reception, lighting up the hall with reflected oranges andyellow-browns from the polished wooden floor. There was only my skipping footsteps and the faint, muffled bangs of….
I stopped. As still as a waxwork. Something was wrong. Another bang.

The sun faded and the Reception became colder. This time the bang was a boom that rattled the mirror. I looked slowly sideways at it. The builders were finished. How could there be any banging?

A louder boom and the whole mirror shivered. Daring to look I saw that again I seemed to be standing still in the centre of it while everything else swam back and forth. I was feeling dizzy like that time I had the fever. Something caught my eye. The coat by the door.     It moved.
It grew, like it was standing up by itself. Two buttons formed eyes and a third became a wet, black nose. The pitch black silhouette expanded and I heard big dry lungs sucking in air. To my left the mirror bounced with the third loud boom. In front of me a huge black dog snarled in anger and padded towards me.

There was a creak as the mirror top tipped slowly forward, away from the wall. I was about to get crushed by twenty feet of wood and glass *or* eaten by an enormous dog *or* both!
There was a groaning creak, a loud snapping, and the mirror lurched out. It's top leaning high over me, eagle grinning as it stared down. It dropped towards me, a voice from somewhere cried

"NOW!"

and the dog sprang at me, hurtling through the air as the mirror crashed down on top of me.

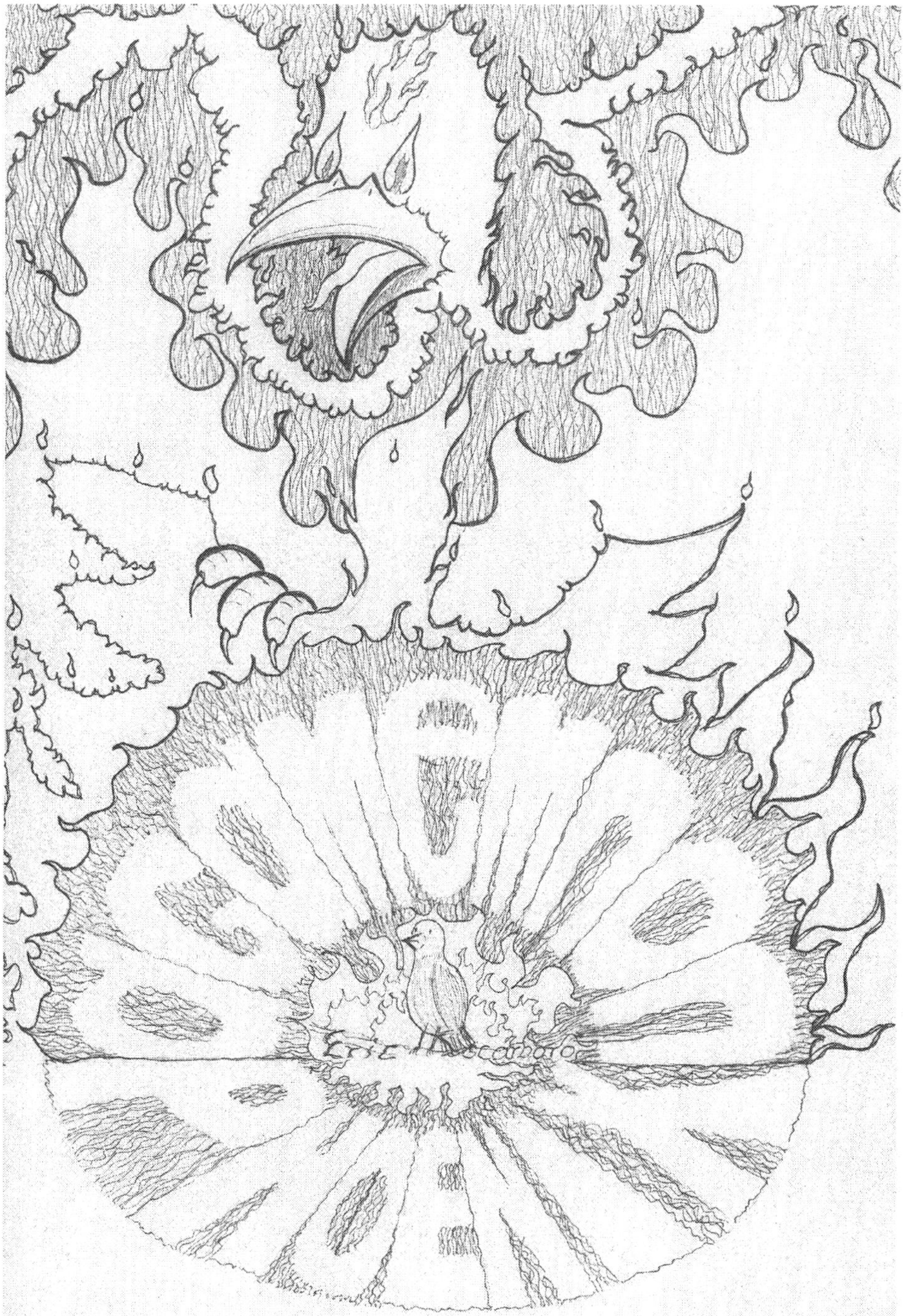

## CHAPTER FIVE

## AN INSPECTOR CALLS

**In which a search is made and a photograph is found.**

**Friday, the eleventh of May, 1956. Time 1.45 pm.**

Everyone in the school heard the crash. Classes were told not to use the reception in *any* event. The caretaker taped off the doorways and began clearing the glass away. The Head was in his office about to telephone Mr Courtney. He looked up from his desk and wondered why it was so noisy in the playground. Investigating, he found that no classes had received the note he had given Tom.

He sought out Mrs Atkinson from the staff room, the first time any teacher could even remember him having been in there.
No one knew where Tom was.
The Head did three things. He sent two top year monitors with a note to Tom's house. He stopped the caretaker from clearing up in reception. Then he phoned the police and reported a boy missing.

Tom's mam arrived just after the police, and all met in the Head's office along with Mrs Archer, Mrs Atkinson and the caretaker, Mr Snade.
No one knew where Tom was.

After a quick, anxious conference they stepped out onto the ruined floor of the Reception Hall. The three ladies watched silently as the two policemen and the caretaker tilted up as much of the mirror frame as they could. The Head crunched forward through the shattered pieces of glass which had spread like a tidal wave of diamonds across the floor. He bent as much as he could, looked under the frame and muttered,

"Good Grief!"

He straightened, ashen faced. Then took a deep breath, bent, and looked again. The tension in the room was unbearable.

"Best leave this to the experts really."

suggested the younger officer. The Head looked at Tom's mam, the distress clearly visible, her smooth young face suddenly heavy and much older. He glanced at the older officer, who nodded. He stood, turned, and crunched over to the wall where the window-hook stood. Despite the continued complaints of the younger policeman, he reached under the mirror with it and dragged out a dark shape.

"A coat! That's all. A child's coat."

"That's *not* Tom's!" Harmony said, with relief.

The shattered mirror was lowered to the floor. An immediate decision was made to search every room and yard in the school., and after that, every nearby street if necessary. A rumour soon spread around the school that Tom had been taken by the tramp, Franky the Fireman.

But no one really knew where Tom was.

There was no blood anywhere, but he could still have been hurt and hiding somewhere, scared or maybe unconscious. Tom's mam was driven home, in case he should turn up there. Several neighbors came out to stare at her as she climbed out of the police car. One even took a photograph, having just come back from the Mount Pleasant flower show. She sat alone in the kitchen, feeding worms to Foghorn as she had named the chick. When the door opened and James came home from work, she was sitting in the dark.

"Is there a power cut?"

"Harmony is there a power cut?"

She shook her head.

"There was an accident at school. We couldn't get in touch with you, you were out somewhere in the van. No one knows where Tom is. We have to wait here for the police."

They sat at the table, gripping each other's hands as she told him of the day's events. A rusty chick in a tea-towel nest chirped away on the table top.

"I should have known something was up. He waved at me this morning as I left. He's never up that early."

He reached into his work bag and brought out a football in a nylon net. Looking desperately for something normal to do, he said,

"Let's wrap his presents up and put them on the table. He could be back any minute. He's sure to be back by tomorrow, it's his Birthday."

There was a knock on the door and both ran to open it. A very serious looking man in a Crombie stood there.

"Mr Hill, Mrs Hill? I'm inspector Gordon. Can I come in?"

Once inside the inspector asked them to sit but remained standing himself.

"We've searched the entire school and the surrounding streets as far as the main roads. There is no sign of your son."

Tears began to fill Harmony's eyes.

"If he crossed the main roads someone will have seen him. Have no doubt about that. We *will* find him."

"Have you checked his friends?         Asked James.

"We've been to all the addresses your wife gave us. Not a big list. I take it he had few friends?"

"Aye. Only Kevin and Barbara… oh and Kenny and Alex!"

"We've asked there as well sir.   No sign.   Did he have anywhere else to go"

"No,… well he loves the park. Saltwell Park. By the rabbits mainly and the swings, and the lake…   Should I go check?"

"Best leave it to us sir.   We need you here in case he wanders back .We need to be able to contact you quickly.   I take it he was…. *happy* here?"

"Well, yes… of course."         insisted Harmony.

"Just I noticed the kitchen seems very new. Would this be the place where the lightning struck last year?"

Despite the fact that the inspector had not seemed to have taken his eyes off them, he had obviously had a good look around the place.

"Well yes, but what would that…. he *is* very happy here inspector." said James, deliberately.

"Well then,  I'd best be off. We *will* find him, I promise. Oh I almost forgot. Can I have a photograph of him? That one on the mantlepiece behind me will do." he added, not having seemed to even glance in it's direction.

"I take it it's recent?"

"Yes. Last summer anyway. He hasn't changed." offered Harmony. "And by the way. One of your neighbors gave us a film this afternoon. Keen photographer. He was setting up at the club for the flower show. We developed it right away."

"He snapped this picture. Of a man he said he spotted in the Mount Pleasant doorway, this very morning. Hanging about. Do you recognise him?" As he held up the photograph, James' mouth clamped shut. Melody shook her head.

"No?  Very well then I'll be off."

As the door closed behind the inspector, James turned to Harmony.

"Sit down Harmony. Sit down, please."

As she sat, James' head dropped.

"I know where Tom is."

A very serious looking man in a Crombie stood there.

## ACT TWO

## THE MAN

**MAN**
ἄνθρωπος
Anthropos

Say; an - throw - poss

Noun :
an adult human male.
synonyms: male, adult male, gentleman, guy, fellow, fella, joe, geezer, gent, bloke, chap, dude, hombre, men folk, gadgey.

# CHAPTER ONE

## IN THE MIDNIGHT HOUR

**In which a journey is recalled and a late visitor arrives.**

**Friday, the eleventh of May, 1956. Time, 4.25pm.**

They talked for hours.

Harmony became angry several times and eventually calmed each time, only to ask the same questions once more and become angry again.

"When we met," said Tom's dad, "I told you that Tom was… special."

"I know, but I just thought…well, everyone's proud of their children, aren't they?"

"Please let me explain. It's *much* more complicated than that. Tom's mam didn't as much die as… well, … disappear forever. It's *not* the same thing.

Her brother Adam has a lot to do with it all. Odd fellow. *Very* odd! You remember I mentioned an Uncle I said was never to be welcomed? He's involved in some malarkey she never really wanted to talk about. Magicians, Druids and Shay-men whatever they are. It was something the family were committed to but she didn't want to be part of. Or at least she gave up when we got together. What I did hear, I didn't like. I only met him a few times and to be honest after the third time I said he wasn't welcome. Venus agreed with me and backed me up. She said he then claimed that he had already decided it was going to be like that anyway, as though it were up to him cheeky beggar. Anyway … when Tom came along, Adam sent us a few things, that clock in Tom's room for one, like they were lucky charms. And in return for him staying away from us, we agreed on a couple of things. Oh my word it's so long ago. Sounds stupid I know, but we agreed to keep Tom away from mirrors, not to have them in the house."

"So it wasn't just superstition, or bad luck?"

"Well yes it was really. He advised Venus not to have any mirrors anywhere near Tom until he was past seven years old. Another thing was never to invite any strangers into the house."

"That's just rude. I always thought so, and I've told you so before."

"No, there's more to it. If it was someone I didn't know, I could say 'I've something inside for you' and walk indoors. If they followed me in it was alright. If they *couldn't* go in without an invite, then they weren't to have one."

"Seems a sure way to have a house full of rude people and very few real friends if you ask me"

"Anyway, because of who Adam and Venus' family were, we had to watch out for Tom until he was eight. After that, he would be fine. So, any day now you could have your mirror."

"Oh." said Harmony.

"What?" asked James.

"Look. Not that I think I've done anything wrong, but…. I sort of already have a mirror."

"What? Where?"

"Well I bought that wardrobe for myself last year. So that we'd have one each?"

"What about it?"

"Well when I bought it, there was a mirror on the back of the door."

"No there wasn't. I checked."

"Yes there was. It came separately, wrapped up to protect it. I never put it up because you don't like them, but… it's in the back of the wardrobe. I take it out now and then to do my hair. Only, you know, special occasions."

"Oh my word. Haven't you noticed? It's been this last year that Tom's been worried… sort of. And acting quiet."

"If you're blaming me, can I remind you, I told you not to go the other night."

"And I told you, part of the advice was, until he's gone eight, if I was really worried about anything I was to go pick up a package that would help."

"Where from?"

"I already said. If Tom was in trouble, Adam would leave something for us, for me, in a box at a railway station. And before you ask I can't remember which one. I remember getting on the train and knowing somehow the right station when it came along, but now I can't remember which one. In the box in the waiting room was the stick and leaves, and the note."

He pulled an old piece of paper out of a trouser pocket, smoothed it flat on the table and read.

"For dealing with large dogs, or small horses, black.

Throw the stick, see if it comes back.

To rush to safety, ask no quarter.

The beast can *not* cross water."

"I don't know if I read that right or not. I don't know if it's made things better or worse. If only I could see Adam."

There was a knock at the door. James rushed to open it. Standing in the shadows was a man in black, with grey temples, propped up against the doorway. He stumbled forward and staggered indoors without being asked, smelling like a bonfire.

"Good evening James and… your good wife.. Eunomia? Adam Abraxason at your service."

His suit was torn and dirty. He looked weak, sick.

"And now if you'll excuse me…"

Then he collapsed on the floor.

"Pick a prize"  "The Beezer"

Dear "Pick a prize" at "The Beezer",

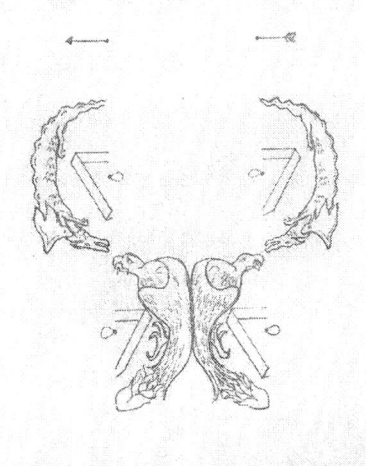

1. Look at the dots on the arrows.
2. Un-focus eyes til the dots join.
3. The dragons and the phoenixes come together.
4. Turn the page sideways.
5. Un-focus eyes to bring together the infinity symbols and triangles.
6. Wobble page to see phoenix fight dragon.

I would like an electric speedboat. I like the Numskulls and Guess What! and Tommy Taylor's Toolbox. However, Guess What! should have a ?, not a !.

11 Ellison Villas, Gateshead. Tom Hill
County Durham

Tom's letter to 'The Beezer' comic.

# CHAPTER TWO

## TEA FOR THE TELLER-MAN

**In which an enemy is revealed as a Guardian.**

**Friday the eleventh of May, 1956. Time 8.45pm.**

Adam Abraxason woke on the settee in the front room which was reserved for guests. As Hermes chirped loudly Harmony thrust a cup into his hands.

"Here, drink this. You've been out for a while."

"What…?" he began

"It's tea, strong and black." interrupted Harmony.

"What…?" he repeated.

"Honey. Two big spoonfuls." she interrupted again.

"WHAT…?" he continued a third time "…are you feeding the chick?"

They both looked astounded.

"Bread and milk." said Harmony.

"No…. no milk. Give it egg yolk, dripped off cotton wool."

Everyone was quiet.

"And chopped up worms."

Adam stared at her.

"What? Now?" she said.

He nodded weakly, but with insistent eyes. She went off to the kitchen.

"Adam, where's my bloody son?" demanded James.

"He's being well fed and looked after."

"Where? Take me to him!"

"First you have to do something. Go to the police Station. Tell them Tom's turned up safe and sound and is asleep in bed."

"Why the hell would I do that?"

"That buys us the weekend. So I can work undisturbed, hopefully. Tell them he has been with me, his uncle. That I found him on my back doorstep. He'd had a fright at school and ran out. Ran to my house in Lady Park. I found him in the back garden when I came home and brought him back."

"Look! Where is he?"

"Do as I've told you. It's the quickest way to see him again."

"Alright. Alright I'll consider it. As soon as you've explained what's going on."

Harmony returned with the chick in the tea-towel nest. All three glad of the warming glow from the fire. Adam took a highly polished silver box from his pocket and stood it by the chick.

"They like to see company." he said.

"There's a job I have to do. A duty if you like, which is passed on through the generations. I don't have a son to pass it on to. I'm sure my sister Venus told you that?"

"Well yes, sort of." confirmed James.

"Well. Someone obviously doesn't want this duty passed down, and seems to think that I intended to pass it down to Tom."

"Is it dangerous?" asked Harmony.

"Yes, ... *Harmony* ? Indeed it is. I didn't intend to involve Tom at all - and I couldn't anyway until he was 'turned eight'. It seems someone didn't want him to be 'turned eight' just in case, and tried to…"

"Kill him? Asked James.

"Or worse." replied Adam.

"On his eight birthday, *that is* the beginning of his ninth year, had I passed this duty to him, he would have come under my protection, but now he has become an enemy of ….. this entity."

"So how was Tom found out?" asked Harmony, cutting through the problem.

"Venus knew the risks of having a child. Even so, she loved you so much James… and thought she would be here to look after him. When Tom came along… oh, she was so proud. That was when we decided that you would move up here to bring Tom up."

"You decided?" asked James.

"Yes James, Venus and I decided. You may think otherwise but… well it really doesn't matter now. The important thing is that you were to have no contact with me. That way we hoped that Tom would be safe. Well hidden. Obviously, somehow, you *have* been found. When you collected the parcel from the station, that did two things. It gave you someway to help Tom, and it sent a message to me, that you needed help."

Harmony stared at him.

"You took your time."

"I have been kept rather busy. No doubt by the … *same* entity who wishes Tom harm. You see, he *was found*, somehow, I don't exactly know how… possibly… by a back-glass discovery spell. A mirror search."

"Mirror search?" asked James.

"Hmm. Like a window hunt. What do you call it? …?"

"…window shopping?" suggested Harmony.

" Yes, exactly. But, can you imagine how hard it would be trying to find someone, somewhere in the world, only by looking through every window in the world, one at a time until you saw them?"

"It'd take forever." stated Harmony.

"Indeed. And how much harder it would be if that person being sought didn't actually have any windows?

"Are you saying this *entity*… looks through mirrors?" asked James.

"Yes. Like you look through windows, and the reason I asked you to keep him *away from* mirrors. It's simple enough, but you can only look through one at a time."

"Impossible!" spluttered James.

"Really? Wait till you see me walk through one. Anyway. The entity kept me very busy. I could only drop in here for a few seconds at a time to check on Tom. I had to be sure it wasn't a trick to get me to reveal where Tom was. So I arranged for someone to keep an eye on him."

"Didn't do much good." insisted James. "He was also being followed by a huge black dog. Your 'someone' didn't do much about that."

"On the contrary. You see, Tom was meant to be crushed under that mirror, or worse! Possibly sent through it in a thousand little pieces."

"And he wasn't?" asked James.

"Oh no. The Pooka, … the 'black dog'… that I sent to look after him. It kept watch on him discreetly and then…. Pookas are the fastest creatures I know… it saved him at the last possible second."

Why would a throat Numskull have an umbrella?

# CHAPTER THREE

## THROUGH THE BACK-GLASS

**There is a bump in the dark as morning approaches.**

**Saturday, the twelfth of May, 1956. Time, 12.35 am.**

Tom's dad returned from the police station in the middle of the night.
"I told the Sergeant and he said he'd let Inspector Gordon know." he said as he took his coat off.

Harmony and Adam were still sat around the fire in the front room where he'd left them.
"I expect they'll be around tomor… well, *this* morning, to check on him - and we *still* don't know where he is!" reminded Harmony.
"Well then, I'd better get busy." said Adam picking up the silver box.
"Can you take care of the …er chick… please Harmony?"
She picked it up carefully in it's nest and carried it into the kitchen.
"I need as much quiet as possible please." Adam asked James.
"What are you going to do?"
"Well this really is quite exhausting. In my state at any rate. I've been fighting the Entity for three days. Is there any chance of asking Harmony for some more honey tea? I'd prefer her not to see this, it might complicate things."
"Things can get *more* complicated, then?"
"Oh yes, trust me *much* more complicated."
James left him for a moment to ask Harmony to make some tea. When he returned, Adam was still talking.
"The Pooka, you see… the dog… doesn't normally co-operate with, … well with anyone. I had to promise her something special. Hopefully it will have kept it's word and rescued
Tom. Run off with him clinging to it's back."
"Hopefully?"
"Yes. Hopefully. They are honorable enough creatures. No reason to doubt it's word. It's just, I've never known anyone ask for it's word before."
"Oh my word."
"So. They run faster than any other creature I've ever seen. Fast enough to snatch Tom out from under a falling mirror, I'm sure. I just hope it didn't get carried away. They normally only take the greedy, vain or foolish, and run until they drop off their backs, dead of thirst or starvation."
"Tom's none of those things." stated James.
"No indeed, which is why I'm sure the Pooka will remember to do as I asked."
"Which is what?"
"To take Tom safely through the mirror before it shattered and leave him

somewhere safe. Of course this would be much simpler if I had a fragment of the actual mirror here. I may have to send you to the school to seek out a piece." He glanced at the ceiling.

"Is Harmony upstairs? Just I'd prefer quiet for this and I can hear her moving around."

"I'll go up in a minute and see." said James.

"Right, I'll get into my fugue. I'll start with the nearest mirrors I can." With that his eyes relaxed, he gazed vacantly into a small mirror he folded out from the silver box.

James left the room and stood at the foot of the stairs. Adam slowly shook his head.

"Not working. Can't even see the closest glass. Tried but just black. Nothing but black."

There was another bump from upstairs. Remembering that he hadn't actually seen Harmony leave the kitchen, James started up the stairwell.

"I think Harmony isn't actually upstairs….."

Creeping slowly up the old, creaking stairs, once at the top of the landing James whispered

"Harmony?     Harmony? Are you up here?"

He switched on the main light in the bedroom and stepped in. He looked around. Nothing.

He was about to step out again when he heard scuffling noises. Listening intently, he heard a panting.  Then a padding.   Then nothing.   He looked towards the wardrobe.       A bump, a groan.

Coming from inside the wardrobe. 'Oh my word,' he thought, 'whatever now. And *here,* in our home.'

Stepping forward, a floorboard creaked under his weight. Sweat ran down his forehead in the cold stillness of the room. He reached slowly for the wardrobe handle and picked up a glass vase from the bedside table, holding it like a club. He saw Adam and Harmony appear slowly up the stairs onto the landing. He raised a single finger to his lips in warning. Lord knows what lay in the wardrobe, but this was *his* home and *he'd* face it.

Just as Adam stepped into the room next to him, he raised the vase above his head, and he flung open the door.

Nothing but coats, blouses, skirts. Then one of the black coats moved, light glinting off what looked like a black button caught his eye. The button moved away into the darkness of the wardrobe, the coats parted and a dark shape fell towards him out of the wardrobe and onto his feet.

Looking down he recognized it at once and shouted

"TOM!"

Then one of the black coats moved…

# CHAPTER FOUR

FACING THE MUSIC

**An awful decision can not be avoided.**

**Saturday, the twelfth May, 1956. Time, 9.15 am.**

The Inspector stood with James and Harmony and Adam, watching Tom through the back window. He seemed to be kicking a football around the yard with amazingly little effort and a great deal of skill.
"Safe and sound. That's the only thing that really matters."
said Inspector Gordon.
"There'll be paperwork of course. Couple of forms explaining the extra men needed and also we borrowed a car and a dog from Chester-Le-Street force. I'll have someone call next week sometime. No rush now is there?"
"No, no, of course not," managed James,
"Can I just say again how grateful we are... for all you did."
Harmony added
"And how sorry we are you wasted so much effort."
"Never a waste Mrs Hill, never. My men flooded the streets in record time, very useful exercise, the public feel reassured we can watch over things, I slept soundly in the knowledge that all possible had been done, *and* we have our happy ending." summed the Inspector.
He looked around the room as he made to leave. Tom was quite certain that in those three seconds he had noted every tiny detail.
"Of course, if you'd mentioned.... Uncle Adam's house...?"
James and Harmony looked at each other, wondering what to say. They hadn't covered this question when assembling their cover story. Adam stepped in before the silence became a problem.
"I'm rarely at home, Inspector. In fact I'm often out of the country entirely. I travel abroad you see, I'm an antiques collector."
The Inspector weighed this statement for a moment as he ran his hands around the rim of his hat, but seemed able to find no fault in it.
"Well then, until next time."
he said, stepping through the door and glancing sideways, obviously noticing the new bricks of the recently rebuilt wall.
"This damage here then...?"
"Er... same time as... as the same storm as... as you know about." stuttered James.
"What? Front and back? And no damage inside?"
"No, thank goodness. We were all very lucky."
"Can I just say then.... odd time of year for chicks to be hatching. Goodbye all."
The chick was upstairs, it's chirping barely audible on the ground floor.

"Thank you again and goodbye." said James as he closed the door. When they were alone again Adam turned to James and Harmony.

"I must say you are taking this well."

"It's just such a relief to have Tom home again. Home safe." said Harmony.

James added

"Of course neither of us are very happy he was in danger in the first place, but… I suppose… Venus did warn me. I never took it seriously enough."

"Well who would?" asked Harmony,

"Magicians and monsters. In this day and age."

"Still, now you have the proof, what with Tom reappearing through the mirror in your wardrobe, how do you feel?" asked Adam.

James and Harmony shifted uncomfortably, not sure they were going to like what came next.

"Feel? About what?" demanded James.

"Well, the next step… Ah! It hasn't sunk in yet. Oh dear."

James and Harmony both fell silent.

"You see. I'm afraid my hand *was* forced. Whatever we think about *how* Tom was found. He *was* found. We can't change that. And before his eight Birthday."

"Which I'd like to remind you, is today."

claimed Harmony, stepping in front of the window, physically blocking Tom from Adam's view, even though, all this time, the real Tom had actually been asleep upstairs in his room.

"Oh of course you shall have as normal a day as possible with him. You must spend time together… before he leaves."

"Leaves? What the hell do you mean, leaves?"

demanded James, catching up with Harmony's understanding of the situation. Adam began to explain, slowly.

"I stepped in to protect him. To save him. Save him from a truly dreadful fate. Had none of this happened…. well irrelevant now really. It *did* happen and so I have automatically declared my obligation of mentor."

At this they both looked puzzled. Adam continued,

"Obligation of mentor? To teach Tom the ways of magical influence."

"We won't allow it." came the reply from Tom's dad.

"No no no. No you can't." He added defiantly.

"Do you *really* not understand? Tom now has *enemies*. Enemies who would harm him. He must learn to defend himself against them."

"But you could just go. Go away and leave us in peace."

"James, I'm afraid if I leave Tom unprotected… well, you really don't want me to finish that sentence… but let's say that you all will have very little peace indeed. Oh he can visit. You *will* see him, perhaps even often. At times. But his life is with me now, if he is to have one. For the next few years at least."

They almost visibly shrank with disappointment and realisation. They sat down together at the table. James suddenly felt cold. A ripple ran up his arms and back and his hairs stood on end. Eventually he could manage to say

"We'll have to discuss this."

"Certainly. It must be done but it is best done with your blessing."
James rallied briefly, not knowing where to turn his anger,

"If you'd just stayed away…"

"Tom would have died under a mirror. Or.." Adam was cut off,

"…or worse, yes we know!"

"I did what I could, years ago. I advised you. Gave you measures and offerings that would help. Ways for you to be defended. Ways for you to be given warning of danger. Ways to send to me for help. Over time I assume you've just forgotten their importance."

Harmony brought the chick downstairs again, and placed it on the table, Foghorn began cheeping away in his nest. Adam studied the bird for a moment then began looking around.

"I've been meaning to ask…."

Suddenly he reached into the inside pocket of his coat. Deep into it. He fumbled around, eventually grabbing something and pulled out an old leather pouch, which looked too big to have been in there. It was held together by leather laces. He moved his fingers over them and pulled the knot apart. Inside was a purple tinted magnifying glass with a silver frame and black handle. He began walking the room, examining random corners and objects.

"What are you looking for?" asked Harmony.

"Traces. Residual traces… of …*sorcery*, … *animation*, … *magic…. fortune, manipulation…* … my word it's everywhere."

He turned to them, suddenly looking very stern.

"And when were you going to tell me, hmmm?"

"Tell you what?" asked James.

"Didn't you understand *anything*? The watch? The clock? The birds? The …"

he turned to peer at the cage, dropped the spy-glass and raised it again in the direction of the chick on the table.

"I wasn't wrong. What on earth happened to Aggamemnon?"

"Aga..? That's it!" chimed James,

"Aggamemnon! I knew he had a long name. Couldn't remember it, just called him Aggy."

"He was already called Aggy when I met James. When we got married." added Harmony. Adam looked amazed.

"Aggamemnon and Hermes? The great defender and the swiftest messenger? What happened to him?"

"Well we lost him." said James, "In that gas explosion."

"Oh my word! A gas explosion! Lots of damage was there?"

"Plenty thanks. Hell of a storm that weekend. At first we thought it was lightning. We were lucky to survive."

"I'll say you were! Why is Hermes still here?"

"Well that's weird isn't it? Aggy disappeared, but Hermes was still in the cage."

"But didn't I tell you to let them out *every* day? Hermes was meant to summon help. Poor little thing. You must have been so frustrated. Aggamemnon…"

he gazed proudly at the chick on the table.

"Well, Aggamemnon did his job heroically as I can see."

The chick chirped madly.

"Oh yes, I, know."

he said calmly to the bird, who sang back at him.

"I'm sorry I wasn't listening earlier, little flameheart. You see, I didn't know."

He chirped again, long and high.

"Ha ha ha,"    laughed Adam

"As I knew you would. Your father would have been very proud of you."

Raising his head to the confused parents, Adam struggled to keep his temper.

"This little creature saved you all. As I was sure he could if necessary. Show me the rebuilding."

They took Adam into the backyard to see the newly-built kitchen wall and roof and the other renovations.

"But look!"

he said, retreating down the yard and up into the garden.

"Step back and take a look."

he said, and when they had done so, added,

"Is it not obvious!"

The kitchen had been rebuilt but the back wall of the house had simply had it's damaged areas replaced.

"Look at the new bricks. And onto the roof, the new tiles. What can you see?"

Now it was pointed out to them it somehow became obvious. The new bricks and tiles marked the path of huge claws which had raked their way up and out of the yard. Adam approached the wall, touching it cautiously.

"A fair sized beast. Of a type I thought to be extinct or banished at least. Aggamemnon really put up a savage defence for you all. No doubt you'll be saving on heating bills. This wall is still a degree or two warmer than the other wall, the new one. Dragon tongue tends to do that, hang around a long time. Still, the heat would certainly have helped Agamemnon's rebirth."

Tom and James looked suitably embarrassed.

"And you thought it a gas explosion?    In a lightning storm? And what of the watch? The clock? The…"

"Well the watch started playing up months ago, " complained James, "One hand started moving backwards can you believe? So I sent it to get mended. It's still there. Watchmaker can't get the back off."

"By the four families." came the exasperated reply from Adam.

"A Delia Quarterpage, designer time-signal and deja-vu detector, and you sent it to be mended!"

"And the clock in Tom's room isn't much better, er… did you say dragon?"
complained James,

" I… anyway… dragon… sorry the clock. I could swear I heard it going off the other night. It's never even been wound up!"

"Everything working fine then!" stated the Magician, exasperated,

"My alarums doing their job, my defender and messenger both alert and heroic…! Only you, not aware of any of it."

The atmosphere had become tense between them. James said eventually,

" I never took this seriously."

Knowing it to be less an excuse, more a confession. Adam relented.

"Well now you must. Don't blame yourself entirely. It's possible that somehow you were influenced by a 'disbelieving', but even so, it's clearer than ever that Tom, simply *isn't* safe here. Surely?"

The pair nodded slowly. Their life had changed so dramatically and so swiftly. The awful state James had been in when they met. Missing Venus, seeming unable to mourn for her. Harmony's own, lost childhood in the orphanage, a dozen foster homes, the illness she had survived only by a miracle. Finding each other like it was *meant* to be, moving north, building a home and family. Then suddenly, all this. Still, at least 'their' son was alive.

All that remained was for Adam to officially declare the sentence.

"Well then. Be good parents. Give Tom a fine Birthday. He leaves with me tomorrow."

## DRAGON
### Δράκος

Say; dra - kos
Noun.
A mythical monster like a giant reptile. In European tradition the dragon is typically fire-breathing and tends to symbolize chaos or evil, whereas in East Asia it is usually a beneficent symbol of fertility, associated with water and the heavens.

Also (in the 16th and 17th centuries) a short musket carried on the belt of a soldier, especially a mounted infantryman.

**Now it was pointed out to them it somehow became obvious.**

# CHAPTER FIVE

## ALL TOMORROW'S PARTIES

### Guests early and late, all are welcomed.

**Saturday, the twelfth of May, 1956. Time, 11.05 am.**

Harmony had been out of the house less than an hour. She had made four telephone calls, delivered a handful of invitations and called at the Front to collect enough buns, cakes and fruit for a surprise party. The timing was military in it's precision. As she was placing the shopping baskets on the dining table, James and Tom were coming out of the front living room. All three met in the passage.
    "Tom and I are taking a walk to the park, said James, We'll be back for one."
    "Well have fun then," said Harmony, "Don't be late." As the door closed she quickly added     "But don't be early!"
    Tom skipped most of the way down Split Crow Road, James' long stride eating up the pavement at his side. It was hard to say who was keeping up with whom. They turned left up Old Durham Road onto the Front. James looked in the doorway of the paper-shop and thought he saw Alex and Kenny. As they passed Batty's he also thought he saw Kevin's dad inside, meaning that Kevin might also be there. 'Everyone seems to be up and about early today' he thought. 'And no-one at the Saturday morning pictures at The Ritz?'. James saw Tom looking.
    "I said straight to the park today Tom. I promised Harmony. We can't be late back."
Tom bounced his new football as he walked.
    " Or early either."
he added, laughing, as his dad held back a smile. They cut down Shipcote Terrace behind Shipcote School and all the way down to the Boy's Grammar. To the right was Shipcote Baths and opposite lay the Little Café, which sold the most wondrous invention of the age, as an after-swim treat: penny gravy dips. To the left along Avenue Road lay the top gates of the park.
    Once inside, it was safe to drop the ball and kick as you went. The main greens were only a few yards away and usually full by one o'clock at a weekend, most families wandering down after dinner. Not being much after eleven, the park was fairly empty. They even saw Franky the Fireman limping away from the park, before it became crowded with kids, although they couldn't say where he had emerged from. It was generally assumed that he wintered in the railway arches at the riverside, where no one really minded an old oil drum being fired up at night-time, and summered in the park, getting his head down in the bushes or in the dene. As he left they heard him having one of his famous arguments with himself and shouting to no-one in particular something about 'having the bloody council do something about Saturdays.'.

Tom had a dozen goes on the big banana slide in only a few minutes, having to share it with only a few other kids. There was no waiting for the swings or the roundabout and no big kids to send it spinning too fast either. There was even a shuggy boat spare. In fact he took his seat at one end, looking back at the lake, and had to wait a minute for a second rider to wander over.

When he did, Tom couldn't see the other boy until his dad had lifted him in and stood clear. Tom looked at him and smiled. Short, fair hair, round NHS glasses. The words popped into his head but thankfully he didn't say them. 'It's…. The Milky Bar Kid!'

This had been the boy's nickname at school but Tom remembered that he hadn't really liked it. He had moved away about a year ago, to Askew Road he seemed to recall, and Tom hadn't seen him since then.

"Allan?" he said, "Allan Coxon?"

"Yes." came the reply, "You're Tom… Hill? Aren't you?"

James' and Allan's Dads, surprised to see that the boys knew each other, sat together on the side benches and began talking. The shuggy boats worked by pulling on two ropes which were attached to the overhead bar on which the boats hung. It's surprising how much talking two boys can do in two minutes of strenuous shuggy-boating. By the time they were both back, sweating, on solid ground, they were as good friends as they would have become had Allan not moved away. Likewise their dads had seemed to have a lot to talk about. When they parted, Allan going home for dinner, he called back,

"Tom! Come next Saturday morning. We're always here early."

This made Allan's dad laugh but Tom couldn't work out why. Father and son spent the next half-hour kicking the ball around the green, building up an appetite for their return home.

Salt well Park lay in the centre of the town, on the hill down to Team Valley and the rapidly expanding Trading Estate. Rumour around the schoolyard was that it was left to the people of Gateshead by Lady Saltwell for them to enjoy a taste of the countryside in the heart of the town.

To the east, a thick, cold, sea-fret was heading towards shore. To the west, across the hills from Carlisle, a thick mist was, quite impossibly, rolling east across the country towards Gateshead. To the north and south also an even ring of thick haar was slowly shrinking inwards. Under the fields of Cumberland, Durham and Northumberland, sods were shifting. Top soil was heaving. Something was breaking through from the clay and rock below. Something*s*. Many somethings.

James and Tom lay on the grass, panting and exhausted. They were near the top of the green and under the shade of the trees that lined the top edge of the park. From where they lay the surface of the lake was as flat as a mirror, most of the boats were in and only a few swans floated around, barely leaving a ripple. Behind the lake, in the valley, all of the factories were quiet and empty, it being Saturday. Only the glassworks smoked a little, the kilns and furnaces being kept warm until Monday.

The walk home was uphill and they took their time, being in no hurry. On

Deckham Front they were passed by Jakey, always a good luck sign. The horse, Jakey, hurried by, pulling the little wood and glass box that contained only a silver urn of ice cream, a scoop, a box of cones and ice-cream seller Jacky. They cut up by the Post Office and were home in minutes. As they turned into Ellison Villas Tom noticed how busy the street was. And how empty. Normally he could hear Kenny and Alex out playing somewhere. Probably British Bulldog or Cups. There was normally only one car in the street, parked outside the Steel's front door. He saw four cars, *and* a delivery van just pulling away. Yet the street was very quiet.

Before they stepped in through the gate James used his extra height to peer over the hedge. As they stepped into the front garden Tom noticed the curtain moving at the front living room window. His dad knocked boldly at the front door, then seemed to remember he had his key all along and opened up. Tom knew what was going on. He stepped into the passage. To the right, was the front living room door, closed. To the left the dining room - empty! The door on the right opened slowly to reveal… Harmony sitting listening to the radio.

"Oh hello." she said, "Here's my two big boys. Have a nice time?"

"Yes Mam."
said Tom, looking around and listening. He had been wrong it seemed. He had been sure they were planning *something.* felt positive that a little party might be happening. His mam interrupted,

"I'll make dinner in ten minutes. Why not pop into the garden. I've left crumbs and crusts on the kitchen bench for Sunblest and the birds."

As he passed through the dining room, he wondered why the curtains were drawn as he paused to place the ball under the table next to the wastepaper basket, which still held the wrapping from his presents, opened only that morning. His attention was diverted for a few seconds by the brand-new radio on the mantlepiece that was playing music. He recognized the tune as 'Tonight You Belong To Me' by Patience and Prudence. Standing up, he looked twice. There was no table. But he had left his new comics on it. Where could it be? He looked around the room, making sure it hadn't been placed in a different corner. His comics and Dad's paper were on the edge of the hearth. They were definitely today's and not just fire starters as he recognized a headline, 'ANOTHER FISHERMAN MISSING'. Still puzzled, he grabbed a few crusts from the *enormous* pile and headed for the back garden. As he opened the heavy, wooden door, sunlight spilled in making him squint. As he stepped out he was deafened by a dozen voices all crying together,

**"SURPRISE!"**
He dropped the crusts in fright. There was the table, in the yard, every inch covered with party food. Around it, smiling were Alex and Kenny, their friend Stephen, Kevin and Barbara and four of their mams and dads. Tom looked down at the crusts at his feet, and wondered why he hadn't been puzzled by such an enormous pile.

"Don't worry about them,"

shouted Kenny's dad, pointing to the table,
"Come and have some proper food!"
Tom's mam and dad appeared behind him, carrying a white-iced Birthday cake bearing eight candles. Tom pushed out his bottom lip, blowing up across his face, making his fringe flick up and everyone laugh.
"No no no,"
said Kenny's dad again,
" You're supposed to blow the *candles* out!"
Every one laughed.
The party began with some racing games Tom's dad seemed to be making up on the spot: to the raised wall and back, twice, with an orange under their chins: once around the garden with a balloon between their knees: up and down the steps while juggling a hard boiled egg.
They were interrupted by a knock at the front door which Harmony answered. Tom couldn't see who it was but he sneaked into the kitchen and overheard what was said. The visitor, who turned out to be a small woman, began,
"Excuse me, is this Tom's house?"
"Yes of course, come in."       replied his mam.
"Just he doesn't get many invites… his temper… I wondered if it was a mistake. He's waiting on the path… while I knocked."
"There's no mistake, tell him to come in. we've just started."
The visitor retreated, to return a few seconds later with… Ronny Thompson! Tom couldn't believe his eyes. His mam broke the silence before it became uncomfortable.
"Tom, here's another guest to the party.  Ronny. Guests are always welcome, Tom, aren't they?"
Tom managed to say,
"Yes of course. Come.. come in Ronny."
He spotted their two mams going off into the front room for a moment, obviously for official mam business, and took Ronny through to the back garden. The sight of Ronny caused a break in the fun until Barbara spoke up.
"Hello Ronny. You're just in time. We've all had a go 'bobbing for apples'. It's your go now."
On a towel on the ground was a round plastic bowl containing six inches of water and three apples, none of them with anything like a successful bite in them. Yet. Ronny walked straight up and plunged his head under, squashing an apple between his mouth and the bottom of the bowl. Once held there he bit into it and lifted his head, and the apple, clear of the water.
"At last,"
shouted Alex's dad,
"Someone with brains!"
Ronny was clearly the winner, but also the wettest guest at the party, and he hadn't been there thirty seconds. A few moments later, Ronny looked around the guests, wondering how they would react to his fearsome reputation.
As Tom went to collect his ball for a few games of 'passy', he heard another

knock at the front door
and answered it without thinking. He could hardly believe his eyes when it turned up to be Allan Coxon and his dad.

"Allan!"

he shouted, bringing his mam into the room from the kitchen to see what the noise was about.

"It's you! How did you know…."

"Ah,"

said Harmony,

"I'm so glad you made it. James was hoping you would. Have any trouble getting here?"

"Well a bit,"

said Allan's dad,

"but luckily we found a guide when we got lost on Harle Street.".

He turned to indicate his pathfinder, who he thought was standing behind him. Hearing the gate clang shut, Tom and his mam leaned out to see who it was. It was the skinny blonde girl from the top of Harle Street, and she was singing,

"Have you heard? The coast of Maine… just got caught in a hurricane? Well did you ever…. "

Harmony called to her.

"Thank you very much. Would you like to come in?"

seeing that the girl was not sure, she added

"We're having a party. You're just in time."

The girl looked away up the street, wondering if she should tell her mam first, then quickly made her mind up, skipping up the garden path and into the house to join the others, making up the nine at the party table.

Tom had so much to tell Allan about. All the things he'd thought of when it was too late, after they'd parted that morning. As they joined the rest in the garden however, Ronny saw Allan and Tom remembered how Ronny had been a bit of a bully. Ronny's eyes lit up and he began to speak,

" It's …"

but then stopped himself. Again there was an awkward silence. Allan himself broke it by completing Ronny's words,

"..The Milky bar Kid!"   Then he turned to explain.

"It's all right! The kids at my new school think I look like him as well."

he marched forward to Ronny, making a fist with index finger and thumb extended and jabbed Ronny in the belly.

"So stick 'em up pardner."

he said, and Ronny laughed the loudest of them all. The napkins were coming off the plates of food however and Tom's mam was ushering everyone into place and making the last minute introductions of the two late guests. Before she went into the house with the other adults for cups of tea, she sat Tom at the head of the table, with Allan and the little blonde girl on each side of him, and Ronny next to them. He couldn't work out why, but this seemed to ruffle Barbara's feathers a little. He wondered if it might be jealousy, but dismissed that idea. 'I mean,' he thought to himself, 'Barbara was hardly speaking to me just the other day. She can hardly complain if I have new friends, can she?'. Then he realized that one of his new friends was a girl. The only other girl at the table. Somehow he sensed that there was a new type of trouble coming over the horizon.

Over another horizon, in a ring about sixty miles across, with Gateshead at it's centre, an impenetrable mist was rolling slowly inwards.

   The food was very colorful, plentiful and tasty. The iced buns and cream cakes went first, which Tom didn't mind at all as this left him with a plate of sausage rolls almost to himself. After that he tucked into a variety of sandwiches including corned beef and tomato, ham and pease pudding and cheese and onion, as did the others but most of them left the onion on their plates. The whole thing was washed down with a couple of glasses of Villa pop. The plate of scones, being plain and without even jam on them, were ignored. Foolishly as it turned out, as we shall see. With perfect timing, Harmony returned just as the last of the bowls of crisps were being emptied. For some reason, Ronny had collected the blue bags of salt that came with them and had them lined up on his plate.
   "They're good luck."
he claimed. Ronny had become very protective of Tom as the afternoon rolled on. In fact, as two hands met, both reaching for the last sausage roll, Ronny intervened, grabbing both wrists.
"Really, we should offer this last one out first, shouldn't we?"
he said, nodding in Tom's direction.
   "Yes, you're right."
said Tom, not taking it, but instead offering it around the table. This wasn't quite what Ronny meant. In fact he reddened up completely when the blonde girl reached for it and said,
   "Why thank you Ronny. Quite the gentleman."
This made everyone laugh and even Ronny himself had a big smile. Tom's mam arrived with a huge trifle, which nobody refused. She then wondered aloud why no one had taken a scone, and insisted that everybody put one on their plate for a game. When they had all done so she announced that the game was to carefully take a bite out of the scones. Kenny went first, biting his in half, before pulling a puzzled face. He reached into the half in his mouth, and pulled out a little, waxed-paper bundle. It contained a new sixpence. Everyone tore into their own, amazed that they had forgotten about this Birthday tradition.
   James was having a few quiet moments listening to Allan's dad, and didn't like what he had to say.  "You know that old ice-cream man that goes around here?"
   "What, old Jacky?"
   "Yes, that's him. We were coming up Split Crow Road from Old Durham Road and there was a right old commotion going on."
   "Really? What happened then?"
   "Well someone said that the horse had been spooked and bolted. Crashed

straight into the wall just past the barber's. Ambulance and everything when we passed."

"What! somebody hurt?"

"Well they said so. Said it didn't look good for horse or driver. They used to say it was lucky to see Jakey, as well, whichever one he is, horse or ice-cream man."

"Oh that's dreadful." said James,

" Don't tell the kids, no need to upset them. Any idea what spooked the horse?"

"Well, woman on the corner said it was a delivery van of some kind. Just came flying round the corner, 'like a bat out of hell' to use her words. She also said that Jakey looked 'a hundred years old'."

The radio was playing on the windowsill. No one had been paying it much attention, until James noticed it seemed to be playing *that* song again. He went over to it and fiddled with a few buttons, but it just got louder. Eventually he took it through to the front room and shut the door on it.

Tom opened his presents reluctantly, but gratefully, never having felt this popular in his life. Kenny and Alex had obviously coordinated their efforts and had given two comics from Battys. Their pal Stephen had brought a wildwest stagecoach with horses and opening doors. Barbara had sent him a magic-brush colouring book, full of pictures of Peter Pan. He had been to see the film last year and hadn't stopped talking about it for weeks afterwards. Kevin had brought him a hoopla game with a Spaceship theme. Ronny had brought a Matchbox car and Allan had got him a starter Lego set. Only the blonde girl didn't have a wrapped gift, as she hadn't even known she was coming to the party. She disappeared into the flower garden and snatched at the air. Tom saw her through the back window and wandered out to see what she was doing. She opened her hand slowly, saying

"Don't breathe."

in her palm was a single dandelion seed - a fairy.

"Put this in your shoe." she said.          "It gives you one wish. Keep it for emergencies."

There was just time for the final game of the day, 'passy parcel' which Kenny won and was delighted when he unwrapped a kazoo, although his parents weren't quite so happy. Harmony looked at the clock just as it crept past three and was fairly pleased at her timing, having reckoned the party would last two hours. So then it was time for every one to leave.

Tom saw everyone off at the door. He had been into his bag of marbles and had chosen a special one for each guest at his party, including the parent's. He had decided to sneak marbles into all their coat pockets for them to find later, hoping it would be a lovely surprise. If only he knew how lovely it would be.

As they were all putting on coats, the boys rubbing swollen bellies and having a belching competition, there was a knock at the door. It was Adam. He tugged along an old, battered trunk behind him and he was holding a bag and a bunch of labels in his other hand. The trunk rattled as though full of old junk. Once inside, he hung his coat up with all the others and went straight to the front sitting room and waited for the guests to leave, rather rudely as James and Harmony thought. When all the good byes had been said, Tom sat alone in the garden. What a day! What a party! Old friends, new friends, girlfriends. He sat back and gazed at the cloudless, blue sky. He wanted this moment to swell up and last forever. Swell up into a bubble around him that no bad thing could ever get through. He enjoyed every second, wanting to be able to remember this warm feeling exactly. He wanted it as a weapon to chase misery away when bad times, in the real world, seemed to stretch out forever. He wondered how many parties you got in your life. Twenty? Thirty? One hundred? He knew that all tomorrow's parties rolled into one could never feel as good as this one had been.

Adam joined him in the garden.

"Tom. I wondered what I could possibly give to a special little boy. What I decided upon was this."

He drew a comic out of the bag he was carrying.

"I've never seen this title." said Tom.

"It doesn't exist. Oh you can read it. Once only though. After that you'll have the memories, but that's all. It's the best comic ever written and drawn, and there will only ever be one of them. This one."

Tom held it in his hands. Taking in the colours, the title, the movement, the smell. He opened it and noticed at once that the paragraph of small print at the bottom of the first page was missing. The one that had the month and year of printing. He muzzled his face up close and drew in a huge breath through his nose, almost tasting the inks. All he could manage to say was a quiet

"Thank you."

Adam left him to enjoy his reading. He explained to James and Harmony that he had been visiting friends, colleagues and those in his debt, all afternoon. He said how he hoped that the party had been a success. He was particularly pleased to see nine children present and also nine adults. He fell quiet for a moment and then asked what was wrong with the radio in the front room.

"The new one?" replied Harmony,

"Why? What seems to be the matter?"

"How could you not notice? It seems to be playing the same song over and over. Come to think of it, it looks brand new. Where did you get it?"

Harmony looked as much affronted as puzzled.

"Why, it just came today, in a delivery van. I didn't think why, really. I just signed for it." Adam didn't like this news and asked them both to

"Come into the front room, quickly." Once there he asked, "What *is* that song? It won't play anything else."

She listened for only a few seconds before recognizing it.

"It's erm… 'Tonight You Belong To Me'. It's by Patience and Prudence, I think."

Tom reached forward to twiddle with the volume, before Adam could stop him.

"Don't do that! Don't touch it!"

"Sorry. Too late. All I did was try the volume. I tried before, but all I could do was turn it up, not down."

"It's one of those new, portable, PAMS."
said Harmony,
"I've seen them in magazines. What's wrong with it?"
"I really don't know."
said Adam.
"May be some thing, may be no thing."
He considered for a moment, then said
"Look, just leave it alone. Just in case. Put it under a few cushions and just let the batteries run out. I'll see to it later."
he seemed preoccupied but managed to add,
"…whatever you do don't let Tom near it."
Around 3.30 Adam said he would leave them to prepare Tom for his departure. He himself had to call at his new base to prepare it for Tom's arrival. Then, tomorrow, he would be taking their son away. He closed the door quietly behind him as he left.
Tom closed the comic and placed it carefully on the table. It had been *wonderful*. It had been like he
always wished comics could be. Clever.

The hero had faced impossible tasks and powerful enemies. He had seemed doomed, with no hope of escape or rescue. Then, amazingly, there was a way to win through. Someone he had helped earlier made a stand against the merciless enemy who would surely stamp on him like a beetle. This tiny gesture of faith and defiance had made an enormous difference. The villain realized that there was one thing that no amount of might or control would ever snuff out. In that instant he was defeated. 'So' he thought, 'stories of the future are much like stories of the past, good people can be relied on to do good things and a situation is never hopeless'. Tom hoped the real world would be just like that but thought it probably took a lot more hard work to have a happy ending.

He helped his mam and dad to clear away the leftovers and mess, then all three settled down on the settee in front of the fire to listen to the radio. Dad listened intently to the football scores and the five o'clock news. Mam sat with her arm around Tom, the chick nestled into a ring of cotton wool inside the tea towel on her lap. James and Harmony had decided that they would explain all to Tom in the morning, if Adam would give them an extra night. Tom read his comics, and although he couldn't find the magician's gift, he wasn't worried. Some wonderful things don't last forever, he thought.

A while later they were considering lighting the fire when there was a loud banging on the door. James jumped up in shock and answered it at once. In the doorway stood Adam. Or someone like Adam. He was extremely ragged, wearing several day's beard, muddy, and with no shoes.
"Bad news, I'm afraid."
he said, and just before he collapsed in through the door he added,
"It seems our time has run out."

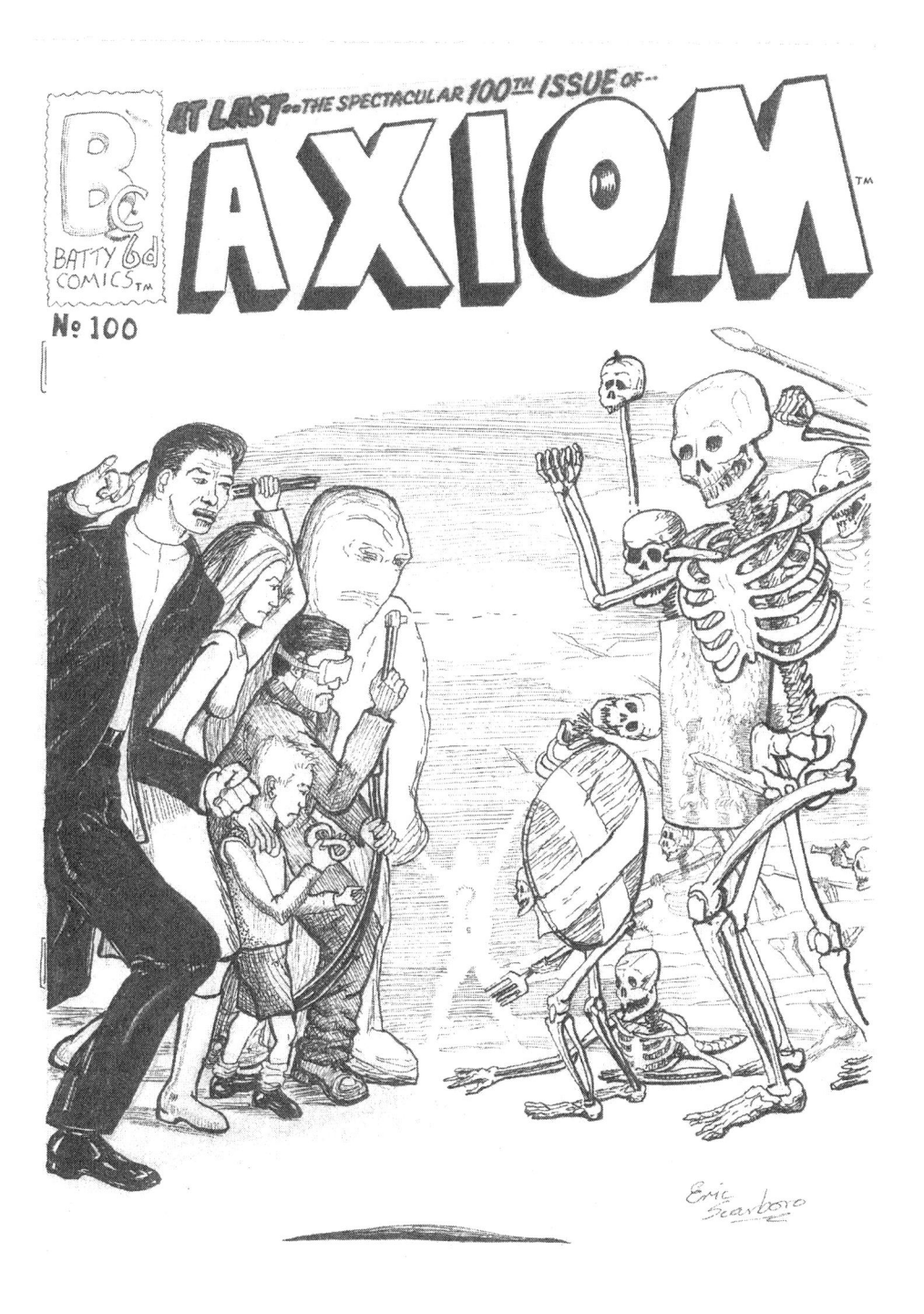

It's the best comic ever written and drawn, and there will only ever be one of them.

# CHAPTER SIX

## ALL OF THAT BAD NEWS TO MY DOOR

### Smoke and mirrors, a warm welcome.

**Saturday, the twelfth of May, 1956. Time, 11.30 am. 11.30 am.**

Tom and James had left to walk to the park. In the kitchen, Harmony, with a party to cater for in an hour and a half, was opening packets of crisps and filling big bowls with them, putting the little blue salt bags to one side. She had put some of the last little blue salt bags from the crisps into James' coat pocket so he could have them for work for his sandwiches.
Adam approached the kitchen door.
"I've taken the ticket from the mantlepiece. I'll collect the watch while I'm out. I'll be out and about for a few hours." he said, "Best to give you some time together today, I think."
Harmony agreed, nodding her head.
"James is a good man. Quick tempered, perhaps, but who wouldn't be, eh?"
"I was meaning to ask," said Adam,
"About him and Tom. Just, you know what sort of people they are, what they like, what they don't… that sort of thing."
Harmony took a moment to consider how much of an intrusion this was.
"I really do need to understand them better, I think. So I can be more use to them."
Harmony relented.
"Well, they're partners in crime those two. Love going off together. Not that they exclude me, mind. Just they really are close. As for them as people well, James as I say *can be* quick tempered, but only to those who get his back up. Tom's very loving. Quiet, studious, incredibly sharp at school but keeps to himself a lot. Not many friends."
She thought a little longer and continued,
"Very good with people, seems to know what they're thinking at times."
This seemed to grab Adam's attention.
"Always very helpful. Which comes in handy what with his dad's memory." she laughed. "Always losing things, but never for long. They always turn up. Thing is they tend to be right in front of his nose all along."
"Really?" asked Adam.
"Oh yes. He'll blunder around looking for his keys, or wallet or whatever, swear he's turned the house upside down. Then we'll ask what he's looking for, and we'll find them first place we look."
Adam looked thoughtful as he said,
"The family inheritance perhaps. An early sign that he has abilities emerging, maybe." "Abilities?" she asked.

"Yes, abilities emerging." he replied,

"Discovered powers… a… proficiency in magic."

Then after a moment he continued,

"You said 'we'?"

"Well yes, that's why I'd disagree with you. Tom has the knack of finding things all right, but I seem to have it as well, so it can't really be called magic can it?"

"Perhaps you can think of a better word?"        he asked.

"Perhaps it's just natural?"

"As is all magic."

"Well… maybe charm is better. Maybe luck. Maybe he's just clever. Observant."

"All of which are qualities very useful to a magician."

"Yes, I suppose they are."

Adam walked down the garden path and out of the front gate. He would leave the family to enjoy their last day together for some time and hoped the party was special. Perhaps he might pick up a gift for the boy and return later, when the party had finished. He held his hand up to the side of his mouth and called

"TAKE-SEE!"

Almost immediately he could hear a rumble, no more than three or four streets away. Within seconds, however, the take-see carriage spun around the corner at the top of Fife Street and into the Villas. It was driven by a filthy, ragged, scowling coachman whose blue-feathered hat suggested nothing more than a spectre at the feast, and powered it seemed, by nothing, the reins and bridle being quite empty. The coachman threw back the brake lever at the last second and the carriage slid to a sudden halt, the huge, spoked wheels sparking on the ground. Adam climbed in.

"To the Tenlock's, Grundy!"

he ordered and banged on the ceiling of the Landau. It instantly raced off at breakneck speed.

Of course what Mrs Rowell, returning from the corner shop, actually saw was somewhat different. A black car with a raised, rooftop Taxi sign, quietly picking up a customer from the pavement.

During the journey Adam had some time to think. He had not planned to take on an apprentice and the time devoted to his studies would lessen. No doubt the nature of his life would change greatly.

He had no idea how much work it would be to bring up a boy into his teens, as well as introducing him to a life of magic. And then there was the travelling! How do you prepare some one for a life of hopping around the time stream? Still, *he* had managed, and the boy *was* family after all.

He needed to organise his day properly, for there was much to do. To Unthank House sometime today, but perhaps it might wait. He would see to making it a base here, a home even, until the boy had completed his Ennia Etos, his nine-years of instruction and familiarity. Sometime soon a visit to Pity Me, Wolsingham, No Place, Hylton even. Before all that he would call in on some of those that owed to him from his visits over the years. He also needed to collect the Delia Quarterpage from the watchmakers and arrange transport of his books and instruments from his home at Greenwich. He was lost without them. In fact he was vulnerable without them. But first he needed to visit to his old friend Rueben Tenlock and have a quick word with some one at Tom's school. Nothing as invaluable as local knowledge and Rueben was sure to know everything worth knowing. He looked out of the window. Already they were surging through Bensham.

All over Northumberland, bony fingers were clawing their way through mud and peat and grass and weeds, dragging up from below whatever was still attached to them. To the west, out to the Lakes, to the south and the hills around Durham it was the same. Even in the North Sea, skeletal hands, long since stripped of any flesh, clawed at the dense seaweed, pulling themselves slowly inland against the tide, inch by briny inch.

Adam was met by Rueben Tenlock at his door as though he was expected him any second, and greeted wholeheartedly as a long standing friend. Rueben Tenlock's study had seen more organized occupants but none as respected among the Jewish community. He himself was a large man, glasses looking as permanent a feature of his face as his long, grey beard. The room was stacked shoulder high with books and unlikely instruments. The only uncovered surface was the top of an old trunk. The only permanently clear floor space was the area immediately in front of a tall mirror. Given his appearance it seemed unlikely that the owner spent much time standing in front of it. Rueben nodded towards it as he said
    "Good of you to use the door."
On what might have been his work desk stood a near-empty whiskey bottle and a smouldering pipe in an ash tray. He had vices and cared not to hide them. Adam looked around as casually as possible but he was obviously looking for something in particular. He tugged at his shirt collar,
    "Awfully hot in here Rueben," he noted,
    "Still… *producing* are we then?"
Rueben had no thing to hide.
    "I keep the kiln warm, out back, just in case."
he said, adding
    "Although it has been quite a while since it was used … in anger…"
he paused here to gauge Adam's reaction,
    "…so to speak."
    "Your ways are your own Rueben, and not for me to question, or for you to explain. I trust you completely."
The old Jew reached for the bottle, but Adam declined with a shake of the head.

Instead, Rueben took up his pipe and puffed it back to life.

"So. Am I to expect to see more of you in the years to come? Are we to become neighbours?" he asked. Adam came straight to the point.

"I have … adopted a local boy. A complicated business but one that can not be avoided. I imagine I will be taking up the vacancy at Unthank House." Rueben's fingertips stroked his beard as he considered this, concluding,

"Close enough. For us to be of some use to each other, I mean. And far enough away to leave me with my own peaceful life here on our little island among the Gentiles."

After a long slow draw on his pipe and a slower exhalation down his nose that filled his beard up with smoke, he added,

"Then I suppose you'll be wanting to reclaim one or two items?"

Adam nodded.

"One or two, yes. In particular the travelling trunk. I have to move most of my … tools to my new home. In fact it might as well be all of them. And the delivery labels will prove useful I imagine."

"Of course."

said Tenlock, then seemed to arrive at a big decision, adding,

"In fact consider all of my collection at your disposal. Rude of me not to say so already, allowing for the help I've received from you so many times."

"You need not worry old friend," confided Adam, ' I do not intend to bring trouble to your doorstep. I do however, appreciate the knowledge you have, that I do not."

"Pah!"

came the quick reply, wrapped up in a blast of pipe smoke.

"You may not intend, but it surely will follow you, as it follows me, although I accept to a lesser extent. Still those around me accept that I am often much more use than hazard. And all flock to my door in time of need. I daresay we will all quickly get used to living in the more exciting times you'll bring."

"So it is then." nodded Adam,

"And if you're going to offer me a cup of tea from that kettle that's just about to start whistling, you can bring me up to date on some local matters."

Tenlock nodded and rose, heading for the kitchen. Adam sat on the large armchair next to Tenlock's straight-backed seat.

"Oh and while I remember, I have a gift to take to a young boy's party. May I use your three P?"

Tenlock peered back around the door frame.

"The Peerless Printing Press? Yes of course. What are we producing for him?"

"Well," came the answer,

"No doubt you've heard of Seigel and Shuster?"

"Awfully hot in here Rueben," he noted,...

Seen from above, the mist that constricted across northern England would have seemed a perfect circle even though it ranged across rock, field, marsh and sea. Inside it, always *just* hidden from view there assembled a bewildered horde. They craned necks without muscle or tendon to gaze around with heads without eyes, amazed to once be more among those they had long since departed - the living. They chattered and shook as though frozen, and eager to march on, held back only by their number who could not walk yet. Those who could only claw inward slowly through the weeds of the North Sea until they reached land. Then as the dreadful assembly found foothold on solid ground, and they picked up speed, the circle would snap in on itself, like a noose.

The walk from Tenlock's to Gateshead town centre was less than ten minutes and Adam had decided to stretch his legs. He soon found himself on Ellison Street approaching the centre of the three entrances to Shepherds Store.

A crowd had gathered outside the store to watch demonstrations, intended to get both children and parents alike up to the top-floor toy department.

The central entrance Adam chose was by way of revolving doors and was manned by Leslie, the Porter, who nodded and said

"Good day sor."

As he entered, Adam noticed a woman leaving by the entrance to the right. She was wearing a bright pink, frock coat and had a lacquered-up Beehive hair-do. Mason's Watchmakers and Repairers was just to the left of the central staircase that led to the other three floors. As Adam approached, a woman dressed exactly as the one he had just seen leaving the store was now walking away from the counter. He passed a small cafeteria area as he made for the watchmakers. His attention was taken by a woman entering from the left doors on West Street at the far end of the store. She was dressed exactly the same as the first two. 'When fashion calls all must follow.' he thought. Stepping up to the counter he paused to allow another woman to move away, having finished her business. Something snatched at his mind. The woman was carrying a red bag. The woman who had just left the counter *and* the woman who had just left the store had both held red bags. He glanced over his shoulder at her. *She* was also wearing a pink coat. Same hair-do. Time began to slow around him. The sound of the diners, the lifts, the feet on the stairs, all began to stretch and distort. He knew he had little time... no... little opportunity... little space... to act. He leapt back to the Cafeteria tables, grabbing two shakers of salt and spinning the tops off them. In one movement he dropped to a crouch right in front of the watchmaker's and spread a ring of salt around his feet. All around him the store was operating at about one quarter speed, and falling slower all the time. 'A pocket, or a loop?' he asked himself. It was difficult to believe that he was getting tangled up into someone else's Deja Vu experience. It would have to be someone with a lot of natural magic experience or perhaps someone very close to him, someone family to him. He would recognise the symptoms of either sickness of the time streams and eddies, loop or pocket, but could feel his own awareness failing him. His own thoughts beginning to slow. No accident then, there was a malevolent and deliberate power behind this. He was safe within the ring, correction saf*er*, but for how long? He looked around, hoping to see someone unaffected, perhaps standing still. Or maybe someone observing him, aloof to the distortions of the flow, anything, anyone, unusual or … disengaged… anything!

A man on the stairs, his arm raised as though looking at his watch? His attention actually on three women near the jewellery counter. A store detective then.

A young woman with hankerchief raised to her face? No. She emerged from the hairdressers, pungent smell that burnt the back of the nose so perhaps just too much perm lotion.

Two identically dressed young girls stepping out of the lift doors, rainbows drifting in the air around their heads? Twin girls just down from the toy department, both blowing soap bubbles.

Through the large, plate-glass windows he could see a young man moving past without moving his legs - gliding! And another who had a spinning, flashing ball of energy moving from his outstretched hand, colours dancing in the sunlight. No, just the demonstrators with a yoyo and an American stand-board.

He saw Leslie the Doorman leaning forward and nodding. He mouthed something slowly to someone who was approaching. Craning his neck to look around the frame of the revolving doors he saw a figure in black coming closer. Himself. Any second now *he* would step into the store and *he* would be snared in a *loop* there was no escaping from. Moving in slow-motion to synchronise himself with his surroundings, he said

"Mmmiissstttteeeerr    Mmmaaaasssooonn."

to get the shopkeeper's attention and held up his ticket towards the counter. The watchmaker took it slowly in what might well have been a bad-tempered grab in realtime. The watch was luckily near to hand and it was passed to Adam with the minimum of fuss. The hands were spinning furiously, but as soon as Adam held it they slowed. When running normally Adam quickly fastened the watch to his left wrist, dial on the inside on top of his pulse. He slowed his breathing as his mind readjusted. As the rest of the world around started to catch up he stepped from the ring of salt. Pink coats, red bags and beehive hair-dos synchronized themselves with no-one the wiser and with no harm done. Yoyos whirled back into hands, stand-boards sped along pavements and bubbles drifted to polished floor tiles, the lucky ones landing gently and forming half-domes for a few more seconds of fragile life.

When all seemed normal, he stepped from the ring and up to the counter. The watch was secure in his hand, dials slowly revolving backwards. He decided to not show this, or let anyone else handle it.

"Five shillings!"

barked the watchmaker.

"Or four and six in Shepherd's Money."

"This shop has it's own money? Whose face is on it?"

Reaching into his pocket Adam withdrew five shillings exactly, at the first attempt.

"Give you much trouble, did it?"

"Trouble? Nothing but! Joke is it? Some magnet trick or something?"
Adam asked what he meant.
"When I got the back off, there were no insides…"
Adam interrupted quickly, not believing what he had heard.
"You got the back off?"
The repairer looked ready to hit someone.
"Eventually, yes! More bother than it's worth. Where did you get such a thing? No insides, no mainspring I could find, no anything!    Five shillings!"
Adam paid him and retreated to the sanity of the street outside to consider. It was a Delia Quarterpage, and he got the back off it! They never went wrong. Came with a Life's Time Guarantee. But obviously it had gone wrong ..or… something *else* caused it to fail. One or the other had caused the loop. All in all he decided he would be glad to get this weekend over and be surrounded by all his familiars, his books, instruments and routines. Pocketing the watch, and with much to ponder over, he opted to walk, to next call on Tom's headmaster.

Adam was surprised by the speed at which his knock on the door was answered. Almost as if he was expected, he wondered? Mr Fleetwood answered with a simple, quizzical
"Yes?"
"Mr Fleetwood. I bring good news. We have found my nephew, Thomas Hill. I just thought you would want to know."
Mr Fleetwood's face brightened at the news.
"Really? Oh that is good news, come in, please come in."
He was shown into a study in the front of the house, with model aircraft in various stages of construction on almost every available worktop. Adam explained the concocted circumstances of Tom's safe return, which the Headmaster gladly accepted.
"All's well, as they say."
he concluded, then seemed about to say more, but hesitated. Adam filled the gap, encouraging him to continue.
"You know the boy well then?"
"Quite well. Recently,   .. I have been keeping an eye on him. Partly at his father's suggestion, when he first came to us. In some respects he's an outstanding scholar, brilliant with numbers, patterns, tables, money… that sort of thing…"
Adam sensed a doubt forming. "
"But…in other areas?"
"Well, he's a devourer of facts, eats up books at an astonishing rate, just, well he is only a boy, but he tends to the imaginary far more than to fact. Aesop, Greek Myth, Norse Gods, Egyptian Legend, some science fiction as they are now calling it…"
"All to be commended as good upbringing surely?"
"Oh yes, undoubtedly. First class parents, always interested. Boy is naturally curious. Never a problem. Could do a little better."

Realizing that the head was slipping into the safety of School Report phrases, Adam reached into his inside pocket and withdrew a small, silver box, snapping open it's lid in one smooth action.

"Don't mind if I ... do you?" he asked.

"What? Oh snuff? No, not at all. Haven't seen that for a while. Quite an anachronism if I may say."

Adam took a pinch, lifted it to his nose, faked a sniff but then blew the dusty powder into the air, snapping the lid shut to cover his actions.

"So then you were saying"

The Head was aware that some of what he had to say was confidential, yet he suddenly felt compelled to trust Adam.

"Yes, his reading habits. Influenced by his mam I think. Had quite a chat with her about literature one day. I remember she told me she had quite a collection of modern fiction, The Hobbit, The Lion, Witch and Wardrobe, Peter Pan, Wizard Of Oz, Silverlock, The Book Of Ptath, Gormenghast, Three Hearts and Three Lions, a Canticle For Liebowitz, .."

Adam interrupted quickly, his tongue-loosener working too well.

"Yes, yes I get the idea. How does he feel about these stories?"

"Well, I know for instance that his class were being read an adaptation of The Time Machine, last year. He insisted on telling Mrs Atkinson that no such thing could possibly exist..  … yet."

"So you'd say he had a good understanding of practical aspects of life *and* the more exotic?"

"Well, yes. I suppose. You could say that he knows how many shillings there are in a pound, seems very interested in history and nature, and *also* has ideas about exotic science. On top of that his art shows promise although it can be difficult to understand, a little Picasso for my liking and he has this tendency to draw ever repeating patterns which he calls… what was it? Fractions? No. Fratterns? No not that either…. Fractures?… "

"Remarkable. You *do* know him well."

interrupted Adam again, quickly.

"Lately I've been keeping an eye on him. Thought it best to after the… oh dear!"

Adam leaned forward, staring into Mr Fleetwood's eyes.

"After the *what*?"

"Well, really this is something and nothing… and if it mattered at all,… of course I would have told the parents…"

"Of course you would. Can I just assure you, anything said here is strictly between we two."

"Well. It's some time ago. And the story is only as I recall Mrs Atkinson telling it to me… but... well…. one afternoon last year we had a strange event at the school. Mrs Atkinson had been preparing for last afternoon lessons at break, when she had a visitor. Smartly dressed man, she remembered, looking very official. Said he was Ian Foreman from the Education office and had she got the note from the head? She couldn't remember getting one and said so. However, when she looked at her desk, there it was. At least there she said it was. Later, we couldn't find it."

The head shifted uncomfortably in his seat. He had obviously been wanting to talk to someone about this for some time. Only professional discipline had prevented it.

"Please go on."
insisted Adam.

"Well he said something about … spot checks, record keeping analysis, and to be fair to the woman, she did think that I had agreed to it by note. So she co-operated. He picked a desk entirely at random and asked about the pupil who sat there. Mrs Atkinson gave a frank appraisal, a professional analysis of the child's capabilities. He thanked her and left abruptly."

Adam considered these facts briefly.

"The child was Tom?"

The head nodded.

" And then…?" asked Adam.

"Well, something just didn't seem right to her, so she came to see me at the end of that last lesson. She explained how she had had a visit from Mr Ian Foreman, and did I know him well?"

"And did you?"

"Oh yes, very well. I'd come across him a dozen times in meetings and such. I then explained that, although there was indeed a Mr Ian Foreman at the Education Office next to the Shipley Art Gallery, just down from the Boy's Grammar, he most certainly had not been a visitor to the school that day. When she insisted, and was on the point of becoming argumentative, I simply placed that day's Evening Chronicle on the desk in front of her. My word you should have seen her face."

"And what information exactly did the newspaper contain?"

"Why, only the obituary of one Ian Michael Foreman. He had died tragically that previous weekend."

As Adam thanked Mr Fleetwood and stood to leave he saw the sunbeams break through the window and light up the motes in the room.

"A little dusty in here sir, perhaps an idea to open the window a moment?"

Mr Fleetwood agreed saying he'd decided to earlier but his memory had let him down.

At the front door, the sun had quickly disappeared and leaves were blowing around on the step.

"Speaking of memory, now I have it."
"Have what exactly?"
" Fractals!    He called his drawings Fractals."

After visiting a few more old acquaintances, the journey back to Tom's house took only seconds. Adam intended to visit briefly, mainly to give his gift to Tom and to reinforce to James and Harmony that the parting must come soon. He had left a last couple of things to do later so that he could leave the family together again once the guests had departed. He also had his instruments to leave and his trunk so that Tom could take with him any bulky items he didn't want to be without.

All this done, Adam summoned his carriage. He had one more visit before he went back to Toms, hoping the party would be over when he did. His last call this afternoon would be to Unthank House, his new home for the near future. However Grundy could have him there and back in no time so there seemed no urgency. How wrong he was.

## NEOLITHIC
νεολιθικός

Say: nee - ol - ithi - cos.
Noun and Adjective: Period relating to 10,200 - 2,000 BCE.

# CHAPTER SEVEN

## IN A BIG COUNTRY DREAMS STAY WITH YOU

**Over the hills and faraway.**
**Saturday, the twelfth of May, 1956. Time 4.45pm.**

The carriage skidded on the gravel to stop outside the door. It's arched top guarded by a large, carved, sharp-eyed scavenger-bird. Adam's hands pulled and pushed at invisible ropes and levers, never quite touching the door, until there was grating thump and he turned the handle once.
"You will wait here." he said to the coachman.
Surprisingly the miserable driver didn't offer a groan in return, as he usually did. The entrance hall was wide, with doors on each side to ante rooms. On the left wall stood a full length mirror with wide, sturdy frame of old, dark wood. He picked up a lantern which stood on a side table and struck it up with matches from a box next to it. Although the place was not well lit, there was enough light to see by without it. The main hall held only what looked like a few pieces of furniture, covered in sheets. The ceiling had a central arrangement of some sort which seemed to be letting in a little light. To each side there were large, arch-topped windows, covered by heavy curtains. 'This will do.' he said to himself, 'This has everything I will need to make a start.' At the far end the hall contained a doorway, which most would assume to be a rear exit, given the length of the building and the size of the hall. He opened it and walked down a corridor that shouldn't have been there, which contained several doors, stopping and entering the last one. There was a pause of several minutes. Then voices could be heard, muffled, distant, voices. Saying words too distant to be being spoken just the other side of a door. They ended suddenly and within moments Adam emerged looking ashen faced. Looking like someone who has just heard the worst kind of news possible. News that somehow he believed he should have prevented. He knew that he had to hurry back to Tom's side. That he might be in great danger. Greater than he would have thought possible. And *much* quicker than he ever thought could be arranged. He ran up the corridor, through the hall to the main door. Bursting out of it he was amazed to see... no thing. The carriage had left without him.

He brought out his Guy's Eye glass and looked through it to scan the horizon in front of the house. Gone without trace. How could that possibly be? Who could threaten his coachman with *anything*? He himself held the man's entire fate and future in his own hands. Could there be an enemy so strong that this contracting spell had been cancelled? He turned back to the doorway. He would use the mirror. He would mirror-walk. Try to reach Tenlock's. He began to focus his mind on the image of himself stepping out onto that clear space in front of Tenlock's mirror. From there he could be through the streets of Bensham then quickly up the hill to Tom's. He stopped in mid-stride. All around was a perfect quiet. He strode to the side of the house. All along the hills to the north, from

horizon to horizon, down came the edge of a solid, dense mist, hiding every thing it rolled over. He instinctively lifted his glass, trying to focus on the fog. He saw into the interior and recoiled in shock. A ghostly, long-dead host stumbled forward, their boney limbs lit like neon tubes at a fairground. Their eyeless heads looking from side to side, as though taking in a countryside hidden to them for centuries. Rotting bodies still wearing scraps of leather and metal, one a helmet with hole punched through to match the gap in the skull beneath. Another with spear still lodged between ribs front and back.
Adam turned and ran as the mist ate up the house behind him and rose up in his wake, pursuing him like a living thing.
Over the hills Adam raced, covering a couple of miles rapidly with the mist still toiling behind him.

It was contracting at a slow, steady pace. The wasted army brought it forth with them. It was good fortune for Adam that some of the circle was over the north sea and the drowned and damned therein were crawling at a crab's pace along the sea-bed. By the time he crested a hill south west of Unthank House, he had gained a few hundred yards lead. He was heading for Villian's Wood, or rather the Cup and Ring Stones that he knew would be on the hill above there. Cutting through the wood he lost some of his lead, the mist fingering its way through the trees as he struggled across the uneven ground. Worse, the hill lay ahead of him and the mist seemed to march at an even pace, whereas the slope would slow him even further.
Climbing the grassy meadows, scattering sheep and lambs as he went, the edge of the enormous circle gained steadily til he could almost imagine it wafting at his heels.

As he approached the stones, still bearing the rings and runnels carved into them around twelve thousand years ago, in the beginnings of the Neolithic, he was almost completely out of breath, 'Just *exactly* what I need!' he thought. He reached into his pocket, feeling for anything that might be of use. Standing before the largest stone he pulled out his hand. A white and blue marble and a few little blue bags of salt. The stone was flat on top and into it's surface were carved several shapes: rings, cups, slots. Several rings were connected by one looping slot. He opened a bag of salt and sprinkled it into this connecting slot as it left the smallest circle, then flicked the marble across the surface of the rock. It bumped and rolled it's way over the uneven face and stopped in one of the indentations. The mist had reached up the hill behind him. Inside it, unseen, there rose a clattering, rattling sound, getting louder as it approached. Adam tried to calm his breathing. Tried to take full advantage of his almost exhausted condition. His eyes taking on a glazed, unfocussed look. He called across the stone,

"Who wants to play?"
The mist rose up the full height of the bank, swelling up in volume, as though building the strength to climb further, or possibly waiting for something inside it to crash down upon Adam himself. Then it was spreading forward again like a tide across a beach, the clattering from inside almost like stones rolling in the

waves, except that this was no soothing sound to daydream to. This was the snatching uneasiness of a terribly important job, forgotten about. The nagging mumble of a nightmare waiting to descend.
Adam called again,
"Who wants to play?"
The mist sagged a little, barely twenty feet from him, as though it was alive and looking around for something, then it began rushing forward, surging at him. Unseen toes sliced through mud or scratched on rock like nails on blackboard. For the third time, mist almost at his back, he called,
"Who wants to play?"
The rattling stopped. The mist halted in the very act of sweeping down to engulf him, like a huge wave about to crash on a beach, in an instant, frozen solid.
Adam opened his eyes. Stepping through the grass came a barefoot, ragged, scruffy young boy with long, uncombed hair. He smelt of sheep. Eyeing Adam's shoes he declared
"I'll play you. But beware, for this is my gamestone,… and I'm rarely beat."

The stone was flat on top and into it's surface were carved several shapes: rings, cups,…

# CHAPTER EIGHT

## THE FOG ON THE TYNE

**Footsore and weary, plans must be made.**
**Saturday the twelfth of May, 1956. Time, 6.25pm.**

James and Harmony helped a very weak Adam inside and laid him on the settee. James was the first to speak.

"What on earth happened to you? You're freezing. You've only been gone… what? An hour or two. Where did the beard come from? Where the hell are your shoes? What the.."
James halted here to examine the arm he was holding and then Adam's waist.
"…you're thin as a rake!"
It was Harmony who interrupted.
"James, let him rest for goodness sake. He needs more than questions just now. Tom get some blankets. James put the kettle on and get me a hot-water-bottle. As soon as that's done, you two get to practice your breakfast making skills. He needs to be warmed up and he needs a hot sweet drink. And plenty of toast, with butter and honey."
The boys quickly swung into action.
Adam lay on the settee, the tea and toast working small miracles on him and colour returning to his face by the second. James and Harmony retreated to the kitchen to talk. Adam's eyes opened as he swallowed another mouthful of tea. He leaned to Tom and whispered some instructions,
"Go to the trunk. Bring the bottle. Open trunk. Like this."
He made a couple of sigils in the air with his fingers. Looked at Tom and repeated them. Tom went off to the trunk. He returned moments later, clearly impressing Adam with the speed with which he had mastered the secret lock on the trunk. He took the empty bottle and wrote on the label 'Popsi'. Then he flipped back the wire releasing the stopper with a pop. Brown liquid fizzed out of the neck. He raised the bottle and drank.
Minutes later he was sat upright, astounding James and Harmony at the speed of his recovery. James asked the obvious question.
"What on earth was in that bottle?"
"I couldn't begin to tell you the recipe… it's a secret but, haven't you heard…" asked the patient,
"..of coming alive with Popsi?" He regained his bearings and shook his head.
"I was wrong to leave things as they were. I should have acted at once, as soon as I arrived.
Not wanting to upset you… and thinking we had more time… well it appears that we are almost certainly in very great danger."
James began to speak but Harmony hushed him, urging Adam to continue.

"It seems we are being surrounded by elemental forces under someone's direction. Powerful elementals. I can only assume that they intend to harm Tom, myself or possibly all of us. I escaped from an ambush some miles north of here, when my … transport… was sabotaged, leaving me in the middle of the Northumbrian Countryside."

James thought this was quite far enough to go without asking a question. Harmony didn't disagree.

"What do you mean transport. Have you a car? And how did you get back then?"

"I'll tell you what I can. You'll have to trust me with the rest. Agreed?"

They all three nodded.

"I was visiting a house my family has title to, to the north, past Rothbury. My transport was… stolen, I suppose is as good a word as any. A powerful force raced after me as I escaped. A mist. An elemental mist of confusion. Had it caught me it may have taken my wits away."

"But you did escape. So that's all right then, isn't it?"

insisted James. Harmony sensed that there was more to come. Adam continued,

"I believe the same force, or worse, is on it's way to encircle us. And before you ask, you won't understand but I'll tell you anyway, just as an example of when to trust me and when to waste time asking questions. I escaped through the cup and ring game carvings, the stones scattered across the hills and leys. They mark sites where travellers met and payed respect to Hermes, and others. I had to win my passage from site to stream, crossroads to causeway, across the countryside and the centuries. On the way I met many souls, some trustworthy, some not. Hence my lack of shoes."

James still doubted some of what he was hearing, perhaps even most of it. He stared at Adam's beard.

"And how long did this take you?"

he asked, disbelieving. "In your time, an hour or so, as you said yourself. In my time I travelled for weeks. I feel sure I covered several hundred miles, and many more years. I met with and played against, Romans and Reivers, Saxons and Shepherds. At last I have learned the fate of the missing legion. This trap has been well set and well sprung. The nearest site I could return to,

eventually, had been moved, to Throckley Bank. I raced back as quickly as I could. Doubtless many others have been interfered with, to lead any users such as myself astray, or turned on their side to make them unplayable.   So. There you have it."

Harmony reached the next conclusion first.

"So. We are to come under attack, you believe. How long do we have? And what can we do about it?"

"I doubt we have more than an few hours. Five or six at a guess. This mist will have us ringed in all directions. It is targeted at us. No one else need be involved. All who fall inside it will be unaware of what develops. Of course *we* have no real idea what our intended fate is either."

"So we can run away? Get on a train or borrow a car…"

Adam cut James off.

"This is targeted at us. You might as well run away from the sunrise." No one spoke. The situation *did* look bleak.

The mist of confusion swept inwards, racing towards the town like two great hands choking around an invisible neck. From inside came a sound of boney heels striking road, climbing fences and walls, clattering along in unison, getting louder, falling into step with one another as they converged on the major thoroughfares, the Great North Road, the Great Lime Road, the Morpeth Road, Durham Road, Hexham Road. As they went, skeletal hands snatched at berries on roadside bushes, withered jaws chomped up and down, the berries splattering down onto ancient ribcages and hips. The Disenchanted Dead were marching.

James and Harmony thought for a while, he trying to control his anger, she becoming grimly determined. Harmony spoke first.

" We thought our son to be dead or disappeared, yet he was returned to us. We have been attacked before, so you say, right here in our own home. And whether by luck or not is regardless, but we survived. And this time we are forewarned. There are more of us and we will not be taken by surprise. I say…. as if we had any choice… it's time to fight back!"


## FOREWARN
προειδοποιήσουν
proeidopoií_soun

Say; proy - do - pwee - son
verb
inform (someone) of a danger or possible problem.
synonyms: warn, warn in advance, give advance warning, give fair warning, give notice, apprise, inform, alert, caution, *put someone on their guard.*

*A ghostly, long-dead host stumbled forward,*

# CHAPTER NINE

## NORTHERN SOUL

**Spirits of the past, bones of the present, what of the future?**
Saturday the twelfth of May, 1956. Time 6.45pm.
Adam looked around the room. Himself and a few random instruments. James, Harmony and Tom his nephew. Against an enemy so powerful he had remained hidden, even to him. An enemy striking at Tom nine months ago, without anyone realizing it. Someone who could break his spell of 'contracting' with the coachman Grundy. Someone who could spring a trap of these proportions, commanding the weather and beasts of legend. It seemed that someone knew him inside out. And that knowledge was giving someone a lot of leverage.

He had been a fool to go easy on the family. For their own sake he should have simply marched in, explained the seriousness of Tom's predicament, and spirited him off to safety. For all their benefits. Still this was his mess and he would get them out of it… or die trying.

"Harmony, you and James will make a list of anything you have that may be of use to us. Simple instruments, weapons even, tools, chemicals, foods, but also old items like jewellery, good luck charms, horseshoes….. Any art or writing or anything you yourselves have created may be beneficial… anything solid *or* magical *or*… well… *anything* you suspect might be useful. Particularly pairs and opposites. If you can find both the qualities in two objects all the better, sameness *and* difference, then wonderful. James, I need to talk to you about our situation. You have been protected too long and must face reality. That done we meet around this table again in five minutes. Then I will begin your crash course in the ways of managing natural magic."

James managed to look determined and organized as he sat down at the table with Harmony, but really he was struggling to contain his anger. The saving grace being that he didn't have a target to direct it at. Yet. Adam and Tom went through to the front room to talk.

"I imagine, you'll find this all a bit bewildering. Scary, in fact?" began Adam. Tom was holding up well.

"I know something's happening. Something strange and unusual. I suppose it's too dangerous for me to stay here then, is it?"
Adam was surprised at the boy's maturity. Inside, he must be wanting to sob his heart out.

"I'm afraid your life is going to change. No one is at fault. It's *just circumstances."*
Tom seemed to accept this so Adam continued,

"You come from an extraordinary family. Your … *mam*, my sister, was an exceptional woman. She tried to protect you. Now, you have James and Harmony willing to defend you to the bitter end."

"But why?"   he asked,      "Why me? What's so special about me?"

"Some one, some where, believes you are very valuable. Or possibly a danger to them. I don't know which yet, but I *will* find out. I also guarantee that I will see you safely through this. From this day forward, you are under my protection, for the next nine years. You are so eager to learn, and I have so many wonderful things to teach you and to show you."

"I don't want mam and dad to see me upset."

"I agree. It will not help. Let's just concentrate on getting through this night, this one, single night, and then every thing is going to be all right."

James and Harmony had just finished the list, and several items were already collected in the living room. As Adam and Tom approached Harmony looked up.

"Here you are, have a look at this, tell me if I'm going in the right direction."

Adam inspected the list and the assembled goods.

"Domestos, Daz, Jiff, sand, salt, sugar, rat poison, liver salts, soap, pepper, polish, calamine lotion,…. and the 'tools', knives, forks, saw, hammer and tongs,… why did you pair them together?"

Harmony answered,

"Well, you said pairs that were the same and different? Well these two go together, everyone's heard of hammer and tongs haven't they? Yet they are different."

"Because why? How are they different?"

"Well one holds, which is gripping, making safe. Secure! And the other is striking, hitting, harming! Isn't that what you meant?"

Her understanding was intuitive and surprised him.

"Yes, that's exactly the sort of thing I meant. Well done."

James made a suggestion.

"How about my gas bottles then? They feel cold on the outside, even on a warm day. But they contain gas. Through the torch, that gets incredibly hot!"

*Adam nodded,*

"These are all good ideas, bring me more, there is no telling what might be useful, what might save the day."

Taking a moment to reflect, Adam fell into a seat and called the family to him.

"But first you are entitled to some answers. Please be seated for a few minutes. I will tell you what I can, but as I say, some of it will make no sense and you will have to trust me on
these points."

They all took seats and listened intently.

"Where to begin….?     All British magic that we know of, starts, more or less nine or ten thousand years ago. At one time it was a messy, unorganized business, with much of the effects being felt at random often with one person benefiting while many others suffered.  Not all of this deliberate. Much was due to ill-informed dabbling by enthusiastic…. meddlers. Four great, old families decided to become curators of 'natural magic'. To study each an area of magic, an aspect if you like. In an attempt to … not exactly introduce order, magic withers when ordered,   making books of magic virtually useless… more to promote understanding and trust. The Kwantickes, the Quarterpages, the

Constantines and the Abraxasons. My family decided they were most interested in the study of passing magic. Of spells acting over time and the continuance and history of magic. Inappropriately, we were common-named The Clocke Stoppers."

"You were like museum-keepers?" asked Tom.

"Exactly. Exactly like museum-keepers, Tom. Except that we *use* our knowledge and artifacts all the time. Correcting mistakes. Helping good people find the right path, hindering evil wherever and whenever we can. We draw strength from the buildings and places that have survived longest. Castles and mountains. Places where the use of magic has soaked into the brick and stone. Places of power. As of the other clans, of course there is a good deal of overlap between the families, and usually, a high degree of co-operation. We are after all, all in the same business: dignifying and altruistically using magic. It is something we merely safeguard, a force of nature, not something we can own, like a pair of shoes or a wallet."

Harmony had something to ask here which couldn't wait.

"But haven't I read that magic *is* owned, usually by Grandwizards or very old witches, or Merlin types who live for *thousands of years? I mean I know it's only fiction, but the stories must come from somewhere, mustn't they?"*

"Many of the stories being told today originated in fact, though by now highly distorted. Of the true events that they came from, yes many times people became obsessed with what magic could bring them, neglecting to ground, or banish, themselves after evocation. Almost always to their own detriment and downfall. You know of Canute, no doubt?"

All three nodded in agreement.

"What greater folly than to think a man could control the tides, and just to prove the fact, for his own vanity. He was lucky to not have nature rebel against him, lucky not to drown in a tidal wave of disobedience. As I told him."

"You met Canute?" asked James, being the first to realise the implications of what Adam had said.

"Yes, and many others like him. I had to step in. imagine if the amateur meddler had succeeded! Oh I see what intrigues you. The small matter of him living nine hundred years ago? More on this later. Another reason for you to survive this treacherous night."

"Speaking of which," interrupted James,

"… what exactly are we up against?"

"Ah, yes indeed. What are we up against? To tell the truth. I don't know. Oh I know the immediate threat. But I know nothing of the force or person behind it all." Harmony once again saw the reality of the situation.

"What must we do to survive? Or at least to protect Tom?"

Adam considered his words carefully. He must be honest. He must lay out the facts, explain how difficult this was going to be, and yet, he must inspire them. They must *see* themselves emerging into the dawn, unscathed. Or as Harmony had put it, to see that Tom survived until morning, even if they did not.

"The bad news first. Then the really bad news."

There was no laughter but it did not matter. This was the gallows humour that serves it's purpose in it's uniting of a congregation. It's affirmation of the challenge and the likelihood that none would survive.

"I am isolated from most of my instruments. The tools which would normally defend us. The means by which we would strike at our enemies."

"What about our friends, our neighbors? Will they be all right?"
James and Harmony had rarely felt prouder of Tom. That he could think of the people innocently caught up in this, and at a time like this. Adam noted that this was yet another quality the boy was showing that would surely make him an excellent magician.

"The practicalities are that we are being surrounded by an elemental force. What I took to be a mist of forgetfulness. This however, seems to be much more than that. There is a stoppage in the flow of time, where it passes. I was unable to cross it. It seems to bypass all others. No danger is directed at anyone but us. Inside the cover of this mist, an army is assembling, perhaps by now many thousands strong."

He paused to let this sink in. He had sharpened the blade before their very eyes. They were bearing up well, none wanting to be the first to crack, to let the rest down by showing weakness, by showing that they realised how impossible their task was. What a powerful force this bond was. Adam was struck by the thought that the greatest invention to ever benefit mankind was the solidarity and strength of the family. It was time now to sink the dagger in.

"Regrettably, these are no ordinary mercenaries. These are the remnants of the dead that have lain in unmarked fields across the north for years, centuries probably. Some even the missing Ninth Legion four thousand strong. They are protected by no ceremonies. No one mourns them as no one knows where they came to rest. They have no flesh we can strike at. These are animated skeletons. We are facing the bone horde."

James asked Tom to look in his toolbox which he had emptied onto the floor in the back of the kitchen. When he had left, James closed the kitchen door and turned to face Adam, looking suddenly old. Powerless. Lost.

"It looks bleak then?"
asked James. Harmony's head also dropped slightly, for the first time. Adam knew this would come.

"Bleak?"     said Adam.

"Bleak? We are fighting for your son. What greater prize could you wish for? Yes the odds are stacked against us, but do you not wonder why I am not distraught? Look at what we *do* have. A fine young boy, honest, brave, conscientious. A magician, possibly two. I expect to be able to arrange at least a couple of surprises. Two proud and determined parents. You yourself were born and raised here before your family moved south. Can you not feel the strength of the country around you? This is your place of strength. There is not a place in England I would rather be marooned or besieged than here. The counties are rich with tradition and legend. There are more castles here than anywhere else in Britain. Why, the Cup and Ring stones that have already aided my escape are networked across this county as nowhere else.

Magic is soaked into the soil of the land and the bones of the people."
He could see them rallying, if only with the force of his enthusiasm.

"This region is admired across the civilized world. Famed for people of discovery and passion that have inspired me for centuries: Arthur Holmes dating the earth itself; George Airy weighing it, giving time to the world from Greenwich; Bill Fox travelling half the earth to become Prime Minister of New Zealand *four times*. Women every bit as remarkable and wonderful as Harmony herself: Mary Astell the first women's rights campaigner; Ellen Wilkinson; Emily Davison; Lord above how can you not be inspired by Grace Darling?"
The fight was returning to them now. Tom came in to see why Adam was raising his voice.

"Admiral Collingwood, the true hero of Trafalagar. Your country's highest honour the VC awarded to Thomas Kenny, Richard Annand, Adam Wakenshaw… and dozens of others. All over the world people say 'nail your colours to the mast' celebrating Jack Crawford the hero of Camperdown. Earl Grey, the Stephensons, Saint Cuthbert, Bede, bringing civilisation to Britain, making Northumberland the centre of the universe. And what of Beowulf? Across those fields rode Edwin, first king of England. At Sewingshields Craggs ruled Arthur himself in pre-history."
Adam looked around the table. In other circumstances he might have expected a round of applause. What he received was better. James standing, arms around Harmony and Tom. Looking him in the eye, saying,

"You're right. We will not fail that tradition. Tonight we carry on where they left off!"

The first suffocating cloud of desperation. He was only human.

## ACT THREE

## THE TASK

TASK
εργασία
ergasia

Say; er - gas - ee - a
Noun; a piece of work to be done or undertaken.
Synonyms: job, duty, chore, charge, assignment, detail, mission, engagement, occupation, undertaking, exercise, business, responsibility, burden, endeavor, enterprise, *venture*.

# CHAPTER ONE

## INTO THE VALLEY

**Ssaturday the twelfth of May, 1956. Time 7.10pm.**
Adam sat them down again at the dining room table, Harmony, James and Tom.
"And now," He said,
"You'll tell me what's great about this town, this region, this country. One thing each, now, without stopping or thinking. You first Harmony."
"The sense of Pride?"
"Sense of humour!" added James,
"…The Park." suggested Tom.
"A good start. But more. Anything. Doesn't matter. There are no wrong answers."
"Friends." "Family." "Battys!" "Countryside."
"Football." "Sunblest." "Saturdays." "Working hard."
"Parties." "The Tyne Bridge?" "Holy Island." "Us together!" "Grey's Column." "Shipley Art Gallery."
"Feeding the Rabbits!" "Shepherd's Money."
"Shipyards." "The rivers."
"The bridges." "The boats." "The coal," "Gateshead Green Glass."
Adam raised his hand.
"That's enough to be going on with. What a lot you are proud of. Somewhere in that is our salvation. I just have to find it."
He thought for a few seconds and asked,
"Have any of you had… well that feeling, you know, that you've heard or seen something before? Or been to a place for the first time, yet somehow you've known all about it?"
"Déjà vu ?" asked Harmony, in a faultless French accent.
"Yes. That's it. Have any of you had that in recent months?"
All three shook their heads.
"My theory is that, when a tragedy occurs, ripples of distress and grief follow through the time stream. However they also flow in all directions and therefore go backwards. Obviously they can't be for a death that has not yet happened. Can they?"
Tom took up the idea quickest.
*"So you think that they affect us as déjà vu instead?"*
"Amazing that you should pick that up so easily, but yes, that's right. And if none of you have had any of those feelings…"
he waited for one of them to put it into their own words. James made the connection and said,
"Then… no one close to us is about to die? Is that what you mean?"
They needed as much confidence building as possible, but Adam wanted them to

start to think more positively *and* differently at the same time. They had to keep open minds. It could be the difference that saved them. Some thing else came to mind.

"What have you done with that radio?"
James raised his eyebrows.

"Oh that! I'd forgotten about it. It's under a pile of cushions in the front room, as you said."

"James, you've already handled it I take it?"
He nodded in answer.

"Then you can bring it in here. Place it on the table, please. And no one else touch it!"

When that had been done, Adam examined it closely. It was still playing the same tune.

"It seems to have gotten louder." he said.
James replied

"Yes, it is louder than when we left it, despite it being under the cushions.
And earlier, it wouldn't turn down, only up. I don't understand it. But, thing is, the tune is growing on me. I have to say, I really like it."

"And you say you signed for it Harmony?"
She nodded, adding,

"And I really, really can't stand it."

"Classic tactics, divide and conquer. Just what I would do in the same circumstances. Well, the propaganda war has begun. I imagine that it would be quite impossible to turn it off now. Even if one of you took it to the front door and threw it out. Would anyone care to try? James. Make a special effort."
James stood, and lifted the radio in one smooth motion. In four strides he was at the door, opening it with one hand and swinging it out into the street with the other.

"There," he said, " Job done!"

*It seemed to have gotten louder.*

However, when he crossed the room to sit at the table he gasped in disbelief. He was amazed to find the radio sitting there in the middle of the table, exactly where he had picked it up from. Adam, appeared not to be amazed.

"Just as I thought. No point in removing the batteries either. If it had any batteries they would have run down hours ago."

"But it'll just get louder and louder all night. It'll drive us mad, won't it." asked Tom.

"Exactly, Tom. Exactly as it was meant to. And the title? A not-very-subtle message.         However I propose to take the initiative back. We shall be the singers not the song, both patient and prudent."

He considered the situation.

"Should we have some fun with it?"

When everyone nodded he asked Tom to bring him his bundle of delivery labels.

"Now then. Some magic in action. You haven't seen nearly enough, not used for good anyway. And this will cheer us all up."

The labels were a piece of string attached to a long, thin strip of card, which was half twisted and rejoined with itself so that it formed a loop. But a loop that turned inside out and back again.

"This is a delivery label. But a special one. I call it my Listing Loop. Others know it as a Mobius Strip."

He began writing on the label.

"Our enemy, has decided to demoralise us with this gift. How will he feel if we do... *this*... fingers in ears every one. James open the door, quickly."

Adam tied the label quickly to the radio. He then stuffed two wads of paper into his ears. Standing up, he swiftly made for the open door, turning the volume up to deafening levels before hurling it out into the street. He slammed the door. The racket ended instantly. He removed the paper from his ears and the family removed their fingers. They all stared at the table. No radio.

"What have you done?"         asked James,         "What did you write on that label?"

Adam chuckled to himself and was delighted to see Tom was enjoying the joke as well.

"It was a special delivery label, as I said. A Listing label. It will deliver any object, within reason, to any destination. I simply sent it back where it came from. I hope it's owner appreciates it's return."

"But how could you do that?"

asked James, not understanding why Magician and Apprentice were so pleased with themselves.

"You don't know who sent it or where from. You didn't have an address"

"Easy. We have struck a blow back at our enemy without ever having even met him. And we are calling a new tune now, aren't we Tom?"

Tom could barely keep his laughter under check.

"Yes we are,"

he declared, and began singing,

"Return To Sender.... Doo-Doo  Doo-Doo… address unknown… "

It was getting late on that Saturday evening when the little blonde haired girl looked down across the Tyne valley, from her front garden at the top of Harle Street. The view normally extended some fifteen miles to the lighthouses at Blyth and Newbiggin, and beyond. Now though it ended abruptly. A dull, grey emptiness that curved from the north out to both sides, east and west, beyond which there was simply nothing to see. It was as if the world were a biscuit, being eaten in all directions around the outside, each nibble bringing it closer to the final bite that devoured the centre. She watched as the farthest lighthouse blinked once and then ceased.

Having raised the spirits of the group, Adam decided he could leave them briefly as it was time to put in place all his applications. He had stripped all the trivia away from the situation, arriving at the following appraisal: an unknown enemy; with unknown strengths. He, largely, and cleverly, distracted and isolated from his instruments and places of strength. The task then, nothing more than survival of this night. The siege would not last long. The enemy would strike while fear and confusion were at their height, while preparation was at a minimum. Having considered the situation, he had concocted a three step plan with several distractions and embellishments. He could arrange a couple of 'stitches in time', no more. Normally he could simply use these to walk himself and Adam to another timeplace, but morally this was not even an option. What of the others? What of Harmony? And this trap, this strangulation of space. It seemed to be distorting time in a way he had never seen before. Oh, but once he was back at Greenwich, with all his resources, then…  Meanwhile Tenlock could help him to manipulate some local knowledge to confuse, bewilder and confound. But as to his determined strategy, he would need an army,  a number of nine and finally, a hidden ally.

He looked around the room, the house. Not a bad place to stage a final defence, but not perfect. The Guy's Eye, had shown him that the house was largely saturated with magical power, a mistake then to drench this place in magic energy and then trap them here. Powerful instruments could be made from… the brickwork and wood soaked with the residue of the Dragon attack, the slow leak of the time-pieces, the residing presence of Hermes, Agamemnon and… something else? Adam's brow furrowed. What was it? Something hidden from him, possibly? Once again reaching for and using the Guy's Eye, he searched the room. Another magical presence? But where? And how had it been hidden from him? He concentrated until a headache developed. He never had headaches. This was the telling factor, the giveaway. He had to believe the almost impossible; that he, Adam Abraxason, had suffered a 'disbeliefing'. Who could place such a spell on him? There were only a half dozen people in the world capable of such a feat. He trusted them all with his life and indeed he had already, many times. He needed to sidestep the spell. Needed one of the family. Harmony? No, the boy. He had shewn many auspicious traits.

"Tom," he called,

"… come over here a minute. Hold this glass and look through it."

The boy held it up to his eyes.

"The trick is," began the magician, "to let your eyes swim into a kind of un-focus …"

Tom interrupted him abruptly,

"Oh. I can see… what is it?"

Amazed, Adam answered,

"You can see something? The tracks of magic?"

"Well yes if that's what they are. Different colours, glowing like a… well like a lighthouse in the fog… or something."

Adam was perceptibly shocked,

"Without any tuition. He can see the … syzyrgies? The Pleroma? Incredible!"

Tom wandered the room, seeking out the traces and their sources.

"There's one that looks like,… well I don't know how, but it looks like Hermes."

"And the other?"

"Well, that's obviously Aggy, but, well he's here now, on the table. The chick!"

"Tom, Aggamemnon *is* the chick. He always was. Amazing that you can see that so clearly. The Guy's Eye takes such a long time for the uninitiated to master. It took me weeks…"

Tom was distracted now, searching for something else, clearly on the trail of another colour.

"What is it boy? What do you see?"

"Another glow. A colour I can't describe. It's like … not purple, gold, no none of that… just different."

Tom followed this trail along the skirting board, into the kitchen, around all the walls, always keeping close to the corners, and finally out to the back garden. Here the trail led to the base of the garden wall eventually disappearing into a little hole that Tom knew well. He reached for a left-over sandwich from the wall top, and crumbled it onto the ground.

"Sunblest?" he whispered, "Where are you?"

## DÉJÀ VU
ἤδη δει

Say; evee - the (as in theta, not as in thee)
Noun. Already seen.

# CHAPTER TWO

## MARCHING MEN

**A fable, a twist, a trip into town.
Satururday the twelfth of May, 1956. Time 7.15pm.**
"Pontikos!" cried Adam.
"Little Pontikos. Of course! Nemeios Illioloustros. How odd that you should call him Sunblest. This little mouse is known as the sun-kissed Lion. I remember now. I placed him here with you after... after something....it's gone. No matter. We have one more to our number and the nine will be easier to assemble."
The mouse skittered around on the tabletop, familiarizing himself with his new surroundings and appearing quite unafraid. James asked,
"But how will a mouse help us. How on earth..."
he trailed off, not understanding the situation.
"And how exactly do you think a bird fended off a dragon? Or do you still doubt my word? This little fellow has a great heart in him. Read your Aesop!"
James was looking very tired. He yawned loudly, unable to stop himself. Knowing that yawns are contagious, and seeing Tom and Harmony not follow suit, The magician asked,
"Is any thing the matter James?"
"What? No, not really, just tired. I feel like this day has lasted a week."
"Of course." replied Adam, "The effects of the constriction of space. Harmony, Tom, how are you?"
Bizarrely, they both felt fine, 'fresh as daisies in fact' as Harmony had said.
"The time flow is not only squashed, but twisted, looping around itself. Even in a space as small as this room, this house." concluded Adam.
"The Eddies will have something to say about that!"
Tom was playing with the labels, idly running them through his fingers, following the inside as it became the outside and then the inside again.
"Uncle Adam?" he asked. "How does it work? I mean is the ... power... the strength... in the loop, the twist, the card or... I don't know... the string? ..is it in the ring. Is it more powerful with a bigger loop?"
"The 'power' comes partly from the ring, being both inside and out at the same time, like I said about ...duality. The sameness and the difference in the same object or pair. A ring of salt can sometimes protect, or an unbroken ring of iron..."
he halted as though a toy, run out of battery power. Tom was on to some thing, even if he couldn't quite say what it was. The boy's potential power was frightening. With no instruction at all he had just planted an idea in Adam's head which he couldn't express himself, having no knowledge or language of the concepts involved.
"That's it Tom. Exceptional thinking. Take all the labels, cut them like

this,"
he demonstrated,

"...and stick them back together. Use them all until you have one enormous loop. Enormous. With *one* and only one, half twist in it. Don't write *anything* on it until I say so!"
Tom began the task immediately.

"This saves us considerable time, at *any* rate. I'll cancel my trip to Tenlock, send Hermes with a message instead. I should be able to use the extra timespace that buys us to place a couple of stitches in time. With luck I can summon our army *and* our ally."

He made for the front door, picking up all the discarded pieces of string from the labels on the way.

"James, close all the windows and curtains. Harmony, when Tom is finished accompany him."

"Where is he going?"   she asked, a trace of worry in her voice.

"Just outside. Just for a minute. He'll know what to do."
He turned to Tom.

"When everyone is back inside again, this is what you write on the label, Tom."

He handed a scrap of paper to Tom, who looked at it and smiled.

"My favourite place!"   he said.

"Yes."         said Adam.      "And what better place to make our final stand? Within *two* rings of iron. See you there, within the hour."
he added. Just as he was about to go, Harmony appeared, holding out a paper bag filled with sandwiches.

"After the state you came back in last time," she said "I've made you a piece."

Adam struggled to remember what that meant, until she volunteered the information,

"A piece! Some bait!"
Now he remembered.

"Oh, sandwiches?   Food?     Thank you."
he said as he stuffed the bag into a pocket.


Adam set off at a fair pace, not used to as much exertion as he'd had recently and still feeling weak from his recent travels. He really missed his carriage. In minutes he had sped down the steep bank of Cromwell Street and along Cobden Terrace at the top of the cemetery until he reached Old Durham Road. From there he had a gentle slope down all the way to the Tyne Bridge, and was able to look over at the quayside as he dashed along. The threat from the north and much of the east and west on the north side of the river, would bottleneck here, on this very bridge. The other bridges being much lower, much closer to the river, or narrower. Plus, this bridge was where all the major roads led, having been the main crossing point for many years. If the Bone-Horde were being directed by an intelligence, they would be sent this way, the easiest, widest carriageway across the river. The enemy was not going to allow him to bring in awesome friends of this city like Posiedon. Therefore the bone horde would take this bridge south, high above the river Tyne.

All around him people passed about their business, unaware that soon they would be enveloped by a mist of forgetfulness, suspended in a fog of confusion while a great battle raged around them. Once across the bridge Pilgrim Street lead him up to Northumberland Street and towards the Haymarket. He was about to summon to his aid, the most unloved army the city had ever seen. And then, if his luck held, he would take a tram south, to ask the help of a giant who didn't yet exist.

Back at Ellison Villas, Tom had completed his task. He had wrapped the house in one, long Mobius strip. Now making sure that everyone was inside, he knelt to write on the label, stepped inside and closed the door.
James and Harmony looked at each other, then James asked
"Now what?"
"Well Dad. If I'm right, prepare yourself for a shock and have a look out of the window." He laughed as his mam and dad approached the window and yanked aside the curtains.
"What the hell!?" his dad managed to splurt out, before standing back and then making quickly for the door.
As he gazed out he could barely manage to catch his breath for several seconds. Eventually he quietly said
"Oh my grief, I don't believe it."
Taking Harmony's hand and resting his other arm on Tom's shoulder, he stepped out of the house. Stepped out to admire the view from his front door. The view *from* the island, across the lake and up the greens of the park.

Arriving at the Haymarket, Adam sat heavily on the steps of the Boer War Memorial needing a moment or two to recover his strength. He turned to face Northumberland Street. He could see from the Tatler Cinema past Fenwick's almost to the Paramount, Newcastle's main picture house, now showing Richard the Third. Another visitor to the region who would casually kill innocents, to gain a kingdom. To his right was the Church of St Mary. To the left the way wandered across the top of the city to the Cooperative store and the Mayfair Ballroom. All this city's buildings clean and proud-standing, not yet having had to endure the years of unending traffic fumes that would blacken it's heart.
Nearby, a flower seller was packing up for the day, outside the Tatler a hot-dog man was warming up his basins for the evening 'pictures' rush. Adam stood at the top of the steps, in deep concentration, one end of a piece of string hanging from his pocket. He felt for the tidal currents of time passing. Because of the strangulation effect all around the area, time was swirling in ways he found difficult to grasp, like an angler, fishing in a hurricane in the rapids. At the top of the steps he should be safe, finding security in the monument and it's continuing presence through the years. Something to hold onto like a rock midstream as he attempted to hitch a ride into the future. The Tatler in front of him swam in and out of focus. This was much more than usually strenuous. He needed an image to

fix his thought onto. He stopped his breathing almost completely, barely taking in any oxygen at all. His mind searched around for an image, an example, an icon, anything to help him focus on the task of drifting into the time stream. All around him motion slowed and ceased, the cars and pigeons frozen as they attempted to fly away from the nearby junction. The scene did not alter for… who can tell? Minutes? Weeks? Such measurements do not have constant value to a 'Clocke-Stopper'.

    The moment continued, unchanged, until there was suddenly movement and music from a doorway a few yards down Northumberland Street. Music that almost every kid in the country would recognise, and a good deal of their parents. 'Da dat-da dat-da da.  Da dat-da dat-da da.
The doors opened, sending a flood of light from the Tatler into the darkening street. Nearby, the frozen hot-dog man's stand started to give off the warming, encouraging smell of warm buns and hot dogs. The steam from the pans, now halted in the evening air, began to waft sideways towards the open door, in unreal, comical fashion, at the entrance making an impossible, right turn into the cinema. Moments later it returned, accompanied by the sound of slow, dreamy, violin strings. A few seconds afterwards, an unlikely image appeared on the streets of Newcastle. Nose glued to the scent-trail of the hot-dogs, a giant blue cat floated through the doors of the cinema and up to the Haymarket. Adam had his icon, the image of the year. He fixed his mind on catching a scent, a smell, the aroma of the future, changing face of the city. All around him, things began to speed up, cars and vehicles became a blur, people followed suit, the sky pulsed like a rapidly living thing, the seasons falling in behind as the years flashed by. Buildings came and went. First the Club-A-Go-Go and then The Handyside Arcade were stolen from the city in a passing, careless moment. A single, brief flame snatched away The Jewish Mother, in an instant a Civic Centre leap up complete with fountain. Behind him the Haymarket Pub crumbled and disappeared. New buildings of more Glass and Steel and Concrete, but less charm, replaced them in the blink of an indifferent eye. A Metro Station rose from beneath his feet. The seasons slowed, crowds swelled and shrank around Fenwick's windows, synchronized with icicles and blizzards, the days and nights returned and eventually the people and traffic gave up their furious dashes, adopting sprints, and then eventually walks, and crawls. The traffic seemed to have slowed too fast, the pedestrians now moving faster than the cars. Adam approached the guarding ring around the monument. A paper chain cast in concrete. Taking the last hand of the chain, he tied one end of the string around it. Along the pavement, workmen from the City Council were unloading demolition equipment from a lorry. 'Just in time, it seems.' thought Adam.
    Back on the island, Hermes was returning from his errand, chirping his arrival proudly. James was having trouble adjusting to his home's relocation, but Tom and Harmony seemed to have settled in, feeding scraps to the swans, who likewise seemed fairly untroubled at having new neighbors. Tom looked out across the lake, which stopped just before the iron safety fence that separated it

from the rest of the park, making it an island within an island. Beyond that the greens led up to the top walk, the trees that lined it and the fence and gates that also encircled them. When locked, they formed a solid, outer, unbroken ring of iron. He turned to his dad.

"Do you think, when all this is over, we might still be able to keep the house here?"

His father realized he had to make an effort to come to terms with his new surroundings, if only for Tom and Harmony's sakes.

"Wouldn't think so lad, we'd have to wait for it to ice over before we could even go for a walk."

The smile returned to his face, broadening as Harmony added,

"Well at least we won't troubled by travelling salesmen."

Adam's return journey was much easier than the outward leg. He stepped back into 1956, trailing a piece of string behind him. The string was attached to the free hand of the first in a line of connected figures, clumping along behind him. They passed a baffled hot-dog man too busy wondering about his now empty hot dog pans on his stall, to pay much attention. The door of the Tatler slammed shut, almost trapping the long, blue tail that had just snaked inside. The last of the late shoppers parted around the strange procession like fish around a rock. A few men sat by the roadside, wondering how their team had fared away to Aston Villa. Adam noticed the papers they were reading seemed to glow pink and gave sporting results. He headed off down Northumberland Street in the direction of The Tyne Bridge, followed closely by the silent, unloved warriors of the future. Warriors who were now to protect the main route south over the river. Reaching the bridge, Adam lined them up near the south entry way. He thanked them for their sacrifice and then left, marching over the bridge to the tram stop at the other end that would take him through to Low Fell, turning for one last glimpse of the brave, unloved Haymarket Lego-men.

### *Möbius strip*
Mobius λωρίδα

Say; mo - bee - us   lo - ree - da  (sometimes ταινία, say tay - nee - a )
Noun.
a surface with one continuous side formed by joining the ends of a rectangular strip after twisting one end through 180°.
"a strip of linen"
synonyms: (narrow) piece, bit, band, belt, ribbon, slip, shred.

## CHAPTER THREE

### GOING UNDERGROUND

**There has to be an invisible Sun, to give us hope when the whole day's done. Saturday the twelffth of Mayay, 1956. Time 8.40pm.**

    Adam caught the tram at the bottom of Gateshead West street, outside Hill Street Station. The first Saturday night drinkers were assembling in The Central Bar across the road. To his consternation trams were replaced by buses in the future. Buses didn't run on tracks in the road and were capable of being steered anywhere, which to his mind, just made them more unreliable. After a few minutes, the tram passed out of Gateshead town centre and by the Church of St George, the Shipcote Cinema and the Springfield hotel and bar, near to the gates of the park. He sat where he was however and continued his journey south, through Low Fell and stepped off at the terminus at the southern end of Kells Lane. He had another five minutes walk to his destination and soon found himself plodding through damp grass towards a rickety, old, metal structure that looked down across the valley to Lamesley and Kibblesworth.

    The old wheel stood black against the sky, now a cloudbank whose fingers reached from horizon almost to zenith. The still puddles of water and oily mud showing it reflected as though belonging underground as much as on the surface. The wooden huts around the outside of the yard were falling to pieces, rusting metal lay all around, melting into the grime and weeds. The site had an unsatisfied feel to it. This had been a place of great endeavour, now not even ticking over, not even resting, more abandoned than gracefully left behind. He kicked at an old box, once securely padlocked, it's rotted timbers simply caved in and crumpled. He reached inside and took out a helmet. Stretching upwards with it in his hand, he caught the last few rays of the sun as it dipped into a distant cloud, somehow finding a way through briefly. The lamp on the top began to glow. He placed it on his head and approached the shaft, looked at the long abandoned cable and stepped out confidently onto the platform that was all that remained of a cage that would once have hung there.

    The boards sagged a little but held. Somewhere a rusted gear wheel slipped free of it's siezure. The cable moaned into life. Recalling the many thousands of journeys the cage had made, he descended slowly to the bottom, secure in the camaraderie of miners now long gone, and taking a tiny erg of sunlight with him.

    At the shaft's nadir there was not even the faintest glimpse of the failing light high above, the rays of the Sun being eaten by the black walls before they could fall even fifteen feet. Yet, invisibly they still warmed the walls, even this far down. The air was dead and lifeless. No breeze blew through these dark corridors. The air was inert. Not even a bad smell could survive this deep. To his right and left he could sense an even darker patch in the air and guessed that the shaft split here, to both sides. He called to one side

    "Swinburne!    Overman Swinburne! Are you here?" and repeated his call to the other side.

His voice repeated once only as it disappeared into the dark, even echoes not able to thrive in the gloom. The walls around him were so hungry for anything from the surface, they lapped up any sound, drank in any light. There was a long silence before he called again

"Swinburne! Overman Swinburne! Are you there?"

A dim glow grew at the left tunnel, bobbing near floor level and slowly rising as it became brighter, illuminating barely anything except the odd puddles and rivulets of dripping, dank water that streaked the walls like veins in marble. Heavy, crunching bootsteps broke the silence. A weak voice trembled through the murk.

"Hev ye brought me piece?"

A fragment of coal was kicked and bumped along the passage towards him, plunking into a puddle. The weak glow stepped right up to him and was almost into his face before he could see the eyes and teeth below it.   "Overman Swinburne?"

"Aye. That's me. What can I do for ye?"   said the vision.

Adam looked at eyes that stared out from almost complete black, struggling to make out any other features at all. It was difficult to have a casual chat with only a pair of eyes and set of teeth hanging before him. He wondered if in all his long life they had met before. Not being certain was a rare feeling for him.

"You are the Overman of the pit? The pit of Allerdean?"   he asked.

"I am that."   came the reply.

"You watch the pit well, Matthew."

"Aye indeed, somebodie's got to dee it."

"And all the men well?"

"Aye, all my men well. Never lost a man, me."

"A proud boast, Matthew. And yet still you stand guard?"

" That's not to say no man hes ever been lost here mind. Just never in my time. They still need watching after, though."

Adam looked up, pretending he could see to the top of the shaft.

"The heap's gone now then."

"Aye, but it's only a heap, like. Easy enough built up again..."

The eyes cast down briefly, as though actually looking around for the first time.

"... *when* the work comes back."

Adam took a moment to consider his words.

"*If* the work comes, Matthew. If it comes it might be a different type of work.

The world might need other things more than coal."

"Why, lad, what are ye talking about?"   The ghost replied, chuckling.

"What is there that the world could need, more than coal, like?"

I will remain

"A good point, Matthew. However... in the unlikely event that ... perhaps someone decides to open a pit somewhere else first or... maybe... doesn't rush to resurrect Allerdean...?"

The eyes dimmed slightly. Adam realized as never before that here was the mirror to the soul. A pair of eyes dimmed, in almost total blackness, betraying the realisation that only dim hope kept this spirit tied to the world of the living, keeping his lonely vigil at the bottom of a forgotten well of darkness.

"Even in that case. That ridiculous case, should people ever be *so* stupid,... A watch is a watch. And not to be taken lightly.    Or abandoned."

"And so do you intend to remain?"

"Aye lad, I intend to remain. I intend to remain for *someone* must remember them. The men who built and powered these engines of ours. Those who gave their lives to put food on tables. Men who never let anyone down. Aye lad, I will remain."

This was all that Adam needed to know. That someone would be here to carry his message into the future. Someone who would not leave his post. He thought that this admiration, though complete and richly deserved, was, by itself a poor reward.

"How's the sky, the day?"

"The sky's the most delicate duck-egg blue Matthew. But there's a lot of cloud to come in later, I think."

"Aye, still, you've had the best of the day."

"Can I tell you what I think?"

asked the magician. Seeing through the eyes, that the Overman had nodded, he continued.

"I see that this place, as you remember it might one day cease to be here. I see however that this spot will be chosen as a special place. A place of pride and smiles and laughter. Families will gather, children will run and laugh in the sun. I see that a marker will be laid, a glorious, wonderful marker will stand on this spot. A huge monument, an Angel with a heart of steel, forged in a furnace of coal. A guardian to mark this site as a place where men of honour and trust are remembered. I see also, in that day, your vigil will be over. I see the giant taking the burden from your shoulders and thanking you for your guardianship."

The silence lasted a few moments. Then Adam felt a hand, lightly on his shoulder. The eyes nodded in agreement.

"Thank ye."

"And in that day of your well earned rest, pass this onto him. It is a symbol that he can follow. That he will be needed when I call him."

He handed to the spirit the watch he had collected earlier that day. Came the reply,

"It's in safe hands lad.  A watch is a watch.  Safe hands."

Adam felt his other pocket, the bulge, the sandwiches Harmony had given him. Handing over the paper bag he said

"In answer to your first question, Matthew.     Yes.     Here. I have brought your peace."

He turned to leave and, considering the immensity of his host's devotion to his chosen task, suddenly felt as small and helpless as a candle flame in a storm.

## MINER
ανθρακωρύχος
anthrako_rýchos

Say; anth - ra - cory - cos
Noun
a person who works in a mine.

## GUARDIAN
Κηδεμόνας
ki_demónas

Say; kee - thay - moan - as
Noun
a defender, protector, or keeper.
synonyms: protector, defender, preserver, custodian, warden, guard, keeper, conservator, curator, caretaker, steward, trustee.

# CHAPTER FOUR

## PARK LIFE

**Saturday the twelfth of May May May, 1956. Time 9.30.30 pm m.**

The park-keeper was just locking the gates as Adam hurried down from Durham Road. As the gates were being swung closed, he stepped behind the parkie and through the gates, drawing as much attention as if he were invisible. He looked down across the greens to the lake. Behind that, and over the Team Valley, Lobley Hill was disappearing slowly as a full and heavy mist crept down it. There, on the island before him, was the house, just visible through the trees. Already James was rowing out to meet him. The greens were sectioned off from the path by a fence that ran along most of the top of the walk. He decided he would ask James to use his gas-cutting equipment to cut away a piece of this internal fence and block the side path with it, creating only one way onto the greens from this top gate. He had no idea of the numbers of the bone-horde, but he could control their flow into the park should they breach the gates.

James was just tethering a rowboat up when he arrived at the water's edge. The gates were locked all around the park now making a solid ring of steel. James nodded to the trees at the right of the lake.

"There's a fellow waiting for you over there somewhere. Odd looking type. Old-fashioned Jew by the looks at him. I wouldn't row him out to the island until you had vouched for him."

"That was the wise thing to do, James. However he is an ally. I'll talk to him in a few minutes, but first, let's get onto the island. See how Harmony and Tom are doing"

James rowed them across, so Adam, facing backwards, was able to see Tenlock walking the greens, sprinkling something from an old pouch at his waist. Harmony and Tom met them on the island bank. Both looked remarkably well given the unknown situation and uncertain future they faced. When Adam had explained his plan for the fences, Tom and James rowed back with the gas-cutting gear to get the job done. Harmony dropped her guard, and her smile, now that Tom and James had left. She seemed relieved at the opportunity to talk to Adam, on his own.

"Something bothering you?" he asked.

"You mean apart from the fact we might all be dead soon?... *or worse,* as you might say."

"Yes, forgive me, I meant is there something *new* bothering you. Something you need to talk about?"

"Well.... I didn't mention it... not to the boys.... Didn't know if I was going mad, to be honest."

"It's all right Harmony. You are a remarkable woman, in an extraordinary situation. You're doing just fine. And you are *not* going mad. Tell me about it."

"....at the party. I was going out with more sandwiches. So... I put the tray on the bench, to open the door. It was horrible. The kids were all there, in the yard, but it wasn't them."

"Wasn't them?" asked Adam, "How not?"

"Well it *was* them, but it *wasn't*. They were old. Ancient, in fact. Running around as though nothing was wrong, but they had bald heads, grey beards, wrinkled faces. It was horrible!"

"It was meant to be. Someone's trying to upset you, Harmony."

"Well they did that all right. Thing is, the parents were also… different. They were babies, lying in piles of their clothes, on the ground. Only Tom wasn't affected."

"He wasn't affected? Not at all?"

"No. Not him or that little blonde girl. They were just standing there, in the middle of it all, as though it was quite normal."

"And where was James?"

"Well, thing is, I could only look for a couple of seconds. I think I screamed and slammed the door. James came through from the dining room and asked what was wrong. I couldn't speak with shock. He grabbed the door handle and flung it open. Everything was normal again. I just said I'd seen a wasp or something. Didn't want it getting in so I slammed the door. What's it mean Adam?"

Adam knew that it could have been a distortion due to the compression of space, and therefore, also time. However, he had to turn this into something that didn't worsen the situation.

"It could mean a lot of things. What I think it means is that… well, it was just an illusion. Not much of a conjuring trick at all, barely no power in it. It lasted barely three seconds. As a show of strength it's laughable really."

He studied her for a few seconds before continuing.

"It seems to me that our enemy has, once again, shot himself in the foot."

"How do you mean?"

"Well, let's look at it again. It was an attempt to shock us. Yet Tom wasn't even affected. All it has really proved is that Tom is far more powerful than any of us dreamed."

"I suppose so." she said, trying to muster some positive feelings.

"And neither the girl he was speaking to, or you or James were affected. Meaning that Tom's strength is enough to protect you all. There is another possibility, of course."

"Another? What?"

"We are surrounded. Surrounded by a strange, time-distorting effect. Hampering us a little, but mainly preventing me taking us out to safety. And also preventing me from summoning help."

"And this is supposed to make me feel better, is it?"

"Yes. After all if this was an attack on us, it's fairly puny. If it wasn't, well maybe it's a message from outside. Maybe someone is telling us that we'll be alright."

Harmony considered this for a moment, then asked,

"But who could be sending us a message?"

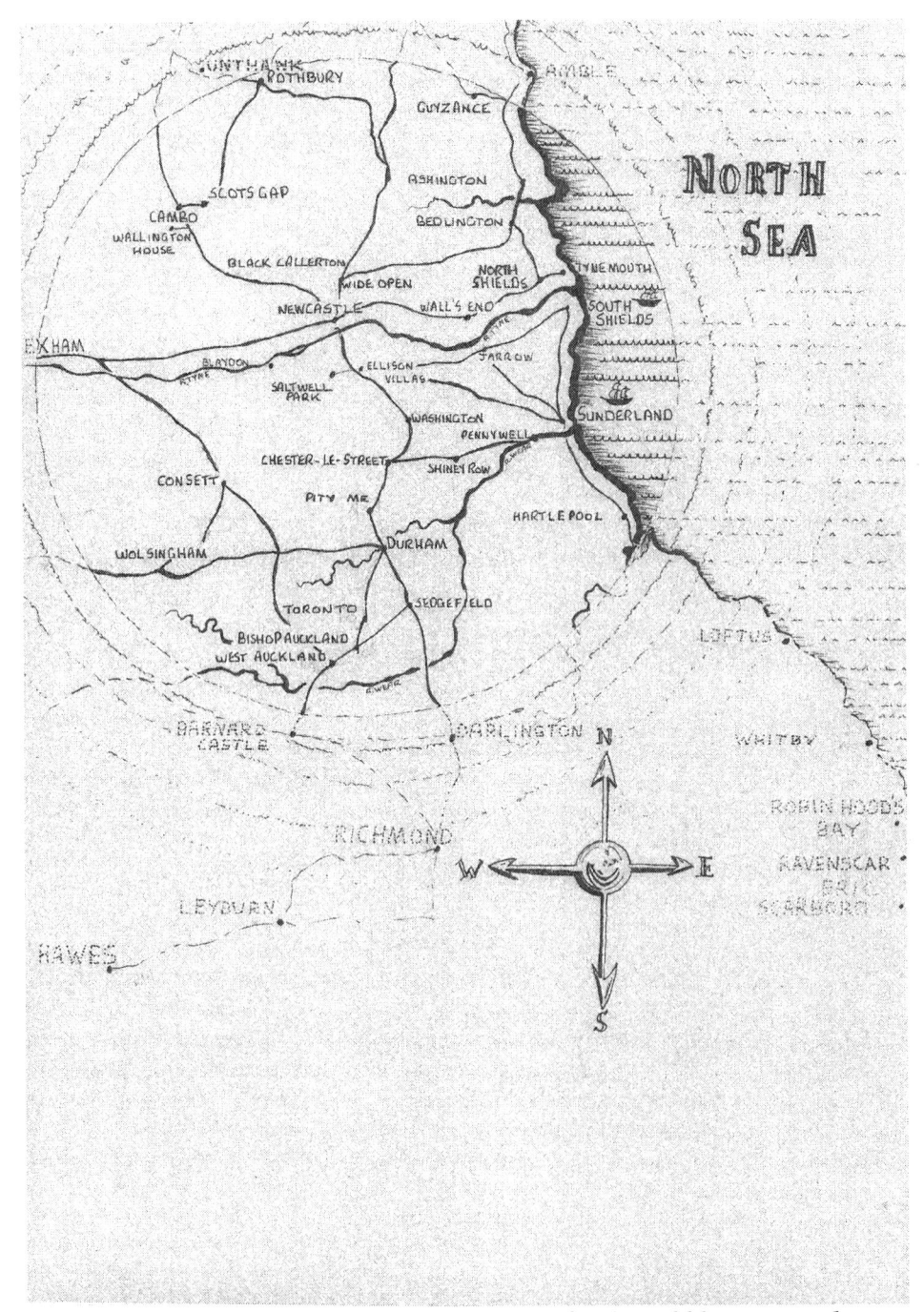

*... the mist that constricted across northern England would have seemed a perfect circle.*

"I think it's a message of hope Harmony. A message the like of which I would send to friends in trouble, if I could. But also, the type of message I would teach Tom to send. From the future."

Tom and James returned from their task, the internal fence now directing anyone who came in by the top gates straight onto the top of the greens. They had hidden their gas-burning bottles and torch in the bushes and trees nearer to the centre of the park. James asked about Tenlock.

" I have asked Rueben Tenlock to go home. He detested me for it, but he knows it is a wise move."
said Adam, hoping no one would realise the implications - that Tenlock was to get word out to the Four Families - if they didn't survive the night. Adam was not sure of the outcome, but he would make sure the enemy was stopped somehow. *And* that revenge was taken. When he said he had *asked* Tenlock to go home what he meant was that he had lied to him about how long they had left to prepare. Tenlock would be at home launching sigils as the mist descended. Adam hoped his old friend would emerge safely if and when the mist was dispelled.

They stood next to the lakeside, just outside the metal guardrail that ringed the water.

"This is our plan, my friends." said Adam.

"We will break the top gates at a moment of our choice. I have made some arrangements to lower the number of the horde that threatens us. However, they will still be numerous. Eventually, if needs be, we can retreat behind the metal ring around the lake, and take a last stand on the island. I also hope to call on the aid of someone very special, should we need him. But for now, our force consists of us. Myself, James, Harmony, and Tom. In addition Tenlock has sent us someone who now waits, out of sight, in the bushes to our left, for surprise value. Aggamemnon is still not ready. Hermes, I will send for help, as soon as there appears a gap in the force that surrounds us. We will soon be joined by a cat and a dog, bringing our number to seven."
James considered a moment, but then asked anyway.

"Didn't you hope to have nine of us?"

"Indeed. Nine would be the ideal number. However, we make do as we are."

He looked around. At last the light seemed to be really fading in this strange, elongated day, where time had ceased to be a straight line for *anyone*. It wouldn't be long now. He wondered how his army on the bridge was fairing.

The ring constricted, squeezing space and time unnaturally. Aircraft left red, white and blue trails in the air above twenty thousand runners. In the Nag's Head on the High Street, Dorothy Stewart danced like a twenty year old, as she had done nearly fifty years earlier in that very room on her wedding night. In Laws the Healthstore's window, jars of seeds sprouted their way out of their glass prisons and began colonizing the shop, drawing a good crowd from Curly's Bar next door. Coming down the High Street was an open topped vintage car called Betsy. In it sat a TV star who hadn't yet been on TV, waving to the crowds that only he and his driver could see, on his way to open the new Shopping City that would replace the Shepherd's store. In which a long haired musician called Gordon was buying a pair of loons. A young man raced down Jackson Street, putting as much distance as he could between himself and the burning 'Sportsday' monument on West Street. In the air above another West Street, Alf Roberts plunged down from a nightclub in the sky. In the Barley Mow a crowd gathered to laugh at a man called The Human Anvil. Cars flew through the air over the long defunct Ritz and Essoldo, on a flyover that wasn't there.

On the Tyne Bridge, THE prestigious way to cross the river, THE only way to make an entrance on Tyneside, a thick mist gathered on the north bank. Bizarrely, it did not drop down to the quayside below, but surged ahead across the bridge, concealing it's hidden clandestine confederates. As it neared the south end, it flowed around, under and through a concrete chain of defenders, hissing like steam out of a kettle lid. In unison, the chain marched forward, step by step, meeting the attackers head on. Skulls cracked, old bones shattered, limbs and joints dislocated and fell apart. Those behind continued their relentless stomp across the bridge, compressing those in front of them against the solid, unmoving barrier. An occasional skull or toe or hip joint escaped the crush, bouncing through the gaps between rows of concrete legs.

Eventually the mass of crushed bone formed a ramp. Some of those at the back were able to clamber over their fallen and desiccated colleagues. Approaching the Haymarket Lego-men, some of them swung old swords or axes, their edges long since blunted by the years, but still carrying much of their original weight. Chips began to fly from the impacts. Chips became chunks. One of the Lego-men became separated from the chain by force of continuous, lucky blows more than designed attack. He climbed ahead of the chain and the brunt of the battle, carving a way through the bony horde. The two halves of the chain followed him, forming an arrowhead that split the attackers in two. The arrowhead ploughed on, lifting the fallen and the still fighting together, and dropping them over the sides of the bridge into the river. Several thousand fell that way, a shower of bone and fractures that hit the water like an eroded, collapsing cliff-face. A landslide of shattered limbs.

Up above, the Lego-men had served their task well. The danger still approached from three directions but the horde from the north had been halted, no more than a handful getting through, to begin their march up the High Street and into Bensham. Fifty years on, no one would mourn the Lego-men's passing. Many applauded their disappearance. The council removal team simply looked bemused at the empty spaces around the Haymarket, took the day off and reported next day that the demolition had gone as planned.

When the crunching, splintering racket had subsided and all was still, a wagon of sorts cruised down Northumberland Street at impossible speed, whipping past the Haymarket ABC, the Tatler and The Paramount, in seconds, and rocketing over the battlefield. This was the Herald. The Herald of the monstrosity that followed.

# CHAPTER FIVE

## PLAYGROUND TWIST

### The Magnificent seven, plus one.
**Saturday the twelfth of May, 1956. Time 9.45555pm.**

The four of them were stood near the playground at the bottom of the green. Apart from a few gable ends on the rows of houses facing the park, it seemed like the rest of the world had packed up and gone home. No street lights snaked away over the hills to Blaydon and Scotswood as they should have. Above, the stars were switching off at the edges of a circle that tightened around them. Off to their left, an eight foot tall, vaguely human shape, steamed as it lurked in the bushes, always just out of clear view. Glancing nervously across toward it several times, Harmony eventually said

"Well, here we are. Our mysterious friend making five. Shouldn't our other two be here by now?"
Adam pointed to the roundabout in the play area.
"Under there, waits one of our allies, though you know him as Sunblest. Another you may see, if your eyes are sharp enough. He pads around impatiently in the undergrowth to the right."

Tom spoke up, having been quiet for far too long and deciding that he had best show Mam and Dad that he was calm and not panicking, even though he knew that he should be anything but calm.
"I saw it before. It's what I think it is, isn't it? And it is on our side?"
"Yes indeed Tom, you have met before. It served a task for me and now is here for the reward I promised it."

The row of houses above the park abruptly stopped being there, followed quickly by the brand-new college. Several funnels of mist poured down the avenues, a dulled but still hair-raising clatter of bony heels the only sound that escaped from inside. The Little Theatre remained stubbornly visible a few seconds longer. Then the mist rose up at the park gates and fences and stopped, as though pressed against a wall of glass. The clattering continued as the hordes in the rear ran up to the ones in front.

The dead men's feet stomped all around, echoing at them from all directions, like a Zulu army clashing spears and shields. Instinctively the family drew in closer to each other, waiting for Adam to dictate the next move. The clattering stopped.
The park was entirely ringed by the disenchanted dead that had survived the Battle of the Tyne Bridge, plus those who arrived from the south, east and west, pressing up to the metal girdle that was all that kept them from storming in and descending upon the trapped family.

Adam looked to the left just as a huge shape lumbered forward, silently, from the shadows of the trees. Rueben's gift. A monstrous, unstoppable behemoth of clay, fresh from Tenlock's kiln, still steaming hot. The Golem.

He was about to speak when there was a commotion to his right. An angry voice called from the greenery. Tom and Harmony instinctively stepped forward, in front of Tom. The voice came again. The bushes shook violently and a grubby arm shot out, grabbing a handful of branch and leaves and hauling the rest of it's body into the open. A ragged, bearded mouth opened to reveal broken, stained teeth, and hollered at them,

"Can't a man get any bloody peace round here? I'll tell the bloody council! So I will!"

Like it or not, their number had just risen to eight, courtesy of Franky the Fireman.

*… an eight foot tall, vaguely human shape, steamed as it lurked in the bushes…*

## *CHAPTER SIX*

### FRANKIE'S TALE

**Waiting for two sons, who are not to return.
Friday the eleventh of May, 1956. Time 7.45 pm.**

Inspector Gordon left the school and headed straight for the nearest Police Call-Box, which luckily, happened to be just around the corner on Durham Road in front of the Boy's Grammar. He called the Watch Sergeant at Swinburne Street to ask if there had been any confirmed sightings in the hunt for the missing boy. No luck. The car had arrived from Chester-Le-Street, with the dog, and the extra two officers were also out on the streets. Newcastle force were watching the streets and parks, but the lad had little history in the town.

This one had him stumped. There was no chance of anyone at the school being involved, his contact at the Education Office had been very thorough in double checking. No new members of staff for six years. A good school. One which teachers didn't often leave. The parents were sound enough apparently and well thought of, with no significant criminal history. Good solid citizens. What nagged at him was The Case. The one he didn't mention, but which was never far from his thoughts. Unfinished business. The one blemish on his career. Well, not blemish. Not exactly. No one could have expected much of a result from **The Case**. No one but himself.

The boy had been on a message to the shops. Just down the bank in Bensham. Davey Davies. Sent round the corner for a bottle of milk. Never seen again. No trace from that day to this. No reason to disappear. No suspects in the area who would do that sort of thing. No recently released criminals. A previously safe area, well lit, busy street sort of disappearing act. The boy would be nineteen now. Not too big to put over his knee and give a good spanking to, should he suddenly step off a ship and declare himself having run away to sea. Last thing he wanted now of course, was another. Another Case. People might panic. When people panicked, accusations flew, tempers rose, people got hurt, police got busier. Crimes didn't get solved however.

He decided to drive between Tom's home, the school and the park. See how many different ways he could find. Let people see that he was out and about. Let the lad see that he was being looked for, just in case he was still in hiding somewhere. Somewhere just out of sight, peering through a fence or under a hedge. Every lap he made, he called in at, or telephoned to, the Station. It was on the fourth call that he heard the news. One of the new bobbies on the force had arrested a man near the Saltwell Park area. He was back at Swinburne Street in minutes.

He swept through the entrance like a man on a mission, nodding only briefly at the desk Sergeant, Bill Morris. Bill shook his head negatively, saying only,

"Interview room two!"

When Gordon reached the room he could hear voices inside. He decided to wait a few seconds, judge where the interrogation had reached, decide when to make his entrance and how to play it. After a few seconds he realized there was only one voice. Odd that the suspect wasn't saying anything. He sniffed at the door jamb. Sniffed deeper and shook his head before entering and saying

"Alright Joe,"

And then acknowledging the officer with a nod.

"You're free to go. Get your things together. And there'll be no further questions, officer. Kindly see Mr Wrigley out and then rejoin me at the front desk."

The officer spluttered something which wasn't quite words.

"Just do it man! This fellow's no harm to any one. See him out. And do it now!"

The arrested man was shown out, nodding his thanks.

"God bless ye, Mr Gordon sor!".

"How's that leg then, Joe?" asked Gordon, his paternal hand-on-shoulder masking the crisp ten-bob note he pressed into Joe's hand.

"Fine, Mr Gordon Sor. No more high-jumping for me though."

At the front desk Sergeant Morris shook his head.

"I didn't think you'd be very happy, but I thought I'd best let you decide."

Gordon drummed his fingers on the desk impatiently.

"Take it easy with him John. He's new to the force *and* from outside the area. A good lad really, just a bit impulsive like."

Just then the arresting officer returned, slightly red-faced.

"With respect Sir. What the hell's going on? He was acting suspiciously in the area between the park and the school. I felt justified in lifting him."

Gordon considered for a moment.

"Todd isn't it? Michael Todd? Yes lad, well done I suppose. You weren't to know."

"Know what Sir?"

"The man you arrested is one Joseph Wrigley, also known rather unkindly, as Franky the Fireman. Had you been here any time in the last five years you might also have arrested him on suspicion of starting several fires, what with him being in the habit of being found in the area of the last six fires we've had in the town. You'd have been wrong then also. Joe is completely harmless. The man couldn't possibly harm a fly."

The officer accepted this at face value and made to leave the station. Gordon added,

"Next time, stick to procedure and telephone it in. Get back-up if you can, *before* you approach someone you think might be dangerous. Oh and, chin up son. Good coppering."

As he drove back out of the police car park, he couldn't get Joseph Wrigley out of his mind. His fascination with fires earned him his 'Fireman' title.

He wandered the streets all day, watching for fires, listening for fire engines. Hearing one he would race after it, pestering the firemen, could he help with anything, could he handle the hose, did they need anyone to dash inside for a rescue?

A decent man, working himself to the bone to provide for his wife and two boys. Putting in seventy hours a week. Wanting better for them than his parents had been able to provide for him. Salt of the earth. Wife working hard as well, barmaid at The Cromwell four nights a week. She still blamed him apparently. Never spoke to him since and vowed she never would. His crime? Absolutely knackered one Saturday night, he nipped to the fish shop to have supper ready for her coming home from the a shift in the pub. Left the three year old in charge of the five year old who had a fever. Told him not to touch the fire or the lights or the oven, where the plates were warming, Dad'd be back in a minute.

When he did return to the house, it took four neighbours to drag him from the doorway and hold him down. Four men as big as boxers to stop him pointlessly running into the flames to his own death. He was held there on the cobbles, his hair and clothes still smoking, looking up at the window, screaming, when the fire engines arrived.

The house had been condemned as a tinder-box, some years before apparently. Landlord didn't care. The council had nothing to offer them so they had just stayed where they were. A normal, happy, little family with a garden. So now Joe wandered the streets, looking for his two lads, blaming the council for anything he could, and following fire engines around. Bedding down in the arches or the park, slowly losing what he had left of his marbles.

Gordon saw a lot in common between Joe and himself. They'd grown up on the same estate at Beacon Lough. Went to the same school. Were both well known in the town. 'Where do lives diverge?' he thought. Joe Wrigley breaking a leg at school, high jumping, while he himself went on to play for the Grammar School Rugby team? A throw of the dice, nothing more. One becoming a joker by necessity, one being left to follow his own course. And now of course, they were both the same again. They were both looking for lost boys. Gordon just prayed that he was not as doomed to failure as certainly as Joseph was.

He had long since clocked off. Regardless, he turned right up the High Street, instead of left to go home. He would make just a couple more laps of Deckham. Maybe three. As he passed the Holy Trinity Church which his dad still called 'the infirmary', he saw Joseph on the opposite pavement. 'Franky the Fireman' was emerging from Woolworth's doorway and having an argument with a Belisha Beacon. Gordon had seen terrible things in his time. Horrible injuries inflicted on loved ones *by* loved ones, un-survivable car crashes, men stretched thin and sharp by greed, and too many broken bodies to count. With the briefest glance in his mirror, he was very thankful for a twist of fate.

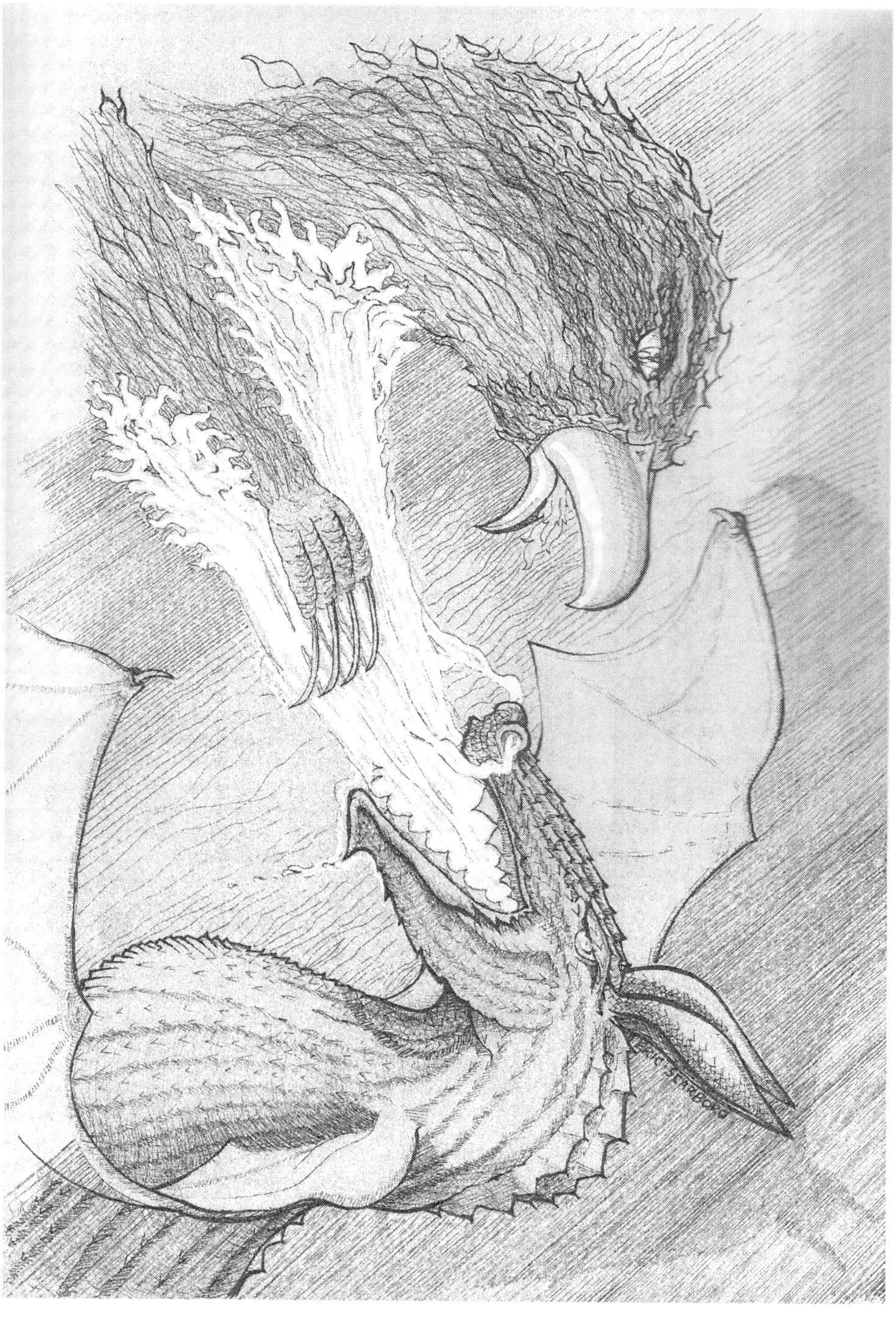

# CHAPTER SEVEN

## PARTY FEARS TWO

**The gates are down, let battle commence.
Saturday the tweeelth of Maaayy, 195666. Time, 9999.555pm.**

The horde from the north had been reduced to almost single figures on the Tyne Bridge. Adam had known that bridge would be chosen, and had positioned his defenders at the south end. By the time the Bone Army met with resistance there would be thousands of them jammed onto the bridge with no way to retreat. The other three points of the compass however had supplied almost as many troops. They had swarmed in along the A1 to the south and down Lobley Hill to the west. Those recruited from the depths of the North Sea descended on the park along Sunderland Road and up onto Old Durham Road. The combined forces now thronged around the park fences, the solid ring of iron holding them back. They thrashed and battered all around, seeking a weak link. Adam was soon to supply it.

James spoke first.

"You're Joe Wrigley, aren't you?"

The old tramp ceased his rant and stared at them, seeming to calm in a few bewildered seconds.

"You… you know me?"

"Yes I know … well at least knew of you. You worked with a friend of mine for a while. Old Charlie Richardson. At Clarke Chapman's. Clarkies."

There was no immediate response. Joe Wrigley seemed to be trying dreadfully hard to remember, but having little success.

"Charlie Richardson you say? Clarkies? That was me?"

"Yes. He always spoke well of you. You weren't a close friend but he said you always were cheerful. Hardworking but happy. A good fitter, good with tools. Easy to get along with."

"Well, yes, that sounds like me."

"Of course that was before the accident. Before you…. "

Joe's eyes were suddenly clear and bright, as though a deep mist had lifted.

"Before I became like this?"

He gazed around the gathering slowly. Then he took in his surroundings as though realizing for the first time that he was in the park. Then he looked further and it dawned on him that he was with a group of strangers, in the park, *at night.*

So what's going on then?"

Adam stepped forward.

"I'm afraid you've been caught up in some *very* unpleasant business. Some great harm is intended to this boy and we are his protectors. There is no easy way to say this, so… I'm afraid you have nowhere to go. You can't leave the park, and I can't help you. I suggest you find a safe place to hide and stay there until morning. Stay there quietly."

The tramp considered his options, seeming to dither for a while before fixing his gaze on Tom.

"So... ...this boy?   Someone wants to harm this boy? This canny lad?  I had two once. Fine boys. Fine bairns.My William would be about his age now.... Little   William. No one harms this boy tonight. Over my dead body."

Joseph Wrigley stepped forward to stand in line with them. Stepped forward with no idea of the dangers he faced, or his chances of survival. Stepped forward with no need to know them. Stepped forward just for the joy of making a decision again and because it was the easiest decision he ever had to make.

Harmony watched as Adam and James stepped forward to shake Joe's hand. What chance did they have? An army of thousands of the dead, or undead, or whatever they were. According to the magician some strange help *might* arrive but, until then.... It was just them, and this cat and dog Adam had promised. What she couldn't understand was the calm she felt. The calm that they all seemed to feel. Was Adam *making* them feel confident somehow? Was something else happening that she couldn't quite see? She certainly felt fine. Clear-headed. Rested even. All this despite the situation being quite hopeless. This then was resignation. A feeling of great relief. All other worries shook loose from the mind, leaving the body strong and relaxed. She looked along the line. A boy, his parents, a magician, a cat and a dog, a clay man and a half-mad tramp.

"Still, chin up everybody."    she said, breaking the silence.

"It's not all doom and gloom. Any minute now the Keystone Cops might arrive."

Everyone laughed heartily. She had caught the mood just right, confirming to herself that the others felt exactly as she did.

Adam reached into his pocket, and pulled out a lock marked TWINPAD.

"They've marched all day. We are ready for them. I say we do this ... now!"

With that he turned a key in the padlock. Simultaneously, at the top gate, the identical twin clicked and fell open. There was sudden silence as the thrashing died down. The gates swung lazily open, an enormous lack of oil on hinges groaning through the still air. When the gates had clanged into place, fully open, the silence held for a few, eternal seconds. The mist sagged, dropped and flowed into the park along the path. There was a crescendo of chaos as the Bone Horde swept in behind it, heels slapping pavement, thigh and arm bones clashing in the squeeze to invade. Many of the older bones desiccated in the crush through the narrow gates.

Once inside, the Dead Regiment fell into step with each other, ten across, devil knows how many deep. The re-positioned fence funneled them onto the top of the green where Tenlock had wandered only an hour before. On reaching the green, they broke into a run, washing down the grass like a rip-tide. There was a blurring at their feet. None of the defenders knew what was happening, until Adam spoke.

" Now we see the value of Tenlock's work. As he sowed so shall we reap."

The blurring was now a flurry of green. Shoots of grass and tendrils of something else whipped up out of the ground. In seconds they were strong enough to trip the ones at the front of the charge. Soon after that they were grown thick enough and moving quick enough to snatch at those not yet caught and haul them back into the marauding mass behind them. More like octopus tentacles than branches, more grappling hooks than twigs, the rush of the green seemed eager to reclaim the recently-risen bodies and drag them back underground.

"Remember!" called the magician, "What we believe in has power. What we don't believe in can not harm us. Remember also that words have power." He looked straight at Tom.

"Tom, give us some wise words if you please."

Tom was both aware of the awful situation, and how simply ridiculous it was. He raised his voice in reply.

"One fine morning in the middle of the night…"

Smiles spread across their faces and they joined him for the rest of the verse.

"..Two dead men got up to fight.
Back to back they faced each other.
Drew their swords and shot each other."

Adam continued with the other version that he had heard.

"One dark night in the middle of the day,
A bony army got up to play,
Swapped and swiped their bones around,
Ran like dogs back underground."

Behind the trapped and entangled, bony fingers clutched aloft sticks, clubs and the occasional sword or axe. The weight of numbers rushing in behind them, prevented any of these weapons being used to cut through the now rich and thick growth that squeezed and cracked bones and skulls.

"Not too bad a start then, eh?" asked Adam.

"Watch how they move. What do you notice?"

All stared, but none had much to say. Only Tom volunteered,

"They're stupid." Again the assembly laughed.

"Expand on that, Tom. Tell me more. What do you *see*?"

To their left, the Golem strode stiffly onto the green, free of the shadows. To their right, there was a scuttling from under the roundabout platform. Sunblest made an appearance, rising on his tiny back legs and twitching his head from side to side as he sniffed the air. There was a boom that turned into a roar. The first shook their ears making them clutch hands to the side of their heads. The second sent a shiver down their spines. When they dared to look again Sunblest was gone. In his place, reared up on powerful back legs, roared a golden ripple of fur and muscle, lighting up the play park in reflected radiance. There, baring teeth and claw stood Nemios Illioloustros. The Sun-Lion.

At the top of the green, sheer weight of numbers was sending some of those at the back stumbling over fallen comrades. Soon Tenlock's defence was breached and a sizable legion spread across the grass. From the rear emerged a much larger figure, standing head and shoulders and more above the rest. It was hefting an axe and a spear. Those in front parted for it to pass until it reached the centre of the front ranks. With right and left flanks now reinforced, Adam strode forward to meet this 'leader'. The others followed a few steps behind. He walked right up to it, stopped and turned his back to it.

"I ask you again Tom, what do you see?"
Tom instinctively said the first thing that came into his head.
"They march like a legion."
"Good work lad, my thoughts exactly."
Turning back to the horde he raised his voice for all to hear.
"This is no attack force. This is an army of puppets. When one marches, all march. There is but one mind behind this, not a thousand."
Despite this, or to prove it, he addressed the newly appeared giant.
"Why carry axe *and* spear, warrior? What use to you is a spear up close? Or an axe from the back of a battle?"
He turned his back in contempt. The giant shifted it's shoulders, swept back an arm and brought the axe up, across and down at Adam. He stepped to the side just as the axe swooshed past and bit deep into the ground. The giant stood there, bowed forward, still gripping the weapon. Adam stepped up and brought his right foot down through it's wrist, snapping it instantly.

"These bones have been too long underground and snap like dry twigs."
He snatched sideways, grabbing the spear from the ogre's other hand. Raising it up above his head, he thrust it down through the ribcage and into the soft earth, pinning his adversary there. Joe strode up behind him and swung the fence-post he was using as a club. With a coconut-tapping BONK! A huge grey skull flew over all of their heads and landed forty yards away in the lake.

"Tell the council about that, bonny lad!"

The horde continued to pour in through the gates, bottlenecking at the top of the green and spilling forward a dozen at a time, but a dozen at time that seemed like it would never end. Adam, James Harmony, Joe and Tom laid into the troop with whatever they had brought. Harmony holding them one by one with tongs. James demolishing them one by one with his quarter-hammer. Joe and Tom played skull golf. Adam sprayed some liquid that smelled like vinegar *and* salt from squeezy bottles. The Golem and the Lion prevented any flanking maneuvers while staging their own, very different assaults. The Golem seemed unstoppable and to have an appetite that couldn't be satisfied, rolling up the green squashing and absorbing anything it could reach and grab hold of. The lion simply hauled down the enemy one at a time and ripped them into pieces. Still the mist and bodies flowed into the park. It became hard to see, thick mist blocking areas of grass. Adam sensed his company tiring and wondered how much longer before they were overwhelmed completely.

Out of sight behind them down the hill at the bottom of the park, it arrived, panting heavily, near the Salt Well. It had very little idea why it was so out of breath. Hadn't it been running long enough? Why was it not far away from this place? It had supped from the Temperance Fountain at the kind invitation of the inscription 'for ye goode of thirstie dogges' before racing up the hill through the dene. The magician had made a promise. Where was he? What could he provide him with here? He crept towards the greens, laying low in the dense bushes. He smelled something new. Perhaps this was why he could run, but get nowhere. He did not like this new feeling. This not running. He would wait. The swiftest of all beasts, he would lay still and be… patient.

The defenders had been keeping Tom at their core as much as was possible. Suddenly the youngster found himself separated from the others. In seconds he was surrounded by a flailing of bony arms. The rest lost sight of him for a few seconds, hidden by a billowing mist that seemed to have a purpose of it's own. Hearing him yell for help, all tried to run towards the voice, Joe, despite his mangled leg, made it first. He swung wildly left and right, high and low, decimating the throng. Tom stumbled free and scrambled clear of the mist, Harmony snatching him up and James leaping in front to prevent further attack. Joe was lost in the sweeping mist. And still the Bone Horde poured in through the gate.

" They weren't hurting me…" shouted Tom.

"They were trying to snatch me!"

Adam decided the time was right. He snatched up a familiar looking bundle of stick and leaves, and hurled it through the air into the bushes to the middle of the park. The group of them formed a circle around Tom, retreating to the centre again, feeling more secure between their two magical allies. They kept staring at the bushes. No thing happened. They retreated and huddled together, too tired now to battle further, protected only by the Lion and the Golem to either side. The horde pressed down on them, relentless. They fell back to the edge of the lake, feeling the metal guard rail against the back of their legs. They would have to retreat behind it and across to the safety of the island. But what then? The iron ring of the rail would protect them but… something nagged at Adam's mind. Joe. Joe's weapon. The fence post he had been swinging. Where had he gotten it from? To the side James stepped back and slipped, almost falling into the water. Adam looked across at him and realized the rail was broken. Joe had taken a stave from the fence.

No one had told him not to. Now the inner ring of iron was broken. There was no point in retreating. The horde would follow them onto the island, where they would be trapped.

Then, to their right, there was a brief gap in the fog. Near the bushes something moved. Something big and black and quiet padded from the undergrowth. It sniffed the air, stretching it's neck and legs as if just awoken. Then, faster than the eye could follow, it raced into the horde, visible only by the damage it left in it's wake, ripping and snapping bones apart. They fell like a spray from a garden hose, all across the greens.

James tried to catch sight of it's impressive progress.

"Our saviour the Pooka, I take it?"

"Yes indeed, James. Better late than never, but we should not have had any doubts."

There, baring teeth and claw stood Nemios Illioloustros. The Sun-Lion.

"What made you so certain it would show up then?"

"Didn't you wonder? When I made a pact with it, to have Tom rescued? Didn't you wonder what I could possible have offered it? Hah ha ha. And now here it is, the most fabulous dog of legend, let loose in the world's biggest bone-yard!"

"The battle swings our way then?"

"Momentarily, at least. However I fear there are further acts to be played."

The tide had begun to favour them. Their fabulous allies making enough of a difference to allow them a moment's rest. The mist and the horde, however, continued to tumble in. Through The foggy air they felt something on their faces. A change in air pressure, a slight change of compression on their ears. Something surged in the air above the battle. A bow wave of pressure pushed the mist apart. A flash of blue rushed at them as a carriage spun to a halt and sprayed the air in the paddle-pool before them.

Down from the seat hopped Lucas Grundy.

## REDEMPTION
εξαγοράς
Exagorás

Say; ex - a - gor - as
Noun
the action of saving or being saved from sin, error, or evil.
synonyms: saving, freeing from sin, absolution retrieval, recovery, reclamation, repossession, return; exchange, paying back.

# CHAPTER EIGHT

## MAGIC NUMBERS

**What's that coming over the hill? Is it a monster?**
Sat Sat Sat Saturday Titheme twepmlth 11.11.11.11.
The coachman rushed forward and prostrated himself at Adam's feet.
"Lord forgive me sor, lord forgive, I didn't know what to do. I couldn't stay. I couldn't stay. Save me from him, please save me from him…."
"Grundy man." called Adam,
"Stand up for goodness sake. Pull yourself together man. What the hell are you babbling about?"
Grundy crept forward, not quite risen, but no longer flat on his belly.
"I saw them coming sor, I saw them coming and I didn't know what to do. I can't harm anyone sor, I can't harm him and that's your fault. I couldn't fight back and that's your fault. I didn't know what I could do. But now I'm here sor, returned now to fight by you, if you'll have me."
"You mean at Unthank House? When I left you outside?"
"That I do sor, that I do."
Seeing that his master hadn't taken a whip to him or delivered any of the imagined punishments he thought he might have faced, Grundy began to calm slightly.
"You went in sor and left me. I saw them coming. Coming over the hill. It was your fault. I couldn't harm them, couldn't harm anyone. Couldn't leave the carriage, couldn't warn you, couldn't do anything. Your fault. Your fault, all of it."
"So what did you do Grundy? What did happen?"
"I had to flee sor. Hope to find you later. Come back and find you later. But he found me first sor. He found me first. Said I was his herald sor, would announce his coming, when he chose it."
"And so now we *are* nine."
"I'll fight by you sor. I'll die by you sor. I'm a good soldier sor, you just ask Napoleon. Just don't let him take me. I've seen the madness, seen what he can do. Seen what he plans for the boy. It's not right, not right. Let me stay here sor. Let me stay…"
Adam looked around the debris of the battleground. Grundy had not flickered at any of it. The horde were pressing forward for one last assault. On last attempt to claim Tom from them. The remains of a long-dead army marched through the rubble of countless thousands of smashed, fleshless bodies, and he hadn't batted an eyelid at any of it. A battle-hardened man. Yet some one or some thing approached. And that some one or some thing had Lucas Grundy terrified.
"You make your own choices tonight Grundy."
Grundy, rose at once. Without hesitation, he leapt into the carriage seat and spun his vehicle into the green, ploughing through the skeletons that marched towards him, cutting them down like a scythe under a ripe harvest-moon. Cat, dog,

clayman and carriage demolished an army that night, on the greens of Saltwell Park, and barely a drop of blood was shed.

Around the greens something had changed. It took a while for any of them to realise what it was until Harmony spoke up,

"They've stopped coming!"

All eyes swung to the top gates. At last the multitude that had thronged the park had been exhausted. Relief spread across their faces, briefly. For to their left the Sun Lion simply disappeared. A tiny shape scuttled toward them through the grass, barely bending the sheaves. Adam summed this up succinctly,

"The hour of the Sun Lion is gone."

The Pooka, high up on the grass, seemed to decide that he had done enough. The bones were old, barely worth a puppie's lick never mind a good chew. He stared down at the ragged, exhausted band of them momentarily, then sauntered off and out of sight into the bushes. His game was over.

At almost the same time, the Golem began to move more stiffly, each step slower than the rest. Within five paces he had petrified completely. The heat and the desire it had fixed within him, now totally exhausted. Adam had no need to check his watch or ask the time, meaningless as both gestures would have been anyway in the circumstances.

"He could not walk into a new day. I suppose that means we are more or less at midnight."

The last tattered band of the dead legion stopped their funeral march. They turned eyeless sockets to each other for a few seconds, and then dropped, lifeless and unanimated, dead again.

In the silence, only their heavy breathing gave a pulse to the night.

Somewhere, a long way off, an old horn blew.
It blew again.           Closer.

Adam's eyes covered the greens, searching for some one or some thing. He saw, for some unknown reason, that one of the Shuggy boats was missing. Then he abruptly turned to them.

"Grundy, take Harmony and James to the island. You'll be safe there. Release Hermes when the moment is right."

Reaching down, he swept up Sunblest and dropped him gently into the rowboat.

"Tom and I must stay here."

Something about his tone told them there would be no argument. Grundy stood up by the rowing boat and held it to shore as Harmony and James stepped in. With a push and a hop they were off into the still lingering mist, toward the island and the temporary security of their displaced home. Adam turned to face Tom.

"There is one task to be done, but first we must meet our tormentor."

They stood together, magician and apprentice, not knowing what they would face, but fully realizing what was at stake for each of them. The images in

Tom's mind whirled at him ceaselessly. Mirrors, reflections, dogs, lions, skeletons, magic words and…. strangely, parties. He flushed them to the back of his head, retaining only the party. Adding to it one by one, his friend's faces, his birds, his comics, the park in happier times. He imagined the sun coming up in the morning, filtering through the leaves on the trees, birds singing, fish leaping in the lake, rebuilding his world the way he wanted it to be, step by step. He glanced up at Adam. He realised by his calmness and slow breathing that he was probably doing something similar.

"Faithfull guardian of Allerdean, I call you back… "

Adam was interrupted by the first blast of the klaxon now suddenly close, deafening, painful. Clutching hands to heads they both spun around to face the top gates. There the mist was banking up, rising higher than the gates, the rooftops, the trees. He called again,

"Guardian of Allerdean. A Collier's son needs you. I call you back… "

The blast continued, echoing back at them from all directions, the reverberations impossibly louder than the original that gave them life. The mist parted. A woman's golden face forged through it.
Emotionless, it lifted up and crashed forward in a swinging, rolling loll as it rose over the height of the gates and lunged down into the park. The mist spread to each side, parting like water, revealing the sides of a long, thin boat, golden and glittering, following behind the Figurehead. Over the sides fell oars, sweeping up and down and back, together, perfectly synchronized. Their oarsmen keeping heads low, not daring to look up for a second. At the back of the boat, spread on a golden fleece, something moved. It was hard to focus on the figure. It shifted, altered it's outline, melted and flowed from one shape to another. Sometimes it appeared to be black with white, pupil-less eyes, sometimes white as snow with no visible features, sometimes striped, spotted, metallic, gaseous and all states in between. Sometimes it seemed to wear a helmet, sometimes it seemed naked. The one constant was the awful laughter, smug, self-satisfied, indulgent, the chuckle of a shark.

The ship cruised up before them, gliding to a halt as if meeting shingle on a make-believe shore. Several huge men lowered themselves to the green. The figure leapt to one side and dropped to the grass. The second he made contact there was a flurry of activity, the grass swelling, browning and dying. Adam held his arms open wide and said,

"Well, well, well.         Opera?         This far north?"
Behind Adam and Tom, there was a swishing sound from the treetops. Branches stretched and swelled, leaves burst into bloom, blossom sprang out, flowered and died, fruits inflated and ripened. They found themselves in a hail of helicopter seeds and cherries and falling leaves. Looking up they could see only the Milk Moon of May, high above in it's small, round window of night sky, everything else funneled out of sight and beyond reach. The ghostly oarsmen stepped down, still not raising their eyes to the horizon. A makeshift crew of fishermen and mariners from all ages. Some dressed in long gone styles, some like they'd just stepped off a boat at North Shields Quay.

Adam scribbled something and handed it to Tom, under cover of the sudden, unexpected autumn leaf-fall. Then he strode forward, stepping up to the boat and giving it a couple of solid slaps.

"As I thought. Wood. As for the rest, smoke and mirrors. What, no perfume? No burst of sunshine? And what of the new-born? No birds do sing, my un-named friend!"

The shape-ful man spread his arms, a collage of skin tones, human and animal. In a stentorian, demanding voice, he bellowed,

**"I AM KNOWN TO YOU WELL, MAGICIAN. BETTER THAN ANY OTHER. ONLY YOUR WITS DO NOT REVEAL THE ANSWER YOU SEEK. UNTIL YOUR SENSES RECOVER, KNOW ME NOW... AS THE FRACTURED MAN."**

"And what might I do for you this fine night, apart from get you to a hospital?"

**"YOU WOULD SEEK TO ENTERTAIN ME FIRST? DELIGHTFUL! BEGIN YOUR SONG AND DANCE, JESTER, AND WHEN YOU ARE DONE, THE END WILL BE THE SAME. YOU'LL GIVE ME THE BOY."**

Adam's distraction had allowed Tom to steal a few steps toward the fabulous ship under pretence of fascination. He quickly attached something to the boat and then he stepped back abruptly, laughed, and said

"Done!"

They watched as the ship wobbled on it's keel. Slowly it rose. Gradually it picked up speed and suddenly soared straight up into the tiny circle of sky. The fractured man howled with rage. His oarsmen backed off, huddling together. Fracture reached for the sky symbolically attempting to drag his vessel back to earth.

**"WHAT HAVE YOU DONE? WHERE IS IT GOING?"**

"Look around you. Where have you left me to send to? Mare Tranquillitatus if my spelling's correct."

Fracture span his hands furiously above his head, the moon wheeled out of sight, the tiny patch of sky brightened, briefly a sun appeared, then the sky darkened again, introducing the moon once more. This cycle repeated, again and again, gaining speed.

**"GIVE ME THE BOY!"**

"Or what, exactly? A light show in that tiny dinner plate of sky? I might half-heartedly applaud if you could manage to fill the horizons, but dear me, you seem to expect a standing ovation. For a Penny-Behind-The-Ear. Oh I can't help noticing, *we* haven't aged!

Parlour tricks! What next? Fireworks? Rabbit from a hat?"

Fracture, his skin bubbling like boiling water, turned to the remnants of his crew,

**"OBEY ME! BRING THE BOY TO ME!"**

Before they could move however, Adam shouted,

"Take-see!"

His coach and coachman rushed up, settling between him and the oarsmen and he ordered,

"Get in!"

The crewmen scrambled forward, squeezing in to the carriage, despite the impossibility of them all being inside at once.

"Grundy, one hundred slow laps of the park. That should be long enough to take care of our friend here, but don't bring them back until he's gone. On your way!"

The carriage sped off, leaves and branches whipping along behind.

**"WHY WOULD YOU DENY ME, MAGICIAN? CAN YOU NOT SEE THE BOY SHOULD MAKE UP HIS OWN MIND? WHAT HE CAN BECOME, IF ONLY HE WILL BE ADVISED BY ME. DO YOU NOT SEE WHAT LIES INSIDE HIM?"**

"Oh I see it clearly. Every day, every second, he grows stronger, amazing me, surprising himself. But what will you do for him? I notice you haven't once spoken to the lad. He's just property to you. Nothing more than a possession. You need him *now*, while there's a chance you can terrify and control him, like those poor souls who row your boat. Those poor souls who I have just liberated. Like my coachman you tried to manipulate. Oh and it looks like you're walking home tonight!"

The anger was readable to all the senses now. Fracture's silhouette shook, his skin now appearing to be made out of storm itself, a whirlwind of fury. Lightning flashed across his chest. There was a smell, a taste of ozone, a sudden heat radiated out to them. Inside the park the mist rose all around, the ground shook with several claps of thunder, the air slapped their ears, lightning rolled all around them, illuminating the banks of mist. Under cover of this Adam managed to say a few words to Tom,

"Tom, what do you see?"

"You must be a big danger to him. Why does he not attack you?"

"Show no respect. Keep him talking. If we infuriate him he may use all of his power."

"Why would we want him to do that?"

"Just trust me. We need a signal, a beacon. A marker for someone to follow to us."

Once again he called,

"Guardian of Allerdean, follow the path Overman Swinburne laid at your feet. I call you back a third time… "

Then he turned to face Fracture,

"Dear me, don't you know anything? It's supposed to be lightning *and then* thunder. I'm beginning to think…"

The sentence went unfinished. Fracture shook his fists at the sky. There was a change in air pressure. Hairs stood up on Adam's neck. He bellowed at Tom,

"Tom! Run! Now!"

Everything went white.

His ears hurt and fizzled. He smelled smoke. Then he realized that the smell was himself, his clothes, his hair. He lay on the play-park between the swings and the slide, grateful for both of them. The lightning had hit him, or near him, but thankfully had fled away to ground through the metal sculptures, leaving him burned, but alive.

He rolled onto his side and could see Tom disappearing through the trees. Hopefully he hadn't seen what had happened, wouldn't come back for him. He turned to Fracture.
"Now *that* is more like it.... "
His eyes closed. He needed rest. 'Just a few minutes, then I'll get up.' he thought, 'just a few minutes.'
Fracture approached.
**"YOU MADDEN ME INTO VIOLENCE AGAINST YOU. WHICH I HAD TRULY HOPED TO AVOID. I DO NOT KNOW WHAT WILL HAPPEN NEXT."**
The magician was down. He could finish him off with his bare hands now. A joy filled him at the thought of some good, old-fashioned throttling. However he held back a second. He hadn't noticed the arm that thrust out from under a pile of broken bones nearby, just seconds ago. His own devastating lightning strike had hidden the sound of a man crawling out from where he had been buried after running to Tom's aid.
Kneeling over the magician now, Fracture cracked his knuckles, distracted as he placed one knee on Adam's chest. Joe Wrigley trailed his club behind him, leaving a meandering track through the grass. Reaching the edge of the play-park, he hefted it above his head. One step, then he dropped it back over his shoulder. Two steps, he shifted his weight onto his back foot. Three steps, he swung the bar straight at Fracture's head. A helmet flew off, battered, but in one piece. The kneeling man-shape rose to both feet and stared at his attacker. In anger he roared into Joseph's face.
**"THAT BLOODY HURT!"**
A cold wind blew up from across the lake, in seconds it formed a water spout as it headed for land. By the time it was above Joseph it was a whirling funnel that plucked him off the ground and flew him straight up and out of sight.

There was nothing that Adam could do to prevent it. He barely had the strength to stand up and stagger away out of sight, hoping to catch up with Tom. As he made his way through the trees he heard branches snapping above him as someone crashed down amongst them from higher above.

Tom stopped to gain some breath near the Old Salte Welle. What was it Adam had told him? About when he had travelled the Cup and Ring stones? He needed to get *into* that breathless state to be *able* to call forth the game-player. 'Why me?' he wondered. 'Why do they all think I'm so special?'
He searched his mind, his memories, looking for a way to attack, to fight back, or a means to hide, even though that would mean leaving them all behind. Calming himself by willpower wasn't easy. In fact he was surprised to find that he could

do it at all. The enemy wanted him to think he was trapped, surrounded. Adam wanted him to know that this was not some all-powerful demon. Somewhere between all of this there was a … message. A signal. He couldn't say how, but he just knew it was there. He used his mind to break the trap. He sent his thoughts out, through the mist. Over it and under and around. But also… past it, somehow. Into a time when it hadn't been there, and then into a time when it was gone, thoughts forming, not a protective bubble around himself as he hoped, but behaving like a star, radiating out in all possible directions, even ones he couldn't describe.
The air halted. The grass, the trees, the wall, the well, they whispered to him. Time froze. Even the tendrils of loose mist stopped dancing lazily in the space above the greenery.

Loose unconnected sounds came to him. Gradually, they threaded themselves together to form a pattern. He could taste the pattern, fresh, orangey, clean. He could smell the music, hear the leather, the cars, the… travelling. He could see the words, bouncing, innocent, free. All sensations melted together in his head until he was left with one lingering word.        Elvis?

Down the path, someone came to him, walking slowly, leaving no trace or sound on the gravel. A face he thought he should recognise. Too old to be a boy from school, perhaps twice his age, almost a man. Long, fair hair. A confident smile. Clear, trusting eyes. Tom heard the words without seeing the boy speak.
    "You can get past this, you know.        It's all up to you.

    You just have to pull everything together.     Find a new place to dwell."
The figure faded like chimney-smoke in the breeze. Seconds later, Adam came tumbling along the path and dropped at his feet.

    The magician was clearly in no condition to help. He was struggling to stay conscious, obviously in pain, his clothes still smoking and ragged, almost hanging off him. He propped the magician against the well. The Fractured man would be here soon. He knew he had a few seconds to think and then it would all start again. The trickery, the madness, the deceit. He closed out all and everything. He found a small, quiet spot in his thoughts and retreated there.
    'It's all up to me' he thought.
    'I just have to pull it all together.'
    'Obviously I don't have to do something impossible.'
    'I just have to find something I can do.'
    'Something I haven't been able to do yet.'
    'Something new.'
    'Something different.'
    'Something new.   A new place…'

    His mind imagined a mirror. What size was it? Enormous. So big it's edges could not be seen. It reached away to both sides and disappeared out of sight. It stretched above and below without end. What was in it? Anything. Everything. What was behind it? Nothing. What did it show? Himself. This was *the* mirror. If he could master it, it would take him anywhere. If he could step, not into *it*, but into *the reflection.*

He stood back and looked again. The mirror was only one frame in a story. One panel in a comic-strip. It connected with all the others. It led from one, to another. And all the panels were relevant to it, forming it's past or future. The last panel was blank.

He stood back. The comic was being flicked through. Hands held it. The pages flickered as they flipped from one side to another between the pressing of finger and thumb, like a flicker-book. The pages fanned a cool breeze to his face. His nose caught the distinctive inks.

He stood back. The flicker book flashed across a large screen in a dark room. A boy in green swooped down on a blustering pirate, sticking him with his tiny sword and then swooping up and away again, delight cracking his face.

He stood back. The boy flew through the air over a house. The house had many rooms. In one he saw a boy looking out of a window. The room had a radio and a clock. The radio was silent but the clock was speaking to him, whispering it's magic word.

He stood back. The boy was looking down on a party. The guests beckoned him to join them. He ran down the stairs and out into the garden. A girl gave him a gift. He put the gift in his shoe. He was brought a cake full of candles, which he blew out, but the wish he kept. He looked up. The sky shook as the jets thrust the rocket up and into space.

He stood forward. He stood forward and looked up. He thought of the mirror, the past the future, the story, the boy who lived forever, the rocket, the wishes, the clock, the magic word.

At the far end of the path, the tree branches swept aside as Fracture stepped through the gap they made. A coldness came with him expanding across the grass and the gravel, whitening everything. Snowflakes fluttered through the air. Above them, the funnel that was all that was left of the sky was filling with little, white, drifting stars. As they fell, they drew Tom up and into them, though his feet were firmly planted, causing his head to swim. He didn't trust his balance to keep him upright and his hand felt out behind him, searching for solid wall.

There was a movement at Fracture's feet as he walked, blades of grass elongating, wriggling, slithering like snakes under his step. His skin took on the texture of paper, images flowed across him.

"I DO HOPE THEY HAVEN'T POISONED YOU, BOY, WITH THEIR LIES.

IT MUST BE SO HARD BEING SO YOUNG. WANTING JUST TO LIE DOWN SOMEWHERE. NEEDING NOTHING MORE THAN TO BE SOMEWHERE WARM AND SAFE."

His eyes sparkled, suddenly clear and visible and trustingly blue.

"YOU CAN SEE NOW, I'M SURE, HOW THEY WANTED YOU ALL FOR THEMSELVES. YOU'RE A BRIGHT BOY. I'M SURE YOU DON'T NEED ME TO TELL YOU HOW THEY'VE LIED TO YOU."

He stepped closer, hands now open, welcomingly.

"AND ALL THE TIME, TEARING YOU IN DIFFERENT DIRECTIONS, SPYING ON YOU. THE HEADMASTER, YOUR DAD, YOUR SO-CALLED MOTHER, ALL OF THEM, THE MAGICIAN, YOUR SUPPOSED FRIENDS.

A smile grew across his face.

"AND EACH OF THEM HOLDING YOU BACK. STOPPING YOU HAVING WHAT YOU WANTED. STOPPING YOU BECOMING SOMETHING WONDERFUL."

He stretched a hand out.

I CAN GIVE YOU ALL OF THAT. I CAN SHOW YOU HOW TO BECOME ANYTHING YOU WISH. COME. COME WITH ME."

Exhausted, Tom stepped forward. He couldn't take his eyes from those that stared down at him from Fracture's face. Couldn't blink. Something caught at his foot. Something under his sole. He took another step forward. There it was again. What could it be? The eyes widened. Widened until he thought he might fall into them. What was under his foot? He blinked, looked down. When he looked back, he saw Fracture for what he was, betrayed by his own skin. When the enemy spoke now he did so from a smaller self inside another, inside another, like Russian dolls there always seemed to be something else hidden underneath. Tom reached down and removed his shoe. Something tiny sticking through his sock into the soft skin under his arch. He felt underneath, rubbed his fingers around. Something came loose, fell into his palm. A seed.
A gift. A wish. 'For emergencies' she had said.
He had the wish in his hand. His eyes met with Fracture's who was slowly shaking his head.

"IGNORANT BOY! HAVE YOU NO GRATITUDE? OH WHAT WE COULD HAVE BECOME TOGETHER. NOW OF COURSE, I'LL BECOME THAT ALL ON MY OWN. SAY GOODBYE."

There was the same feel in the air again. Tom had little time to think. He had the two wishes now. He had the little thing that hid behind his imagination dancing and shouting to be free. He had the awake / still-sleeping feeling in his head. Sacrifices had been made for him, lying unconscious in the park and behind him. He had all destinations laid out in front of him. He, like Adam, had the power from the constriction of space and time flowing all around him. For months he had lived and played and slept in a house soaked in magic. For years in fact. Mentally, he reached into the clock, pulling out the soldier, the special one. The one with the brains. Wondering if his 'passport' card could take him away. Starting to realise now what it was... but then... Shutting the clock back, he saw in his mind, the plate on the inside of the door as it closed. Saw it reflected against the shiny brass workings inside.

       M     O     I     X     A.
          Em - Oh - I - Ex - A.

The letters formed a word. It came to his lips just as Fracture raised both hands above his head.

          "EM OH I X A!"

Lightning broke from the skies.

A charge of electricity filled the air. The forks of lightning split above Tom's head and fell in stuttering bolts in a wide arc around him. He wasn't alone. He stood at the centre, unharmed, Adam lying at his feet. He felt so full of energy that it leaked away from him as he moved. Realizing that he controlled it all, he stepped toward Fracture and smiled.

    In the valley below the park, the mist clung to every feature of the landscape, rising and falling with the hills and troughs, suffocating every building.

    To the south a ripple formed. The mist bulged, concealing but revealing at the same time. Something moved. Something *very* big moved through the blanketed streets, closing in on the park. An enormous head and outstretched arms pushed a bow-wave of fog before it as it stepped over the east gates.

    Adam raised his head and tried to focus on his surroundings. He could see Tom moving away from him and beyond that Fracture retreating, cowering. With an enormous effort he managed to whisper to Tom,

    "The Dene. The south gate.    Take him there."

    It was easier than that. Fracture tried to run to ground of his own accord, seeking a cave or underground tunnel or sewer, he naturally descended the winding path into the Dene. He could not hurt Tom and had no idea if Tom could hurt him, but he suspected so and did not want to gamble otherwise. Something had awoken in the boy. Energy was all around him. The boy was full of awful energy and surely could not control it. He was likely to boil someone in their skin just by looking. Fracture needed to escape. Hide somewhere, rebuild his forces and his strength, see about liberating the rest of... his musings were cut short by the groaning of metal that rang through the Dene. Somewhere, a huge iron door was swinging open, as though a ferrous giant's chest was being unlocked. He forced ahead, splashing through the stream, desperately wishing he could see where he was going, not wanting to look behind. The sky seemed to darken a little as though under the shade of an enormous tree. Or perhaps the sides of the Dene were closing in and he was nearing an underground opening of some sort. The water ahead must run underground somewhere soon. He ran, he ran, he ran, imagining his footsteps as thunderous, heavy and shaking the ground. He ran until he thumped into something solid and cold. It was now much darker. And

A charge of electricity filled the air. The forks of lightning split above Tom's head …

getting darker still. He grasped around the solid metal wall in front of him looking for a break, feeling the air compress slightly as the last dim light disappeared behind him. Too late he turned. Too late to stop the gap closing closing around him. Too late to do anything except scream as the two steel edges of an enormous Angel's ribcage came together with a ringing, echoing clang.

"**NNNOOOOOOOOOOOOOOOOOOO**..... ....   ...   ...        "

The mist dropped all around inside the park. It dropped and slipped away into nothing in a circle that widened every second. In the still thick mist beyond the park, a huge metal giant moved away to the south, to retake it's place at the old pit-head, it's obligations met.

Tom felt like he was waking from a dream, suddenly aware how cold he was. Cold and alone and only eight years old in the Dene in the park at night. He stumbled up and out of the Dene, to go looking for Adam and then Mam and Dad, and then Sunblest and Hermes and Aggy and…. and then, try as he might not to, he simply burst into tears.

# CHAPTER NINE

## MORNING HAS BROKEN

**Sunday the thirteenth of May, 1956. Time, 10.55am.**

There was very little conversation around the table. Adam was still obviously in a lot of pain and on the verge of actually agreeing with James and Tom that he *really should* go to hospital. Harmony was trying to inject as much of a normal Sunday as she could, supplying eggs, toast, and hot, sweet tea. She wasn't completely succeeding, what with cooking on a make-do arrangement of gas cylinders James had set up, but then it's not every weekend you meet Magicians, tramps, wizards, magic creatures and walking clay men.

They were grateful that *they* had survived, of course, but the gratitude wasn't enough. They were still in shock. They wondered why Adam wasn't talking about Tenlock, this Grundy character or Joseph Wrigley. And they were keeping the curtains closed, despite the fact that there was very little light getting in through the trees.

They wondered what the council would say about the state of the park. Whether the mist had completely receded everywhere yet. They wondered if the boat would come crashing down out of the sky at any minute. Adam told them he would see to it all, but they really wished he would get started.

Above all, they wondered how they were going to explain how their house came to be on an island in the middle of Saltwell Park lake.

The clock struck eleven. Instinctively James stood up and announced he was going round to the papershop for the Sunday Sun. It took him a few seconds to work out why they were all laughing at him.
Adam said,
"I once knew a boy who lived in Venice, his dad said he had to get a paper-round, but he couldn't swim."
They all laughed. It isn't every day you meet a real magician who really can be funny.
James joined in.
"I knew them as well. They didn't have mice in the skirting boards, they had fish!"
They laughed again. Everyone took a turn and they all laughed. Whether good or bad, they laughed at every joke. Just because they were alive, just because they were together, and just because they could.

*... how their house came to be on an island in the middle of Saltwell Park lake.*

## CHAPTER TEN

## ASHES TO ASHES

**A small gathering.**
**Friday the eighteenth of May, 1956. Time, 12.55pm.**

The little wooden chapel in Saltwell cemetery was packed. It took several minutes for the mourners to make their way out, tearful and blinking, into the open.

James looked around the others gathered at the gate, waiting to be asked to enter to attend the funeral of Joseph Robert Wrigley which would be held next. Less than a dozen of them, Joe having made a thorough job of alienating all his remaining friends over the years. A couple of old workmates Eddie and Bren, James, Harmony, Tom and Adam obviously, and a brother Michael, red-faced at the lack of any other family. What James took to be one of Joe's fellow tramps, freshly scrubbed, de-loused and just released from somewhere, and Inspector Gordon made up the rest of the congregation. Nine. The magic number.

A couple of minutes later they were ushered in and took their places on the painted, wooden pews. An elderly lady entered and began playing a strident yet tuneless and gloomy dirge. Funerals serve many functions. They can primarily stand as occasions for a letting-out of grief. This was certainly that. They can substitute as a last chance for people to feel good about themselves, which this wasn't. They can be to say how much a person will be missed. This was not really that either. The usher glanced repeatedly and nervously at his watch, confirming that there were at least two people who really didn't want to be present. Eventually he decided to come clean and strode reluctantly to the front as the piano subsided.

"Ladies and gentlemen, ah… friends and relatives. We … er, have a slight problem in that the priest today hasn't erm, had much luck with his travel arrangements. I believe that a ceremony has erm, run over at Heworth… possibly. Well…. What with another ceremony being booked in right after us… so to speak…. In short erm, I think it best if I ask if any of the congregated mourners would erm, choose to er … say a few words?"
He backed away then, making it quite clear that whatever the options, they didn't include him.

Several heads dropped then, making sure as to be completely out of any possibility of eye-contact. More in embarrassment than in any enthusiasm, Joseph's brother Michael stood up. He turned to face them and took an enormous breath in and out.

"Well. Not prepared, obviously. So. Maybe I should just say Joe did have many friends but recently, well, people don't keep in touch any more do they?
I remember Joe and I remember all the good things about him. Don't know where to start, there are so many. He bought me my first suit. When I left school, like, him being working, he took me straight down to Jackson's, on Jackson

Street as it happens. 'That'll get you through any interview.' he said. Of course, being Joe, he wouldn't throw in the shirt and tie. Said I had to borrow his best like, and return it washed and ironed. He knew what he was doing. Making me learn how to take care of what I had. Knowing I'd take care of his clobber, do it properly like......

      He saved a kid's life once. Bet none of you knew that! Didn't hardly ever mention it. He were coming back along Split Crow Road from Fred's in a blizzard that awful winter we had, with the eight-foot snowdrifts. Cars and wagons were parked up all along the road. He saw a kid coming toward him, clambering over the tops of them for fun like. Once he had gone a bit further, he looked round to see where the kid had gone. He hadn't passed him, see. Something just told him to go back. He went back and the kid were upside down between two cars, face down under the snow. He would have died there if Joe hadn't dug him out.     Still.     Anyway.     Once at Clarkies he come across an apprentice getting bullied by Dicky Watson the gaffer. Really thumped him like. Joe downed tools straight away like and marched up and slapped Dicky.

      Gaffer turned around and went into the time office. Docked him a quarter off his pay. The lad had an easier ride after that though. That's what I meant to say.    Liked things fair did Joe. He did have two beautiful boys though, didn't he?    That's how I remember him. When he was happy. Before … all the … problems… and such.        Just a shame that there's nothing more recent to say……"

The silence was like a thick blanket thrown over them.

      After a few seconds there was a scraping sound. All eyes turned to see the pianist slowly turning over her page, getting ready for the final hymn. The silence returned.

      There was a sound of shoes on bare floor on the wall end of the last pew. Even the picking up of a dropped hankerchief would have been welcome distraction and heads began to turn to this essential viewing. With brother looking back past work-mates looking back past inspector looking back past tramp, the torch passed to Adam to look right to James, to Harmony and finally to Tom, who was standing up. He placed both hands on the back of the pew in front and coughed lightly.

      Slowly Tom raised his hand. All the others present followed his gaze. Michael said,

      "Oh, here's a little boy who knows the answer.  Yes?"

      "I just wondered if you mind me saying, Joe was very kind to me once."

      "Well that's kind of you to say so."

      "He was kind and brave. You're right. He wouldn't stand by and see anyone bullied.

      I just thought I should say. Because *that's* more recent and you should know. And because people weren't kind or brave back to him."

This seemed to spark memories in the rest of the assembly, or at least to provide them with some temporary courage. Eddie, Chargehand at Clarkies, spoke up.

"He was just about the best apprentice I ever had, for company anyway. First thing I ever did first day on the job in the Tool-room was to throw me chalk-line at him. That limp he had, see? Shattered my hip in the war. First morning he worked with me, I looked back to see him walking behind me, I thought he was taking the mick. He had his head in the clouds sometimes, but, even with the Gaffers cracking the whip and the Boilermakers threatening to strike, he kept laughing, joking.     Made the shift fly by.     A good lad."

Bren smiled. Lifted his head. Took a deep breath.
"Did you hear the one about the rabbit?"
He and Eddie laughed before Bren could say another word.
"Me and him was on sea trials with the winches, five or six miles out. I came up top with the tool kit and there he was, sitting in the middle of the deck with his hands on an upturned bucket. I said, 'What are you doing Joe?'. He said, 'I've caught this rabbit under here………'."
Eddie and Bren laughed again before Bren could continue. And kept laughing.

Thirty minutes later, they were all leaving the cemetery in a group, hoping to find a room in the Nine Pins where they might be able to sit and drink a toast together and take Tom in for a glass of lemonade. Just before they reached the gate, a panting priest came dashing through.
"Oh my word.  Oh my word I'm so dreadfully sorry.     They told me one-thirty you see."
Without any malice, Michael simply said,
"Don't worry about it. We managed just fine."

# CHAPTER ELEVEN

## REASONS TO BE CHEERFUL

**One, two, three.**

Adam sat in the Confluence room at Unthank House. One by one the mirrors brightened and faces were revealed. The youngest asked to speak first and was granted this.

"As regards my sister Melody, and of which we spoke previously. She has relocated to Gateshead, in the North east area, where her soon-to-be husband originally came from. All seems well and I have installed some of those measures which we spoke of. My thanks."

The slightly older spoke next.

"I believe this may be a time of great change and upheaval for you Adam. I propose that we defer all other considerations for our next meeting. Would you care to speak next?"

Adam nodded and then began,

"I have relocated recently, after a severely trying time. I now have all my instruments and books with me again. I will need them here for I have taken on the mentoring rights to a young man for his Ennios Etos. I preferred a policy of remote guardianship, but my hand was forced. By events and by the nature of the catalyst."

He hesitated here, possibly fearing that he was about to admit to failure of some sort.

"There has been a fairly major conflict. Unfortunately, several innocents were involved."

The eldest spoke here, softly and with understanding.

"That is unfortunate. However I'm sure … we're *all* sure, you handled the situation as best you could. There should be no recriminations."

"I thank you for your confidence. However, there are situations which have arisen which require… well, my intervention. I have discovered a severe miscarriage of natural justice.

I ask for leave to address and rebalance the situation."

Again there was silence until the eldest had time to consider his words.

"It goes without saying that there can be no lasting change to the environment. Or to the accumulation?"

"Of course not. I judge that what I propose will be without risk to the continuation. I also believe that Karmically, there will be several benefits. I believe that some other, small, miscarriages of natural justice will be avoided and that there will be several small, social benefits for an isolated community."

"In that case, I believe we can leave the matter in your hands. I add only that… you *are* still learning Adam. There will come a time when you have to know when to turn your back and leave things be. We can't be *everybody's* Policeman. You also face a time to come when you will have to know that you *can* be ruthless."

Adam considered recent times.

"I believe I have taken a major step towards knowing that, in days just gone. I am sure that you would not recognise me as the same man, so great is the change."

The room fell silent again. It seemed that all 'present' knew that there was something else to be said. The next voice he heard came from the next eldest.

"There is another matter to be addressed, Adam. Something you have perhaps overlooked for too long? There is a way that you can reassess the matter. Show some decisiveness, but compassion. It could also be seen as a matter of natural justice. However, it is, as always, up to you.

And beyond that, there are dark times to be prepared for. I can say no more."

Back in the main hall later that afternoon, Tom was staring at the ceiling, amazed that such a small dome could let in so much light. The windows to each side were covered by curtains. Tom walked across to one side and pulled the drape open. He gasped in surprise at what he saw there.

"I did say not to look out there yet, didn't I?" asked Adam as he entered the hall.

"You did.     What does it mean?     Does it ….? Oh, doesn't matter. I'll find out soon enough I suppose."

Adam stepped alongside him and drew the curtain closed. He pointed at the large mirror.

"I've got some research to do and a couple of tasks to see to, but tomorrow, we start your lessons on how to use this back-glass. Remember at all times, keep an open space in front of it clear of all obstructions."

In Gateshead Harmony was positioning the new mirror in the sitting room. She was doing just as she had been asked, placing it in the corner, and with a rug in front of it that she hoped would stop anyone moving anything in front of it. It was full length and in a polished beech frame. 'From a famine to a feast' she thought, stepping back to admire it and to primp up her hair. James was finding it more difficult to keep busy. He was simply missing Tom too much. He had taken to tidying up the garden and was planting bedding plants out the back, in the plot above the yard. Occasionally he would stop, as if to listen for something or someone. Then his eyes would glance up at the claw-shaped new bricks in the back wall and he would just feel grateful that Tom was still alive to visit them.

Inspector Gordon sat in his office on the top floor of Swinburn Street Police Station, gazing at the view of the city centre across the bridge. It was lightening up now, the sky trying on a fiery sunrise for size, and the street lights winking out. He had stayed through the night, reading newspaper reports from previous weeks, looking back through the arrest sheets and desk log, trying to find some pattern in recent events. As such the debris of his search littered floor, desk, bookcase and walls. Flora would forgive him. She'd put up with a lot

during his career, mainly during the early years when he was a firebrand young copper, in a rush to get places. The twenty six years since had seen him rise exactly three floors. Only the view got better. It seemed that people kept finding new ways to hurt each other. A few kept finding new ways to get rich quick, always at someone else's expense.
Which brought him back to Joe.

Too many odd things for a small town like this. Mostly the problems used to find their way over the river into the city, only coming back out to his patch after they'd sorted themselves out. Now the city was getting too big and the overflow had to flow somewhere. He'd seen the plans in the Mayor's office. Swinburn Street would survive, for a while, and the Town Hall next door, but pretty much all the rest of the centre was coming down. There was even a contract out for a multi-storey car park bang in the middle of the town, with a nightclub on top. Madness with maybe only three or four hundred cars in the town. All in the name of expansion. Once that started, he thought, the floodgates are open. He could imagine hard men coming up from London, fresh new turf to be fought over. Bloody stupid place for a nightclub, six floors up. He could see someone taking a nasty fall.
Which brought him back to Joe.

Was there anything else he could have done? Where do people like Joe go to get better? He could have intervened. He had opportunities to have Joe sectioned, locked away for the sake of his own health. Have him looked after. He'd also seen people after the system had looked after them. First cold snap of winter, the cells were full of them looking for somewhere to keep warm, and finding it. The railway arches gradually totted up the score of those who didn't.

He looked back over his shoulder to the map on the wall by the door. Robberies and thefts in black, attacks and violence in red, alcohol 'hot spots' in blue, 'unexplained events' in green. Thing is, the green markers for Joe's last sightings were easy to place, Swinburn Street and the Park. However, if he added the missing boy's home in green, then he had a perfect triangle. It didn't help that, when he traced lines from the middle of all three sides to their opposite corners, the exact centre was spot on Shipcote School. Sometimes the pattern leapt out at him, sometimes it didn't. sometimes it leapt out at him and he was none the wiser. He spun around to the window again. The last of the city centre streetlamps was blinking out.
Which brought him back to Joe. At least his suffering was over. Wasn't that a good thing?

Adam sat in the study room in Newcastle library. From what he had gathered, it seemed as though Lucas Grundy was as much a victim as some of the people who travelled in his carriage. He had come from a large family, born in 1781, the youngest of eight, five of them boys, in the village of Lamesley. His father had too much of a quick temper and his mother not enough time to spare. He had found satisfaction in helping an old man called Avery who bred birds in the High Fell area of Gateshead and would often walk the five miles to get there, shoeless. By age of nine he was working for a man called Bryson who looked after horses of various shapes and sizes for local businesses. By fourteen, the British Army had turned him into a paid killer in the Napoleonic Wars. It seems he had thought he was signing on to be a farrier and ended as a Cavalryman. When his time in battle was done, like many others, he was dumped back in 'Blighty' and forgotten about.

From later conversations with Grundy, he confirmed most of this, and several other matters. His horse had been bought from Bryson, who in turn had bought him from an abusive factory owner. By the time Adam released the beast on the fields of Windmill Hills it was due a deserved retirement, but the visible injuries were inflicted not by Grundy but by the Factory boss.

What none of this changed was the awful crimes Grundy *had* committed. But even here there was mitigation. He had fallen into debt to a local money-lender and thug, in order to buy the horse and carriage. The people who disappeared, initially, were this thug's local rivals. Thugs themselves and capable of many barbarous acts also. Grundy knew if he defaulted on payments then the horse and carriage would become the lender's property, horse likely to be taken to the glue factory that stunk up the east Tyne on hot days.

There was even room to allow, that the act that had brought Grundy his good fortune had been ordered by his criminal master. Grundy would have assumed his passenger to be another parasite the world was better off without. Grundy claimed that there was no choice in any of this, once he had fallen into the debt, other than to tackle the money-lender and his thugs and provide them the opportunity and reason to cut his own throat. Philosophically, he saw the situation as one of removing at least some of the thugs from the city. The one redeeming factor in all of this was that Grundy, patiently waiting his opportunity, had at last taken the money-lender himself on a 'last ride' one dark, drunken night.

Since then, he had expressed genuine remorse at the terrible things his life had led him to. He had wished his life over and asked for release from his 'contract'. Grundy obviously, deeply resented the servitude he was forced into by Adam, but who wouldn't? One fact was undeniable. In the park, *that* night, Grundy had choices. He could come to the aid of his new, faceless master. He could simply hide until it was all over. Or he could recognise true, malevolent, chaotic evil and take a stand against it. Which he had done.

Can a man turn his life around given the chance? Did even the pathetic, wretched Grundy not deserve some compassion? Was there to be no amnesty?

Can a man who *really* wants a chance to change and do some good be denied that?

And if so, who the hell was Adam to be the one to deny?

# CHAPTER TWELVE

## HERE COMES THE SUN.

### There's No Place like home.
**Friday the tenth of May 1957.**

The 'Taxi' pulled up outside of the school in the village of Co-operative Villas, also known as No Place, County Durham, and two passengers stepped out. One a man dressed in black, despite the blazing sunshine breaking out from behind the clouds, the other a young boy about nine. They entered through the main gate, past the overflowing nasturtiums and the butterflies and bees that surrounded them like a haze. The man spoke.

"Now remember, just follow my lead. You're ten years old and we are moving to High Handenhold. I'm your father and I'm looking for a good school for you for when you're eleven. Got that?"

"Got it."

Tom knew there would be some point to this, something to learn if he was sharp enough to spot it.

They went straight to the Head's office and found him reading that morning's Journal. He folded the paper away and commented,

"Damned odd business that. Mill Dam at South Shields being used to house those lost fishermen who turned up out of the blue. Foreign some of them, Seamen's Mission can't understand a word some of them say."

Soon, with very little fuss were soon being shown around the school by a sixth form monitor. They saw the art department, the languages department, the maths department, the history department and the music room. They walked for at least thirty minutes until Tom felt yawns coming on. After several looks through windows into various classrooms, they were back in the Head's office where Adam asked,

"How about your practical skills departments? Could you show us them?"

"What, you mean like Woodwork and Metalwork?"

"Yes exactly. Can you show us your metalwork department?"

"Yes, of course. It's right this way and it's called a metal workshop. Just taken on a new teacher, really knows his way with tools. I tend not to visit. Not being able to knock in a straight nail, I feel I have no business there."

A few minutes later they had left the main building and were standing in the corridor of the workshop block, which divided the rooms into metalwork and woodwork areas. The classes looked out onto the field where two football games were being held. Normally this would be just enough distraction to introduce an element of anarchy into a lesson. Adam was watching the metalwork lesson that was in progress. The class, all boys, were busy in various stages of a project, marking, measuring, cutting, drilling, filing and polishing. All were working hard, most sweating but smiling.

"This is Mr Crawford's room."

volunteered the Head.

"Mr Crawford? A heroic name."

"He's only been here a year. Everybody likes him. Nobody plays the wag when… pardon me… nobody stays off and misses his class."

Mr Crawford stood leaning back on the blackboard. A still steaming mug of tea on his desk. He watched everything that happened in his room, a confident, skillful teacher. Seeing something at the back of the class that needed some attention, he leaned forward and walked around the desks, just happening to be in the vicinity when a boy raised his head, looked puzzled, and asked for advice.

As he walked Adam noticed he had a distinct limp. He hoped that Tom had noticed too.

**Monday the twelfth of May, 1958.**

"I knew you'd be here today."
Said the blonde girl. She was walking down Ellison Villas and met Tom just as he arrived at the gate to his parent's house.

"In fact, I even knew what time you would get here. Isn't that strange?"
Behind them, some kids were running up the street, shouting. There was a loud clip-clopping.

"Here, I got you an ice cream."
she said, handing him his first ever sugar cone.

"But sorry, I didn't have enough money to get your uncle one as well."
The boys spun around and lined up on the pavement as the horse-drawn wood and glass box came to a halt. An old man whose teeth were a bad example to ice-cream buyers leaned out and said

"Right boys, what can I get you this fine sunny day?"
before tipping up the brim on the trilby hat with the blue band that he wore.

**Sunday the thirteenth of May 2007.**

Another bus pulled off the A1 and into the lay-by. A dozen people got out and made their way to the hill, the kids racing up to stand in the iron giant's shadow, the adults fumbling in their bags for cameras. It's hazy shadow fell towards the football pitch, the Thomas Wilson Club Football Team's very own Sun-dial.

An unusual young woman pushing a buggy passed un-noticed as she cut through the pitch in the midst of an actual match.
A breeze blew up momentarily, groaning high in the air as it passed the giant's outstretched arms.

On a blanket near the giant's feet a fair-haired woman was in charge of a small posse of kids, one of whom perked up her ears and asked,

"What's that?"

"Well, no-one knows for sure. But if you press your ear to the giant's foot you can hear moaning. Some people say it means he's got indigestion."

"Indig - gestion?"

"Means he's eaten something that didn't agree with him. Something nasty."

The sky brightened. The shadow sharpened. On a blanket near the giant's feet a fair-haired woman in charge of a small posse of kids said,
"Here comes the sun."
To which they all answered,
"Doo-doon doo doo. Here comes the sun, and I say….. "

***An unusual young woman pushing a buggy passed un-noticed…***

## ILLUSTRATIONS

| | | | |
|---|---|---|---|
| 1. | The fog now so thick he could not see the horse… | Page | 12 |
| 2. | Featureless white… | Page | 18 |
| 3. | … as if something was about to be revealed… | Page | 25 |
| 4. | A page from Tom's Mathematics Jotter. | Page | 29 |
| 5. | After Tom had a fever, aged seven,… | Page | 37 |
| 6. | Dad had said not to, *ever,* because of the mirror, | Page | 40 |
| 7. | Padding toward me, each enormous paw… | Page | 48 |
| 8. | In my room there was an old mantle clock… | Page | 53 |
| 9. | Phoenix. | Page | 62 |
| 10. | A very serious looking man in a Crombie… | Page | 66 |
| 11. | Tom's letter to 'The Beezer' comic. | Page | 70 |
| 12. | Why would a throat Numskull… | Page | 74 |
| 13. | Then one of the black coats moved… | Page | 77 |
| 14. | Now it was pointed out to them… | Page | 83 |
| 15. | It's the best comic ever written and drawn,… | Page | 93 |
| 16. | "Awfully hot in here Rueben," he noted,… | Page | 98 |
| 17. | The stone was flat on top and into it's surface… | Page | 108 |
| 18. | A ghostly, long-dead host stumbled forward… | Page | 112 |
| 19. | The first suffocating cloud of desperation. | Page | 118 |
| 20. | It seemed to have gotten louder. | Page | 122 |
| 21. | I WILL REMAIN | Page | 133 |
| 22. | … the mist that constricted … | Page | 138 |
| 23. | … an eight foot tall, vaguely human shape,… | Page | 143 |
| 24. | Phoenix versus Dragon. | Page | 147 |
| 25. | Nemios Illioloustros. The Sun-Lion. | Page | 153 |
| 26. | A charge of electricity filled the air. | Page | 165 |
| 27. | … how their house came to be on an island… | Page | 168 |
| 28. | An unusual young woman pushing a buggy… | Page | 179 |

Illustrations by Eric Scarboro, Kris Stewart ( @Avery_3000) and Ryan Avery.

# ASPECTS OF THE PLEROMA

"If you want to find the secrets of the universe, think in terms of energy, frequency and vibration." - Nikola Tesla

RHAPSODE.
A **rhapsode**, (In Greek: ῥαψῳδός, *rhapsōdos*) or, today, **rhapsodist**, refers to a Greek, professional performer of epic poetry, adventure and wisdom, as recorded in the fifth and fourth centuries BC (and so undoubtedly from even earlier times).

Rhapsodes notably performed Homer's Iliad and Odyssey but also the wisdom of Hesiod and the satires of Archilocus, Plato's dialogue Ion sees Socrates confront a rhapsode, and is the best source on these artists. Rhapsodes are depicted in Greek art wearing a cloak and carrying a staff. The characteristic dress of travellers, implying that rhapsodes were itinerant performers, moving from town to town.

As they are the first known performers at religious events and festivals to be competing for prizes and prize-money by 'embellishing' their repertoire of tales and histories with jokes and asides to the audience, then they are literally in at the birth of Stand-up Comedy. All they lacked was a microphone. And possibly an unscrupulous promoter. Cheque to follow.

MILBURN HOUSE
First building on Dean Street leading up from the quayside area of Newcastle.

The PENNY UNIVERSITY COFFEE HOUSES, were everywhere during the 1600's and 1700's.

I have found no detailed records of establishments in the north east, but it's inconceivable that major cities and seats of learning didn't have them. The following quote…
"In coffee shops famous and ordinary, one could absorb conversations as stimulating as the coffee, eavesdrop or participate with the best minds of the era from lawyers and clergy to politicians and merchants to students at the university to students of life. In fact, because the price of coffee was usually a penny, and the conversation so acclaimed, the coffee houses came to be known as Penny Universities. Anyone of any means could afford a cup, nurse it for hours, and learn the gossip, the emerging revelations in science, art, trade, and politics, and enjoy the headiness of it all. The coffee house was then, like it is today, a place to see and be seen, hear and be heard, and all for the price of a cup of coffee."
…is from  www.supermarketguru.com/page.cfm/30186
Now it is quite normal to hear conversation in the library.

The internet is a Coffee House in your own home. Cafes have, unstoppably, introduced free internet access, coming full circle.
Until, that is, the internet finds a way to download coffee into your cup at home for you.

Thanks to Phil Lempert plempert@supermarketguru.com for permission to quote the above.

## THE RETRAITE
'Sounding the retraite' became known as 'sounding the retreat'. Le Retraite, is a soldier's call to rest or to bed, and not as people now think a call to withdraw from battle. It was simply a part of a soldier's daily routine.

COFFEE JOHNNY was not as some people think now, a myth. He was a real person and larger than life. A good starting point to find out about some of his exploits is http://www.genuki.org.uk/big/eng/DUR/Winlaton/Coffee.html .

BLAYDON ISLAND or KINGSMEADOW, was an island in the middle of the Tyne, near Blaydon. It's exact size is not known, but it was large enough to have races there, and attract a good crowd. Kingsmeadow School carries on the name and is probably most famous for old boy Paul Gascoigne.

DARLINGTON. An industrial town in the heart of the north east. Linked with Stockton and the birth of the British Railways system.
The events hinted at by Coffee Johnny are told in the second book of this series. Or the third. Or both.

NORTHUMBERLAND COUNTY CHRONICLE
Obviously the idea of a Pink newspaper containing sporting results is quite ridiculous.

THOMAS WEDDERBURN'S HOLE, I have visited myself while walking through Thrunton Woods, just north of Longframlington. There is an excellent website covering the fascinating history of the Wedderburn family at http://perso.orange.fr/euroleader/wedderburn/capnW2.htm#Pitscottie .
The site covers Captain Wedderburn's Courtship, a song in which Captain Wedderburn tries to win the hand of a young lady, by answering the puzzles she sets him. The verses spoken at the entrance to Thomas Wedderburn's Hole being part of this.

WEDDERSHINS
Not clockwise.

DRAGONS
This particular Dragon is very similar to the European Dragon as described by Dr Ernest Drake in DRAGONOLOGY The Complete Book of Dragons (Templar Publishing), which he names Draco Occidentalis Magnus.

DRAGONS IN SPACE
Space Dragon launch
http://www.spacex.com/news/2014/05/30/dragon-v2-spacexs-next-generation-manned-spacecraft

AT THE END OF MY STREET ONE DAY….
http://ufologie.patrickgross.org/ce3/1964-06-02-uk-gateshead.htm

GUY'S EYE
The people of Longwhitton, Northumberland, had three wells which supplied healing waters. They were unable to use them because they could sense that an evil force was nearby. This turned out to be an invisible dragon. In an epic battle Guy of Warwick was able to kill the dragon, thanks to the magic eye ointment he had which allowed him to see the beast. See 'A Little History of Dragons' by Joyce Hargreaves, Wooden Books Ltd. Adam's Guy's Eye spyglass is coated in this same *ointment.*


THE CONFLUENCE ROOM AT UNTHANK HOUSE.
Magicians have many ways to keep in touch with past and future. This is Adam's method. Obviously, at certain times when future information was being too directly related to a past embodiment, to avoid too much forewarning, the appropriate mirror would darken. All sound and sight would cease momentarily. No science can explain the system. It works because Adam believes in it.

UNTHANK
There are many Unthanks in the UK. To get to this one take the A1 FROM Newcastle to Edinburgh. After Morpeth, the A697 splits from the A1 and carries on up to Wooler and Coldstream. North of Thrunton Woods leave and go through Whittingham and Ryle Mill.
Nearest Post Code NE66 4TH
Latitude (WGS84) N55:23:51 (55.397446) Longitude (WGS84) W1:58:40 (-1.977868).

The BEQUEATHMENT OF SALTWELL PARK by LADY SALTWELL, has been told to me since I was a kid myself. It is probably apocryphal. Saltwell Towers was the home of Joseph Shipley who bequeathed the Shipley Art Collection to the people of Gateshead and this is now housed in the wonderful Shipley Art Gallery.
Saltwell Park has been voted the best Urban Park in Europe. However as we all know, Saltwell Park is the best park in the world.
Recently the Dene has been renovated and the water flows freely if slowly through it, down to a dog's fountain at the lower (eastern) gates.
Much inspiration has been provided by this simply excellent site…
http://www.gateshead-history.com/low-fell.html

POOKA
I met one once, with my wife Alison and sons Shaun and Kris, in the woods just across the wire suspension bridge at Low Force, County Durham. High Force waterfall was frozen solid. It was New Year's Day 1991.

## *ALBION*
Albion is an ancient name for Britain, or England, depending on whom you read. In GODS, DEMIGODS AND DEMONS, by Bernard Evslin (I.B. Tauris and Co Ltd.), it's England. Albion was the son of Posiedon and Amphitrite. He traveled to Hera's Golden Apple Tree on the western edge of the world, to pick a gift for his mother. On his way home he found an island covered in mist, just east of the Hesperides. The tribes were blue-painted and worshipped him as a god, for which he rewarded them in return. He taught such a high standard of boat-building and sea-craft that the islanders have ruled the waves to this very day. The land took the name Albion, until it became known as England.

ENNIOS ETOS
Tom is approaching his eight birthday which is the start of his ninth year, just as your first birthday is the start of your second year. Nine is a magical number and equal to three times three, which is also a magical number. It is the ideal time to start his Ennios Etos, his nine years of study.

PONTIKOS / SUNBLEST
Is not to be confused with AION the Greek Lion (or Lion-headed) god of time, whose two keys opened gates which led to eternal lands of the soul, beyond time as mortals understand it.

CUP AND RING STONES
The Northumberland Rockart team at Newcastle University have put together a detailed study of all known Cup and Ring marked stones in Northumberland. HARE LAW CRAGS Rock Art, for example, can be found at http://rockart.ncl.ac.uk/panel_detail_archaeology.asp?pi=14 .
The home page being http://rockart.ncl.ac.uk through which I read of Throckley Bank, Newburn, Rockart and many others. It is a fascinating and very detailed study. Hopefully they won't be too upset that I have decided the purpose of the stones to be gambling and time-travel. It's better than having another casino. Recently these have been awarded World Heritage Status.
http://www.ancient-origins.net/news-general/historically-important-prehistoric-rock-art-sites-northumberland-077892

A FORTY-FIVE
Imagine an mp3 download, made real and fired into a flat, black, vinyl disc.

DEJA VU
I like *this* explanation. Powerful emotional events in life cause waves of upheaval

for some time after they have occurred. The ripples would also flow back in the time stream as well as forward, but obviously you can't be sad for a specific event before it has happened. These powerful waves of emotion affect people in different ways. Some become aware of the disruption in time and experience this as déjà vu. Some people get 'the call'.

## HAYMARKET LEGO MEN
The least loved of all the north east's public art, the lego-men were a chain of concrete figures also serving as a fence between the busy Haymarket Metro station and the roundabout. Normally it would not be possible for a large amount of solid objects to *really* travel in time. However the constricting effects of the trap released huge amounts of energy and created distortions wherein many strange things happened out of sequence.

## THE MISSING NINTH LEGION
Were sent up Northumberland to quash trouble in Scotland in the second century. They were never seen again.

## THE TEMPERANCE FOUNTAIN
Was unearthed recently in the park when renovation work was carried out between the dene and the bottom gates. A water supply for dogs was found and put back into use.

## The PLEROMA
The Pleroma, defined from the Greek meaning, is essentially 'the wholeness'. It can also mean 'fullness' or the 'full extent' (of powers). By implication it has also come to be regarded as the higher, perfect world, of which the physical world is an imperfect copy, or reflection.

The qualities of the Pleroma are, PAIRS OF OPPOSITES, such as -The Effective and the Ineffective.     Fullness and Emptiness.

| | |
|---|---|
| Living and Dead. | Difference and Sameness. |
| Light and Darkness. | The Hot and the Cold. |
| Force and Matter. | Time and Space. |
| Good and Evil. | Beauty and Ugliness. |

        The One and the Many.


## ABRAXAS
I have always understood to be the name of an ancient British semi-god. At http://www.freewebs.com/navanath/seven_sermons.html I discovered the following

Abraxas begetteth truth and lying, good and evil, light and darkness, in the same word and in the same act. Wherefore is Abraxas terrible.

It is splendid as the lion in the instant he striketh down his victim.
It is beautiful as a day in spring.
It is the great Pan himself and also the small one.
It is Priapos.
It is the monster of the underworld, a thousand-armed polyp, coiled knot of winged serpents, frenzy.
It is the hermaphrodite of the earliest beginning.
It is the lord of the toads and frogs, which live in the water and gets up on the land, whose chorus ascendeth at noon and at midnight.
It is abundance that seeketh union with emptiness.
It is holy begetting.
It is love and love's murder.
It is the saint and his betrayer.
It is the brightest light of day and the darkest night of madness.
To look upon it, is blindness.
To know it, is sickness.
To worship it, is death.
To fear it, is wisdom.
To resist it not, is redemption.

THE RABBIT
The tale of the rabbit, popular in the north east shipyards, is as follows. When out at sea on trials of equipment or the ship itself, an upstart apprentice would be selected for the ritual. A tradesman would sit on deck with his hands on top of an upturned bucket. When the apprentice appeared he would be told of the rabbit trapped underneath, and asked to pounce and catch the rabbit as soon as the bucket was lifted. Of course the bucket was lifted and all that was underneath was a turd. Any apprentice not asking themselves what a rabbit was doing out at sea deserved no better.

IAN MICHAEL FOREMAN
Yes, very clever. Well spotted. Spot any more? There are several and also one glaring visual mistake.

VILLIAN'S WOOD = SCRAINWOOD (SCRAIN'SWOOD) as is on the map of Northumberland, giving clues as to it's original reputation.

SYZYRGIES
Here meaning the alignments of magic, where events or circumstances line up or coincide, sometimes producing a colouring or discoloring, to those able to detect such things. Such as those who were born with the power to, or have trained themselves to, see auras.

CONSTRICTION OF SPACE
Our adversary seems to have shot himself in the foot. In an attempt to intimidate,

he evoked the constriction of space in an ever narrowing circle. This altered space *and* time, *and* the relationship between the dimensions, freeing a lot of energy for our 'heroes' to take advantage of.
http://www.messagenet.com/myths/bios/hours.html   is worth reading for the eagle eyed among you.

THE ANGEL OF THE NORTH...
...by Anthony Gormley, has really been taken to the hearts of Northerners. He stands facing south to greet visitors to Gateshead who arrive via the A1 North, the most popular route into the region.

## *THEOGONY*
1)      A way of thinking about the origins of the world.


2)      *Theogony* the initial state of the universe, or the origin (Arche), is Chaos, a gaping void
(abyss) considered as a divine primordial condition, from which appeared everything that exists. darkness in this space), and Eros, a sexual Desire -the urge to reproduce, not the emotion of love as is the common misconception).


3)      A poem by HESIOD, describing the origin of the universe and of the Greek gods and their 'family' groupings: Titans, Gorgons, Cyclops, Hecatons (Hecatonchires) etc.
First there was only Chaos. Concepts such as Chaos, also have personalities and actual physical, bodily existence.
From Chaos came Erebus a place of darkness between the earth and the underworld and Nyx (Night). They gave birth to Aether the atmosphere that the gods breathed and Hemera, the daytime. Therefore Chaos effectively gave birth to Gaia, the world we know.
After that came success generations giving birth to, among others, Uranus (Sky), the Ourea (Mountains), Pontus (Sea).
Uranus and Gaia to created the twelve Titans: Oceanus, Coeus, Crius, Hyperion, Iapetos, Theia, <u>Rhea</u>, Themis, Mnemosyne, Phoebe, Tethys and Kronos (Cronus),
... and three Cyclopes: Brontes, Steropes and Arges,
... and three Hecatonchires: Kottos, Briareos, and Gyges.

Meanwhile, Nyx alone gave birth to Moros (Doom), Oneiroi (Dreams), Ker and the Keres (Destinies), Eris (Discord), Momos (Blame), Philotes (Love), Geras (Old Age), Thanatos (Death), Moiria (Fates), Nemesis (Retribution), Hesperides (Daughters of Night), Hypnos (Sleep), Oizys (Hardship), and Apate (Deceit).
From Eris, came Ponos (Pain), Hysmine (Battles), the Neikia (Quarrels), the Phonoi (Murders), Lethe (Oblivion), Makhai (Fight), Psuedologos (Lies),

Amphilogia (Disputes), Limos (Famine), Androktasia (Manslaughters), <u>Ate</u> (Ruin), Dysnomia (Anarchy and Disobedient Lawlessness), the Algea (Illness), Horkos (Oaths), and Logoi (Stories).

In the family of the Titans, Oceanus and Tethys married and had three thousand rivers (including the Nile and Skamandar) and three thousand Okeanid Nymphs (including Electra, Calypso, and Styx). Theia and Hyperion marry and have Helios (Sun), Selene (Moon), and Eos (Dawn). Kreios and Eurybia marry to bear Astraios, Pallas, and Perses. Eos and Astraios marry and have Zephyros, Boreas, Notos, Eosphoros, Hesperos, Phosphoros and the Stars (for example, Phaenon, Phaethon, Pyroeis, Stilbon.
From Pallas and Styx (another Okeanid) came Zelus (Zeal), Nike (victory), Cratos and Bia (Force). Koios and Phoibe marry and have Leto, Asteria (who later marries Perses and has Hekate). Iapetos marries Klymene (an Okeanid Nymph) and had Atlas, Menoetius, Prometheus, and Epimetheus.
Much of this definition is explained clearly (and taken from)
http://en.wikipedia.org/wiki/Theogony


Κρόνος
Kronos is not just a 'god' of time, but also a negative force, a destructive, ravaging effect of time passing. He is often seen with a harp and a sickle. The sickle he used on his father Uranus, in the most destructive way possible. Some depictions of Father Time and Death also shew them carrying a sickle, or scythe.

THE FOUR FAMILIES OF MAGIC
The Abraxasons, the Kwantiks, the Quarterpages and the Constant Tynes.

MAGIC WORDS
On the subject of which many thanks to Alan Moore, the consistently excellent sage whose works and magic words have entertained for more than 30 years. IN PARTICULAR, thanks for the inspiration for the atomic/cimota duality. When teaching, I always considered that something was learned when the student could repeat it back but in his/her own words. Something thought of can bring about understanding but only sticks once it has been vocalized. Magic words.

MAGIC
Tom's mind has set up various 'Prompting Signals' in his everyday life. These signals can be as simple as favourite colours or smells, or very complex and obscure like hanging upside down in a house that is running on chicken's legs. Whichever is the case, these signals are necessary to spark the mind, body and senses into the state of awareness needed to elicit a response from a person's natural magical ability. For most people it never comes, or they are unaware of the opportunity when it arises. Tom's mind summoned all of the available prompts. In his position, a near death experience, his life was already flashing

past his eyes. This 'arousing' usually happens around the time of puberty.

You can't help but be fascinated by people whose minds operate faster than you can press buttons on a calculator. Even those who aren't anything special with mathematics will admit that the more they practice the better they become. As with everything, magicians find the attaining of the right state of mind much easier and quicker to achieve, the more they practice.

Grant Morrison, a very imaginative writer and practicing magician, explained how he achieves the right state of mind at www.grant-morrison.com and also in The Book Of Lies, edited by Richard Metzger and published by Disinformation. Basically he finds a state of 'no mind' by running or dancing energetically, for example. Understand now why Adam was so glad to be exhausted when pursued across the Northumbrian countryside. No more clues. Magic is hard work and not something to be given away too easily.

Perhaps the answers are in book two? Until then look for Angel Haar website. Begone!

Printed in Great Britain
by Amazon